What Happened at School Today?

PRIS MASTERS

What Happened at School Today? is a work of fiction. Names, characters, places, events, and incidents are the product of the author's imagination or are used fictitiously. Any resemblance to actual persons, living or dead, or to events is entirely coincidental.

Author photograph by Jill Matthews

Cover by Proofreadingservices.com

BENT TREE BOOKS

CINCINNATI

ISBN 978-1-7362802-1-8

Chapter 1

Thursday, March 14th

I sat at my desk after school, trying to finalize the next day's lesson plans. Looking up at the clock, I decided to call it a day. It had been a long one, with Chloe, one of my students who has autism, having a meltdown just as the kids were getting ready to go home.

I raked my papers together and crammed them into my briefcase, then straightened the ever-present piles on my desk, shoving them to the sides a bit so I could actually glimpse the wooden surface in a few places.

I headed up the hall to the office to use the restroom and glanced in the door to see a little group of teachers yakking. I knew that if I went in, I could get sucked into hearing some saga about the disrespect our youth show authority. I didn't need that. I just wanted to get on the road, so I snuck past the office, down the hall to the girls' room. None of the other teachers ever use the girls' restroom due to its high scuzz factor, but I'm in there often because my kiddos (who have multiple disabilities) sometimes need help.

I shoved the restroom door open and was hit by a nauseating smell. There's nothing like the smell of blood, so heavy and metallic you can almost taste it. I didn't even want to guess at the cause. I almost backed out, but what the hell? I was already there.

1

I would just go in quick, breathe through my mouth, pee, and be gone.

My business done, I washed up quickly and cranked out a paper towel. As I turned to pitch it, something caught my eye: a closed door. Someone was in there. For some stupid reason, a quick chill ran up my spine. I guess it's always eerie when you think you're alone and find out you're not. Then I noticed the giant pool of blood in the stall. Weirder yet, I could see by peeking under the stalls that whoever was in there was kneeling in what I think of as "throw-up position," facing the wall.

"Are you okay?" I ventured. No response. I bent down lower and took a better look. She was kneeling in the puddle of blood.

"Do you need help?" I asked as I walked over and tentatively began to ease the door open. As I pushed, she shifted aside but still said nothing. I pushed the door a little farther and poked my head in just enough to take a quick peek. I froze. I have never before felt what people describe as "the blood draining," but I sure felt it then. She hadn't moved of her own volition, but instead had fallen out of the awkward position she must have been propped up in. When I'd pushed on the door, she had been shoved to a new position, jammed between the toilet and stall wall, staring up at me. There was no doubt she was dead. A gash above her left eye had spilled blood all over that side of her face. Her lips were the color of lilacs in spring. Her eyes protruded in cartoonish horror as if she were both shocked and surprised. Her gray sweatshirt was drenched in blood coming from her abdomen, where something was stuck in her. Was that a knife?

I grabbed her wrist, hunting for a pulse. This was clearly a waste of time. No one could be alive and look like she looked. No pulse. I looked at my watch: 4:02. (But I then wondered why I was doing that since she had no pulse. Habit, I guessed.)

You'd think with all the fake deaths and dead bodies I see on TV, with all the murder mysteries I read with their gory descriptions of death, I'd be jaded about seeing this woman. But all those movies and books are pretty removed from me. This was so close. Two feet away from me was a not-long-dead woman with a weapon protruding from her gut. I could not only see her up close, but smell her. And as I looked down at the floor of the stall, I had to be careful not to slip in her blood.

I'm ashamed of what I did next. I pulled my head back out of the stall, hustled back down to my own stall, and promptly puked. Then I began to shiver. Not just a tremor, but a whole series of tremors moved through my body, making me do a little dance of horror, rattling my teeth together. I heard moaning, at first thinking foolishly that it was her, but then realizing that it was me. I clamped a hand over my mouth, muttering, "Hush." I took a couple of deep breaths and went for another peek. Yup, she was dead all right, no question about it. With this peek, I noticed blood on the wall. She had undoubtedly smacked her face on the metal toilet paper holder, (placed stupidly, four feet high in the stall) when she had gone down. I almost upchucked again, but instead I went to the sink, feeling like I was moving in slow motion. I turned on the cold water, rinsed my face, and took a few sips out of a cupped hand. I took more deep breaths. My ears were ringing. Body uncooperative. Again in slow motion, I backed out of the bathroom, keeping an eye on the stall door, the folded legs, and the pool of blood as if I thought she was going to come alive and come after me. I stood outside the bathroom door for a moment, resting my forehead against the door frame and wondering if my legs could carry me, if I could go back to breathing without conscious thought, if my heart could have literally moved up into my throat where it now felt like it was lodged. I engaged in a little self-talk along the "don't be such a wuss" line, and then turned away from the door.

I marched down to the office, where I nearly dislocated my shoulder as I attempted to shove open the locked door. I looked at my watch: 4:10. Of course it was locked. So on I went, down to my room, where I collapsed into my chair. I knew I should call 911 right away, so why wasn't I? I realized I had tears streaming down my face and snot pouring from my nose, and I was almost sobbing. I gave in and had a good cry.

When I was pretty cried out, I looked in a little mirror that hangs at the back of my classroom for my girls to check themselves out. When I checked *me* out, I was startled at how crappy I looked. Eye makeup was smeared all over my face, nicely complementing my puffy eyes and red nose. I cleaned myself up as I took another set of deep breaths. Then I called 911 and spilled it all to a kind, patient woman at the other end of the line. Emergency vehicles would be there shortly, she said. Being the skeptic that I am, I consulted my watch, wondering how long "shortly" would be. I would be waiting out in front of the building, I told her. I grabbed a piece of gum from my purse to hide my yarky breath and got myself out in front of the school, pronto.

She was right. "Shortly" turned out to be four minutes. The first to arrive was a fire engine with lights flashing but no sirens going. Two firefighters got out of the truck and approached me.

Chapter 2

"Are you Hannah Hutchinson?" the taller one asked.

"Yes," I said, stupidly adding no further details.

"Did you call 911 to report a body down?"

"Yes, I did. I called to report a *murder*, I think."

They looked at each other as if they had heard it all before. (Really? Murder?)

Just you wait, I thought to myself. "This way," I said as I turned and entered the building. I was still a bit shaky and wasn't feeling like talking a lot, which is pretty unusual for me. I headed down the hall with the two of them following, our footsteps falling in unison like a little band marching down the empty corridor. When I came to the girls' restroom, I stopped and pointed.

"She's in there," I said, feeling for some reason like I was eight years old. The short, heavy, nicer looking of the two pushed past me. The taller one held the restroom door open and gestured for me to enter, which I tried to do without hesitating noticeably. Once inside the door, there was no need for me to do anything further. I stood aside, refraining from putting a hand on the door handle as if ready to run, or from clamping a hand over my nose, again breathing through my mouth so I wouldn't have to smell the stench of blood in the air. The two firefighters were taking turns trying to wedge themselves into the stall. My guess was they were trying to take a pulse that wouldn't be there, noting her ghastly appearance, realizing they could do nothing for her. They mumbled a few things between themselves. I caught the words *cold* and *lividity*(which I'm pretty sure, from all the mysteries I read, is a technical word for bruising). They did not move her.

The taller guy pulled a radio from his hip and began to talk into it. He spoke quickly and I caught just a few words of what he said. The two of them looked around the restroom, which made me do the same. I would have been *so* disappointed in myself if I had overlooked some vital clue.

"What a dive!" commented one. Looking through their eyes, I had to admit he was right. The restroom is cavernous and ugly. Built for functionality, not beauty, it has horrible old linoleum flooring. The walls are institutional olive. Long row of ancient sinks on the left. Long row of stalls on the right. The sides of the stalls are covered with graffiti done in pencil, pen, and Sharpie, and even scratched into the surface by those who really wanted their thoughts etched for eternity. The metal stalls have shifted over time, so a couple of the doors don't lock. The slits between the metal dividing walls of the stalls are so big, you can almost peek through and spy on your next-stall neighbor if you really want to. All part of the character of an old building, I guess.

The short, cute guy held the door open for me, and we (much to my relief) went out into the hall. I could hear the radio crackling with chatter that I couldn't make out. We both looked up at the sound of approaching footsteps and saw two uniformed Cincinnati cops coming down the hall. So far, I was impressed with the speed of my local emergency personnel. These guys couldn't have been more than five minutes behind the firefighters. The three men spoke to each other so quickly and in such low voices that I could only catch about every fifth word.

The firefighterturned toward me and introduced me to the cops. They politely dipped their heads in my direction, then one of them went in to take a look at the strange scene. I stood in the hall with the other, and he got right down to business, asking me questions and nodding as he listened.

I told him my short story. He asked a few more questions and I thought I handled myself pretty well. I got a little teary-eyed, but none spilled over. Then he got on the radio, telling someone that he was talking to a witness who would be available for further questioning. How did he know I would be available? Maybe I had a hot date to get to. If only.

By this time, Sam, our head custodian, had joined us and was listening with big ears to all that was going on. The cop wisely turned to him, asking where we might wait for the homicide detectives. Sam is the Frazz of school custodians: accommodating, funny, wise, and generally a wealth of school gossip. Seeing the look he gave me now was like getting a hug from three feet away, and I appreciated it. Sam walked us down to the main office, where he unlocked the door and, holding it open, put a hand on my back and then a light pat on my shoulder as I went through.

The main office is in one of the newer parts of the building, and it's well designed. You walk into a large open area that acts as reception. Beyond that is a warren of offices for the principal, assistant principal, and guidance counselors, and a few conference rooms. The area was nearly deserted right then. Andrew Taylor, the principal, poked his head out of his office to see what was going on and joined our little party. I wasn't surprised to see him. The main office door is always locked by the secretary, who leaves at precisely four o'clock, but the principal, assistant principal, and guidance counselors often stay later. Locked in there, they can hide in their individual offices, experiencing some rare solitude and getting work done without anyone bothering them. As it turned out, Andrew had walked in with the police, returning to school after an administrative meeting to do whatever principals do to stay caught up. Already knowing part of the story, he offered his office to use as a waiting area. I sat down, and the two cops hovered around; whether they were waiting for others to show up or waiting for orders, I wasn't sure, but it soon became apparent.

I've never called the police for anything in my life, so again, I have to give the Cincinnati Police and Fire Department some credit here. My 911 call was answered within only a few minutes, and now, within only a few more minutes, I could see two suit-clad men coming into the building. The two uniformed cops went out to meet them, and they had a little powwow outside Andrew's office, with me watching them through the window, trying to read lips. Notes were being made. Heads were nodding. I was sure questions were being asked.

The two suits came into Andrew's office and introduced themselves, their names getting past me without a thought. "Officer Casey is going to give you a ride down to headquarters, Ms. Hutchinson," said the taller of the two men.

"Why am I going to headquarters?" I asked stupidly.

"Because you're a witness, ma'am. We'll process the scene here, and then we'll be down to the Crime Investigation Section to talk to you."

"But can't I just tell you what happened right here? Right now?"

"No, ma'am. I'm sorry, but that's not how it works. We have to process the scene, and then we'll take your report."

One of the uniformed cops came into the office at this point. I heard him mumble something about handcuffs to the taller of the two new arrivals, who now turned and looked at me. A tiny smile crossed his face.

"No, I don't think she looks very dangerous," he said in a voice that I'm sure was not meant for my ears to hear.

Now, why would that piss me off? But for some reason, it did. "How long is this going to take?" I asked in a voice that sounded whiny, even to me.

Without saying another word, the two detectives turned as one and exited the room, leaving their underling to deal with me.

"Hopefully it won't take too long," the uniformed cop said unhelpfully.

"I want to drive down to wherever it is we're going in my own car. I don't need a ride," I said.

"Unfortunately, that's not how it works," he said, shaking his head. "When you've witnessed a crime like this, you have to be *taken* to CIS."

I gave him an exasperated look.

"Well, what if you were the perpetrator?" he asked, spreading his hands apart, palms up. "Then you'd be able to make a quick getaway." He said this with what I interpreted as a sympathetic smile. I felt myself relax just a tiny bit.

"All right," I groaned, feeling like a complaining adolescent. He accompanied me to my room, where I grabbed my purse and briefcase. (As if I were going to go home and do some work. Ha!) He then escorted me out to his cop car and politely held the back door open for me, telling me to watch my head.

I hate to confess it, but it was sort of scary riding in that backseat with the caged divider in front of me and the doors that had no openers. The trip downtown took about twenty minutes. I was still vastly freaked out about the whole dead-body-in-the-bathroom thing and unhappy about having to go down to the police station. My mind was racing unproductively in all directions until the moment we pulled into the cramped parking lot of the Criminal Investigation Section. I gazed up at a very modern-looking building that is attractive from the outside—lots of glass on an arc-shaped building that curves around the busy corner it sits on. The cop who had transported me let me out of the car and accompanied me quite closely into the building.

Chapter 3

My phone was taken away from me, as was my briefcase. For some stupid reason, I begged to be allowed to keep my lesson plan book, and surprisingly they let me. Officer Casey led me into the bowels of the building. After walking past a number of closed doors, we came to one that he stopped at and unlocked.

"Make yourself comfortable," he said as he gestured for me to sit on the far side of a white plastic table.

He had to be kidding. I found myself in an eight-by-eight room, complete with three blue plastic chairs, the table, and four gray walls. Nothing else. There wasn't even the two-way mirror that always appears in cop shows. I was disappointed.

"Can I bring you a soft drink or coffee?" he asked.

"Yes," I answered quickly. My mouth was feeling Saharan. Probably dehydrated from all my crying and puking. "I'll have a diet cola."

He nodded as he left, closing the door behind him. The second he was gone, I got up and checked to see if the door was locked. Yup. It's not like I was going to try to escape; I just wanted to know. He was back quickly, handing me the soft drink and commenting that it could be a while. What's "a while"? I wanted to ask, but I was starting to feel too exhausted to talk, and I figured he might not know anyway. I sat looking around me and found there was one more thing in the room I had missed. In the corner across from me, actually mounted on the ceiling, was a tiny camera, its red light glowing. Were they watching me? Maybe.

I sat sipping my drink with my eyes shut, trying to relax. But closing my eyes was not a good thing. It took me back into the bathroom, back to the sight of the *very* dead woman. I popped them open, looking around the room again. With nothing else to do, I opened my lesson plan book and sat staring at it without anything sinking in. I had my watch on, so I know it had only been ten minutes when I heard the door opening. Good, I thought, this will be over quickly. A woman about my age came in and sat down. She introduced herself as a victim's advocate. She was here to see if I would like to have someone to talk to about the incident I had witnessed. I immediately balked at this. Hell, no, I didn't want to talk to anyone about it—not any more than I had to, anyway.

She gave me a nice spiel about what her job was and that she was there to help me deal with any trauma I might be experiencing. But I dug in my heels and was not willing to really listen. She gave up after a few minutes, sliding her business card across the table to me and telling me I could call her if I changed my mind. I nodded slowly without even saying anything, and she left, telling me that I might have to wait a bit longer.

I waited quite a *bit* longer, I thought. It was really only forty-five minutes, but when you look at your watch two or three times a minute, the time goes at a glacial speed.

Finally, the door to my tiny cell opened again and the two detectives stepped in and seated themselves across the table from me. They asked me to tell them my story from the beginning, which I did, getting through it with only an occasional tremor in my voice. They had both pulled out tiny yellow pads. One of them took notes constantly, while the other seemed to write down just a word or two now and then. When I finished, I sat back, feeling tired from the retelling. They both sat looking at me for a few long seconds.

"Do you know this woman?" asked the more senior of these two.

"No. I don't think so. Her face was pretty covered with blood," I added, feeling my face cringe with the memory. He made a note on his tiny yellow pad, looking back and forth from it to me.

"Did you touch her?"

"No. I mean, yes. Yes. I took her pulse, but of course she didn't have one. A pulse, that is."

"Who else did you tell about this incident?"

"No one. There was no one there to tell. Everybody had gone home for the day. I just went back to my room and called 911." (Was I blathering? I pursed my lips together, trying to get myself calmed down.)

"And you say you found her at 4:02. Are you sure of the time?" He looked up from the notepad and kept his eyes on me.

"Yes, I'm sure," I said, a bit defensively.

"Why are you so sure of the time?"

"Because I looked at my watch."

"You looked at your watch. Why did you do that?" The notepad forgotten, he looked at me blankly.

For a moment, I gazed back at him. I was not too upset to realize I was being sized up, so I did a little sizing up, too. What I saw was a middle-aged guy who looked like he spent more time pushing a pencil than chasing bad guys. He had probably been good-looking twenty years before, with his turquoise-blue eyes and what was left of sandy blond hair. He looked uncomfortable in his suit. His shirt was stretched tightly over a beer-rounded belly, and its collar, tightened by a cheap tie, dug into his oversized neck. Had he put the weight on recently, or over the years, and just never admitted he needed to go up a few sizes? As he sat facing me, it was easy for me to see his badge. It was front and center on a lanyard resting on his ample belly. This was Detective Marvin Kennedy. Unfairly, I wondered how smart he was. As upset as I was, it was sort of funny to me that I was studying this pudgy guy as he sat waiting for me to answer him. I love to look at people. I feel like you can learn so much just by looking. And what did he see as he looked at me? Chin-length wavy brown hair (undoubtedly a mess, because that's how it always is), dark brown eyes (beautifully puffy, no doubt,), a curvy figure, ten pounds too heavy to be called slender, average height. Probably thought I was a ditz since I was having somewhat of a hard time focusing. I felt my spine straighten a bit under his eye.

"It's sort of a habit of mine in an emergency."

He looked either bored or confused.

"Most of my emergencies come in the form of a kid having a seizure. When a kid starts to have a grand mal seizure, you look at your watch. You have to time the seizure. If a kid seizes for more than three minutes, you call 911 because that's too long. Like, it becomes an emergency."

"Okay, okay, I get it," he said, going back to the notepad for further scribbling. "You're a teacher at McKinley, right?"

"Yes. I teach kids with multiple disabilities. So, like, kids with cerebral palsy, autism, Down syndrome—"

"Okay, okay, I get it," he said again, looking at the notepad as if it held answers for him. "What were you doing there so late?"

"It wasn't really that late. I often stay and work on lesson plans and stuff for a while after the kids leave."

He nodded at me, saying nothing.

The other detective, not having said but a few words since our quick introductions, now spoke up. "Did you see anyone after school? Any other teachers? Anyone in the office?"

"No. I was in my room the whole time. Well, that's wrong. I went to the teacher's lounge and saw another teacher for just a minute."

"Who was that?" he asked.

"Mrs. Knight. She's an eighth-grade art teacher," I added as if they cared. My attention now turned to detective number two, and I took him in. He had never been a good looking guy. The too-tight suit must have been a uniform for detectives. His was even tighter. I almost wanted to reach over and loosen his tie. His face was beet red. Probably high blood pressure, but maybe it was just that his tie was choking him. His name, I noted from the badge protruding from his gut, was Appledom.

"Ms. Hutchinson?"

"Huh?" I said. Good God, Hannah. Quit with the mind wandering. I knew somewhere in my brain that I was having difficulty focusing because I was in semi-shock. I pulled myself together a little. "I'm sorry. What did you say?"

"I was asking if that was the only person you saw."

I thought for a moment and answered yes.

"Are you sure of that?"

"Yes," I said a little more emphatically. I could feel myself getting a little cranky, and just then my stomach growled ferociously. No surprise to me. Stress always makes me hungry.

The two men now looked at each other in a way that was almost comical, their heads swiveling toward each other on those tight collars. It reminded me of someone or something, but I couldn't think what. Maybe someone in a book? And into my head popped Tweedledee and Tweedledum. In case you don't remember these two, they are characters from *Alice in Wonderland*. They dressed exactly alike. They were doughy and laughable. They were not bright. In fact, they were downright stupid. Maybe the parallel had something to do with the sound of their names, too: Kennedy and Appledom, Tweedledee and Tweedledum. I tried to squelch my comparison, but I felt a little smile creep to my lips. The two detectives studied me as I worked at wiping it away.

The interview went on and on for what seemed like an eternity. I told them two or maybe three times how I had found her, how she had shifted to the side as I opened the stall door, that I had never seen her before. Finally, there was a little pause as Kennedy paged through his tiny notebook, looking at what he had written, and Appledom sat staring at me. Kennedy spoke up.

"This woman, the victim, had no ID on her. She had no wallet, no purse, not even any keys. There was no car in the parking lot that was unaccounted for. She apparently didn't drive to your school."

I digested this for a moment. It did seem very strange, but I certainly had no guesses as to what it all meant.

"Of course, she could have gotten a ride to the school, and the perpetrator could have taken her private property away from her."

I nodded my head, these possibilities making sense to me. They sat, looking at me. I had nothing else to tell them. I was exhausted and really just wanted to get the hell out of there.

"Can I go home now?" I suddenly blurted out. I had started feeling pretty sketchy, wondering if more yarking was in my future or if I was just starving. Probably the latter as I had gone way longer without food than I'm used to.

Kennedy looked at me, sizing me up a bit more, and maybe he suspected how close I was to falling off my chair.

"Are you gonna be okay?" he asked.

"Yeah, I'll be fine," I lied.

"I think we can let you go home. We may need to talk to you again, but it seems like you've given us all you can for now."

We all got up and finally left the tiny room. Appledom roped someone into taking me back to school, and after a long and silent ride, I got dropped off next to my car in the school parking lot.

I drove home in somewhat of a daze. Around the halfway mark, my car automatically turned into an Arby's that is on my route. With no conscious thought, I ordered a roast beef sandwich and jalapeño poppers. The latter are billed as an appetizer at Arby's, but I love them with a sandwich. I ate them as I drove, burning the roof of my mouth on that first bite of fried pepper and molten cream cheese, and dripping it down the front of my shirt. Damn! I knew it would stain because I already have a little collection of popper-stained shirts in my wardrobe. The food made me feel somewhat better, but I kept revisiting the vision of that poor woman until she almost seemed familiar to me. Maybe I did know her. When even the knife started looking familiar in my mind, I had a serious word with myself.

"Now, that's enough. You're being ridiculous." My voice sounded loud to me in the car.

Once home, I was not much better. I watched as Rascal went through his doggie door, but didn't accompany him down the deck steps into the yard. He turned, looking back at me with his most pitiful golden retriever look. "Oh, all right," I said and plodded down the steps to roam around the yard with him, as was our normal routine. He pranced around, bringing a begrudging smile to my lips at least briefly. Nothing like dog appreciation to make you feel better. Rascal has a lot to appreciate as he is spoiled fairly rotten. Lots of walks and park visits for him, a spot smack in the middle of the bed every night, and a nice view out the window from the couch where I'm sure he illicitly spends most of the day.

I debated going up to see my upstairs neighbor Stella. I certainly needed a shoulder to cry on, but I knew if I went up I'd get stuck up there, plus I was afraid I'd make her stay up all night worrying. I vetoed the idea. Instead, I called Anne and Ava, my classroom assistants, and Dana, my best friend, to tell them my horror story and cry on their shoulders. I ate a few cookies to top off my dinner, finishing just as Andrew, my principal, called to check on me. Why did I assure him that I was fine? Why did I choke back tears and make sure I had no tremor in my voice as I talked to him? Stupid pride, no doubt. I could do this cuz I'm so tough. I could be calm in the face of tragedy. But underneath it all, some inner voice was saying, what a wimp!

I tried to get my mind off the events of the afternoon. I turned on the TV and flipped through the channels. I read a mystery for about five minutes but realized the words just weren't sinking in. I wandered around the apartment, thinking maybe I'd clean up a bit. I didn't clean at all. I finally took Rascal for a walk. It was surprisingly cold out, but a lovely, clear night with stars visible even in the city sky. The walk calmed me down and made me realize how exhausted I was. When I got home, I pretty much dumped myself into bed and fell asleep immediately. But sometime in the middle of the night, I started reliving the events of the afternoon. Not just once but three times I dreamed of opening the bathroom stall door and peeking in. My horrified psyche would only let me go so far, just to the point where I saw her from behind and asked her if she was okay. It did *not* make for a restful night.

Chapter 4

Wednesday, March 13th

I had dressed carefully Wednesday morning, knowing I needed to look professional. I put on a skirt and tights, and even heels, wishing briefly that I owned a suit, but it's just not my style. I left the house early and was sitting at my desk by seven fifteen. I went over Rosie Mitchell's IEP. (In case you don't live in the world of special ed like I do, that stands for Individual Education Plan. It's the legal document written yearly that all kids who get special ed services have. It outlines what progress the child is expected to make in that coming year and how they'll be helped to achieve it.) Finally, I headed for the office conference room. I had been dreading this meeting for a month.

Of course, I had no idea at the time that I would be finding a dead body the next day and that no matter how awful that day went, the next one would beat it by a mile.

Meetings are just about my least favorite part of being a teacher. After all, if you become a teacher, you're doing it to be with kids, right? I am a teacher of *very* special kids, or at least that's how I like to think of it. I am not a specialist who works with kids who primarily have learning disabilities or attention deficit disorder. In our world today, that has actually become the new "ordinary." Kids with LD and ADD form a tremendous portion of school-age kids. Current statistics will tell you kids with learning disabilities make up 5 to 10 percent of the school-age population. That is not my gig. I teach the 1 percent, the kids who are more significantly disabled, those who are very autistic, and those who are disabled in a variety of other ways like cerebral palsy, fetal alcohol syndrome, Down syndrome, etc. I teach kids who have terrific needs, are hard to figure out, and who constantly challenge me.

I teach in a middle school, grades six through eight. Everybody knows middle school is a crazy place. That's because adolescents are just plain squirrely. But please, think back. Remember what it was like to be an adolescent? Trying to fit in, yet be an individual. Trying to be independent, but still really needing parenting. Trying to look cool, beautiful, even sexy, but seeing a gawky, pimply, ugly you when you looked in the mirror. Trying to be a grown-up, but knowing you're acting like a child a lot of the time. But squirrely isn't all bad. It can be entertaining; in fact, it is never boring and is full of surprises. I think that among the general population of teachers, those who teach junior high or middle school are considered sort of nuts. Yeah, right. We go well with the squirrels. But it's a good kind of nuts. Anyway, add the middle school thing to the very special specialed thing, and some people might think I'm crazy to do what I do. But I feel it's my niche, and I'm one of the not-so-many people I know who are actually happy with their job.

I might as well backtrack a bit and fill you in on how I ended up in my chosen field. When it came to colleges, Dad and Mom were willing to foot the bill for one school, the University of Cincinnati. That was really okay with me, but I sure didn't want to live at home. I got a job my senior year of high school, kept it through the summer, and saved enough money to live in a dorm on UC's campus. I can't actually remember how I picked speech therapy as a major. I vaguely remember paging through a shiny brochure of fields of study. I may have done something like close my eyes and point. I liked science. It sounded interesting. Good enough.

When I moved into the dorm in the fall of my freshman year, I found an instant social life with the other girls on my floor, and it was one that centered around bars and parties. I had developed a taste for beer in those early experimental drinking days that most kids go through, starting in late adolescence. So I came to UC knowing what I liked: beer, and plenty of it. I also fell in love with cafeteria food. Having gone off to college as a human string bean, it was okay that I gained a bit of weight. It's the ten pounds I've put on since then that are a little over the top (the muffin top, that is).

I *did* go to all my classes. I am blessed with a good memory for both what I hear and what I read. So I took tons of notes in class but basically never looked at them again, crammed for exams by reading all the chapters in the few days before a test, and squeaked by with an infrequent A, mostly low B's, and an occasional C. That was just fine with me. I was having too much fun to care about my grades. My major being speech and hearing, I had to take lots of sciences: biology, anatomy, physics. This was where I was getting the C's. But by my junior year, I finally got to pick an elective. I had been fascinated by Psychology 101 and decided I would like to take Abnormal Psych (yes, I was too stupid to choose an *easy* elective). But the beauty of this class was that the professor was affiliated with a school for kids with disabilities, and on day one of the class, he offered this: any students who would do four hours a week of volunteer work at his affiliate school would get their grade in his class raised by a letter. What a deal! It never occurred to me that this would involve a far greater time commitment on my part than simply studying.

So off I went every Tuesday and Thursday afternoon to the Drummond School. I was assigned to a class of seven severely autistic adolescent boys. There was one overwhelmed teacher in the classroom, an assistant who seemed scared of the kids, and as far as I saw, no real learning going on. The boys spent a lot of time rocking in the three rockers spaced around the room, pacing while flapping their arms, looking out the window, sitting and doing nothing in a corner of the room, or crouched on the top of a filing cabinet (the favorite perch of a handsome boy named Charlie).

None of these boys spoke a word, and none of them had any means of communication that was anything like a system. Here was the wake-up call for a future speech therapist! I found these young men interesting, a bit scary, and terribly hopeless. But they were also lovable, appreciative, funny, and a fascinating mystery to me. I started lying awake at night wondering about how their minds worked, how they saw the world, and why they did the things they did. I was given a pretty free hand to do as I pleased in the classroom, working one-on-one with the three most severely autistic boys. I developed different degrees of rapport with each of them, but all three of them always seemed willing to work with me. They probably learned almost *nothing at all* from me in the many afternoons I worked with them, although I hope they at least benefited from time spent with a person that they knew liked them. But I learned mountains from them. I dreamed up little experiments to see if I could get them to quit flapping, rocking, or moaning. I learned that when they were engaged, they stopped those idiosyncratic behaviors. I figured out that they, like everyone else, just wanted some control of their world. I learned what they would do when control was taken from them. Yes, I was swatted, scratched, and even bitten once. (Just the first of *so* many bites I have received from kids over the years. I always have to learn the hard way.)

My fascination with these young men led me to sign up in my senior year, when I got to take three electives, for special ed classes, and it took me straight through graduate school and a master's degree in special ed. I knew exactly what I wanted to do, and it was to work with the most severely disabled kids. I do love kids. Doesn't everyone? But if I'm being honest, I have to admit it's not the *love* of the kids that drives me. It's the love of the problems they present, the challenge of figuring out what makes them tick, how they learn, and how I can get through to them. When things go wrong in my classroom, I often spend hours trying to figure out why a kid flew off the handle, shut down, or bopped their neighbor. It's like solving a mystery, complete with clues and even red herrings. What is it that makes a kid bang his head on his desk? Why does a student keep doing the exact opposite of what I ask her to do? I collect evidence, sift through it, hypothesize, try out my theory, and—aha!—I get results. Better behavior. More learning. Happier kiddo. Sometimes. Other times it's me who wants to bang my head on something, and I have to start all over. I try different approaches, fine-tune, and try again. Often I end up just flying by the seat of my pants, and that can yield startling results too. I guess part of becoming a "professional" in your field is developing good instincts. And over the years I've taught, I have found there's a lot to learn from my students. They may have disabilities, but they also have courage, patience, perseverance, and wonderful senses of humor and fun. I've been doing this for nineteen years, and I've never had a day that was boring. How many people can say that about their jobs?

Chapter 5

Now, as I took a seat in the conference room and arranged my papers, Rosie came through the door with her ever-present smile and a "Hi, Ms. H." Rosemary Mitchell is a delightful child. In my mind and in my teaching experience, she is high functioning for a kiddo who has Down syndrome. She reads at a fourth-grade level, can do first-grade math, and has near-perfect speech and great social skills. She is polite, kind, and funny. It's difficult for me to believe she came out of the womb of her witch of a mother.

I clearly remember the first time I met Rosie. It was a few days before the beginning of her sixth-grade year, at a summer open house for new students that McKinley always hosts. It's really just a couple of hours when teachers are asked to be there to meet new kids who want to come in and walk the building. Very informal, and a time that teachers use to set up their rooms. I was working on bulletin boards when Rosie came in with her dad, Nathan. Having previously met him, I naturally knew who she was.

"Well, this must be the famous Rosemary Mitchell," I said.

"How did you know it was me?" she asked, looking first at me, then up at her dad.

"I actually met your dad a few months ago," I fessed up.

"That makes sense because I'm really not famous," she said with a posture that I interpreted as an attempt to look demure.

I looked up at Nathan, feeling myself grin. Rosemary's articulation was perfect, and of course, her conclusion was right on.

We chatted for about fifteen minutes, in which she entertained me with details about her summer, her friends, and her family.

She was animated as she spoke and showed her ability to laugh at herself. She told about a day when she had not come into the house after her mom called her and had gotten caught in a sudden cloudburst. She concluded the little story with "I looked like a drowned rat!" This young lady didn't have a shy bone in her body. She was bright and spoke well. I was excited to have her coming to my classroom.

Of course, the reality became that Rosie only spends about twenty minutes of her day in my room. The rest of her day is spent in regular education classes, but I see her there on a regular basis. My weekly schedule includes times when I spend portions of bells in Rosie's classes, making sure things are going okay for her (while Anne and Ava run the show in my room). Although Rosie is not shy, she tends not to speak up much outside of my classroom. This worries me. It makes me feel that maybe she isn't comfortable in those classes. On the other hand, when she is with us first thing in the morning, she can be quite the blabbermouth.

This morning Gretchen followed her into the conference room, indicating where Rosie should sit as she sat down next to her. No smile from Gretchen. She was ready for battle. Of *course* Gretchen had on a suit. She even had on actual nylons and pumps. Her blond hair brushed her shoulders in a perfect coif. She likes to see herself as a businesswoman, and in fact, she is trying extremely hard to become just that. She has been, for several years, in the process of setting up an advocacy business for parents who need someone to help them out in meetings just like that one. God forbid I would ever have to face her in more than one IEP meeting a year! Not that I haven't had plenty of meetings with her this school year. I have done everything for Rosie except stand on my head and spit wooden nickels, but it's never enough for Gretchen. She can always find a way I'm lacking, some way in which Rosie needs more services we're not providing. The reality is that Rosie is getting more than her fair share of services already. Why? Because the squeaky wheel gets the grease, and Gretchen is *so* good at squeaking.

Rosie's dad was the next one to enter the room. Nathan seems like a pretty good guy. I can't, in my wildest imagination, figure out how these two got together. Gretchen is very average looking, while Nathan is on the handsome side. She seems downright asocial, while he is fairly friendly. I did see him blow a gasket last year when I first met him, over a situation brought up at Rosie's IEP meeting in which she had apparently been bullied. But I couldn't blame him for that. Anyway, I figure Gretchen must be a hell of a cook, really good in bed, or both.

The conference room filled up with Ian Stevenson (who, as assistant principal, always wins the dubious honor of sitting in on IEP meetings), Suzanne (occupational therapist), and Ruthie (science teacher). As OT and teacher gave reports on how Rosie is performing for them, I got a chance to look around the room. Ian sat at one end of the table, an intense listening statue. His eyes were on Ruthie as she spoke, hands folded as if in prayer. (I hoped he was praying for a peaceful and quick end to this meeting.)

Ian has been our assistant principal for two years, going on three. He is a few years younger than me. He is ambitious, generally businesslike, and quite handsome in a tall, dark, and swarthy way. I think a lot of the teachers at McKinley are a bit intimidated by him. He is not an easygoing guy. He's not gossipy, and when he calls a meeting, stuff gets done. The staff think he's too straightlaced. I think maybe they are also intimidated by his appearance: tie straight, suit perfectly fitted, not a hair out of place, beautiful eyes, luscious lips. The guy could be a model. As could his wife. She is a part-time OTA (occupational therapy assistant) in the district. She is more personable than Ian and very well liked. They have two gorgeous little girls and gee, I guess, a pretty perfect life. I have found over the years that Ian is really very human. The perfect appearance is just part of his obsessive-compulsive behavior. His office looks that way too. Behind his desk, he has framed degrees, team pictures, and a picture of his graduating class from UC. He must have put the pictures up with a level. And then there's his desk. I asked him once if he straightened the few things on it so they were at right angles to each other every day before he went home. He grinned and fessed up that indeed he does. He has a sense of humor, but he hides it pretty well. I find him fair and easy to have as a supervisor, even if he is picky about paperwork. His pickiness has saved my ass a few times in meetings with equally picky parents. There are many times when I wish I were more like Ian.

Next to Ian was Gretchen, sitting with that perpetual smirk on her face. Continuing my gaze around the table, I noticed that Rosie had taken out a spiral notebook. Already bored with this meeting, she was drawing, first a house, then three stick people: large, medium, and a small one in the middle, holding the hands of Medium and Large. She added details to the people: clothing, hair, and faces. I assumed this was a drawing of her family. She gave them straight-line mouths, then went back and changed the little person's mouth to a big smile. As Suzanne launched into her report, I continued to watch Rosie. She paused as if in thought. Then she went to the largest stick person and made tiny lines at the corners of his mouth so he was smiling, just a little. She moved over to medium stick's face, paused, then moved on to draw a sun up in the sky. (Wouldn't take a shrink to figure out what that was all about.)

On the other side of Rosie sat Nathan, who was really the only one at this meeting who seemed relaxed. He lounged comfortably in his chair with an ankle resting on the opposite knee, in that position that is classic for men but not fit for ladies.

We worked our way through the IEP, doing the parts that affected the OT and science teacher first so they could get out of there. Gretchen nitpicked a bit, but we made progress. As the warning bell rang to tell kids they had five minutes to get to class, Ruthie said she had to leave but had one more question. When would Rosie be having her surgery? Yay, Ruthie. I would have to find her after the meeting and thank her for bringing this up.

Rosie was born with a heart defect called atrioventricular septal defect. It is a congenital problem common in kids who have Down syndrome and causes abnormalities in the heart's valves. Infants often have surgery to correct it, but Rosie's case was very mild, and it was thought that she would outgrow the problem, as some kids do. My understanding is that she was monitored by a cardiologist for several years, in which time her heart appeared to have remedied the problem on its own. But just recently, she had been short of breath and tired all the time, and long story short, she needed surgery to repair her heart. Nathan and Gretchen had put it off, twice in fact. I can understand their hesitancy about their daughter having open-heart surgery, but the situation has really started to take a toll on her. She isn't supposed to run or exert herself too much in any way. That's no way for a thirteen-year-old to live. Gretchen quoted a new surgery date, three weeks away, and I sat wondering if it would really happen then.

Ruthie thanked them for the information, making a note of it, and she and Suzanne got up to leave.

Including Rosie in this meeting was Gretchen's idea and I had no objection to it, although I'm sure it was boring for Rosie and much of the talk was over her head. I was glad she was now being allowed to leave for class. She gave both parents a hug, and Gretchen, to my surprise, told her that she loved her and to have a good day. She actually looked pretty as she smiled at her daughter. Knock me over with a leaf, I thought. This woman *does* have a kind bone in her body.

I have never had a job in the business world, but I know it has some things in common with education. I'm sure that if I sat in any business meeting, I would be lost in terms I don't know the meaning of. Education also has acronyms and terms that would sound like a foreign language to anyone who doesn't have to deal with the things they represent. So when I say "full inclusion," this is what I mean: a child with special needs (the kids I teach) spends their entire school day in regular education classes, receiving their special ed services there. Rosie is a good kid to use as an example. From the day she started school, she has been with her "typical" peers all day long. When she was in kindergarten, her skills were probably pretty close to theirs. She is a very social child, and kindergarten is a place where kiddos learn to be social, to follow rules, to be part of a group (and lots more too, I know). Rosie was able to fit in there. Fast-forward to fourth grade. By that time, she was two grades lower than her peers in reading ability and even more in math and writing. Now it was becoming more difficult, but specialists could go in and help out in the classroom, maybe pulling her out for remediation now and then.

Now that she is in sixth grade, the gap, especially in math, is vast, and in my mind, a regular education classroom is not the best place for Rosie to learn math. But Gretchen has a very clear plan for Rosie, and it is for full inclusion until the day she graduates. She intends for Rosie to be a trailblazer. Rosie has no choice in this, and I don't think it's in her best interest. I think of it this way: if you sat me down in a class on quantum chemistry and said, "Just learn what you can," I would be frustrated, embarrassed, and bored. Trends come and go in education just as they do in business. My attitude on full inclusion is probably outdated and, to some people, blasphemous. But I can't bear the idea of wasting the time of a child who learns slowly to begin with on a curriculum that doesn't make sense to them.

I won't bore you with any more of the details of this meeting except for its tumultuous end. I am a professional. I have to do things at times that I know will make parents unhappy, disappoint them, and go against what they believe. I had to do it now, and believe me, I didn't want to.

"There is one issue that I feel we should discuss before we all sign off on this IEP," I began. "We've had a few conversations about it during the course of the year, but I feel we need to revisit it." The room was quiet. I had the floor. "I feel very strongly that Rosie should be in a special ed class for math. Her skills are just so far behind those of the kids in her regular ed math class that she can't even follow what's going on. She's lost in there." As I paused for breath, Gretchen jumped in.

"Her name is Rosemary, and that is what I would like you to call her. And she's got a C-plus in math class. She's doing her homework, and she's doing fine on weekly quizzes."

"Gretchen," I pleaded, "she's only doing fine because an adult sits right next to her in class, re-explains everything, shortens her assignments, gives her only the easiest problems, and lets her do them with a calculator. But more importantly, why do we have Rosie multiplying fractions? When is she ever going to use that skill? She needs to be doing things like counting money and using a calculator in more functional ways. She needs to be in a place where she can feel successful instead of feeling confused and embarrassed."

"She needs to be with her peers, learning what they're learning. She will catch on to this math. She just needs a little more time."

I forced myself not to roll my eyes at this fantasy. Meanwhile, nothing from Nathan. We argued back and forth, going over the same old stuff repeatedly and getting pretty pissed off at each other. Finally, Ian came to my rescue.

"It doesn't seem like we're going to be able to resolve this issue today. But it sounds like we've agreed on the goals for Rosemary, so maybe we could think over the issue of class placement and sign the IEP so it can be put in place."

Gretchen agreed to this, as did Nathan. I desperately wanted this meeting to end, but the whole thing stuck in my craw. "I can agree to that," I said, "and I will sign the IEP, but I need to add a sentence saying that I disagree with the placement in regular ed for math."

Gretchen exploded, saying that I would *not* add any such thing to Rosemary's IEP.

I became a mule and said I wouldn't sign. By this time, we were actually yelling at each other. Ian intervened again. We calmed down and, to my amazement, I got to add my sentence about disagreeing and we all signed the IEP, pretty much in stony silence. When Gretchen signed, she immediately got up to leave, huffing her way out of the room without saying another word. Nathan signed, got up, shook hands with Ian and me, thanked us briefly, then left the room.

"Are you okay?" Ian asked me.

Clearly, I was not. I could feel my ears burning, always a sign that my blood pressure is up. "I'm fine," I said while pretending to tear my hair out. "I'm gonna get to class. The kids will calm me down." I gathered up my files and fled the conference room.

Surprisingly, as I walked down the hall, I didn't calm down. I got madder. This bitch had plagued me all year. She had made tons of extra work for me, had nagged me endlessly, and, most importantly, she seemed to be using Rosie to make a point to the world. That was the worst part. This poor kid was working so hard, and she just couldn't do the work that other sixth graders were doing. I knew she was frustrated and miserable in her math class. But her mom had her so well trained that Rosie would *never* complain about it to her.

As I approached my classroom, the bell rang and the kids came pouring out, heading the opposite way for their art, PE, and music classes. I stormed across the room and ferociously flung my files on my desk.

Chapter 6

"Whoa," said Anne. "Bad meeting?"

I stomped back over to the door and closed it so that Ava, Anne, and I were in private. I probably looked a bit comical as I put my hands firmly on my hips, but humor was the furthest thing from my mind. "If I ever thought I could kill another person, I could kill Gretchen Mitchell right now," I said in a marginally controlled voice. "She is the biggest bitch I have ever known in my life."

Ava reacted appropriately with a controlled grin and raised eyebrows. Anne, as always, looked the picture of calm, but I saw a little smirk hovering on her lips. I gave them the gist of the meeting, blowing off steam as they sympathetically listened to my ranting and retelling. Anne is the adult who sits with Rosie every day in math class, so she knows firsthand how bad it is. She actually got her dander up too, and we had fun bashing Gretchen. The two of them got me in a better mood, and finally they decided they needed to hustle off to help the kids in their specials. Naturally, I headed straight for the junk-food machine as soon as they left the room.

As I tried to shake off the meeting and get down to work, I have to admit I was pleased with one thing: I got to add my objection in writing to Rosie's IEP. I knew Gretchen wasn't going to agree to a special ed math class for Rosie. But it was important to me to have it on paper that I thought it was most appropriate for her. So gloating a bit over my one tiny little statement of grievance helped me get over the meeting.

The rest of the day was uneventful, by my standards. Tony was a wild man during social studies. He's *so* tactilely defensive. He just can't tolerate icky stuff like glue. So when we were gluing pictures in a booklet with rubber cement during seventh bell and he got some of the goo on his hands, he sort of went off the deep end, running and jumping around the room, yelling loudly in the midst of our creative mess. Ava managed to get him calmed down enough to take him for a walk. I took pity on him and finished his gluing while he was gone. (Autism is a tough row to hoe. He couldn't help it that the glue grossed him out.) All in a typical day.

As we were cleaning up and the kids were packing up their backpacks to go home, Anne moved to the front of the room and, with her back to the kids, said, "We had an interesting discussion during homeroom this morning." These first twenty minutes of the day are devoted to hearing announcements, checking plan books, getting organized. Most kids are in a homeroom that is also their first bell class, but there are a few exceptions to this. Rosie is one of them. That first twenty minutes of the day is the only time she actually spends in my classroom. We always use five or ten minutes of the time to give the kids a chance to share news, talk with us and with each other a bit, and generally work on their speech and social skills. I had missed the homeroom session that morning on account of being stuck up the hall with The Bitch.

"Oh, really?" I said with interest. "What did you learn today?"

Anne smiled furtively and gave a mock shifty-eyed look around. We are constantly amazed and sometimes horrified at the bits of news the kids will share with the class. The best of all these gems was the time when Basil told us about walking in on his mom having sex with the landlord. We had learned over the year that

April's mom seems never to cook; that Christie's parents sleep in separate bedrooms; and that Freddie's, Rosie's, and Zak's houses are not very secure. We regularly caution the kids to keep some things private, but that's a tough concept for kiddos who may have "mental ages" (to use a bygone term) around five or six.

"Rosie told us all about another big fight her mom and dad had last night. She said they had their bedroom door shut, but she could hear them yelling at each other. She said, 'Dad called Mom a bad name, then he came out of their room and slammed the door, and his face was real red.' I felt bad for her. She was so clearly upset about the whole thing."

"Yeeks. I wonder if that was all about the meeting today? Surely they weren't fighting about that!"

"I wouldn't think so," Anne offered. "Sounded more like marital problems to me."

"Did Rosie say *what* he called her?"

"No. And I didn't want to ask," Anne said with a grin.

I gave a questioning look as we turned back to our students who (oh, yeah) were still there needing our help as we quietly gossiped at the front of the room. We helped them finish getting packed up and shooed them off to their buses, following behind to make sure everyone got up the bus steps and out of our realm of responsibility.

I feel very lucky to have Anne and Ava as my right-hand women. They are far and away the best classroom assistants I have ever had. Both of them would have made great teachers, but I'm very glad they decided to be who they are. The three of us have worked together for six years now, and on our good days, we function like a well-oiled three-part machine.

Anne is four years older than me. At forty-six, she is an experienced mom, dealing well with having her younger of two in our building this year. She is loving and kind and fantastic at working one-on-one with kids. Anne is often the calm in the storm of our classroom. She is so good with adolescent girls, has the patience of Job and a great sense of humor, and is willing to tackle anything I may dream up for her.

Ava is nine years younger than me. At thirty-three, she has three little kids at home and a life so crazy, I don't know how she does it. She is a techno-wizard, which is a good person for a techno-idiot like me to have around. Ava loves the harebrained projects I dream up and always jumps in both feet first to help out. She is also a lover of partying, dancing, and having a good time. Maybe this is because of the three little ones at home. She is good at joking around with the kids, and I'm sure they think she's pretty cool.

I'm sort of the tough-love person in this whole picture. At times I'm surprised the kids even like me because I'm pretty much the enforcer in the classroom. (But there are sure a lot of chinks in my armor.)

Anne and Ava pretty much make their exits right after they get the kids out to their buses. They are paid hourly, not *nearly* enough for all the responsibilities they have and for all they put up with. So I don't blame them for getting out of here as soon as they can. There are lots of teachers who do the same thing, but I nearly always stay for an hour or so after the kids leave, doing all the stuff teachers can't get done during the school day: fine-tuning lessons, grading, updating the endless data-keeping systems teachers are now forced to maintain. Fun stuff.

I moved around the room, cleaning up the minor mess of the day and grabbing my plan book from the front table as well as work the kids had turned in. As I wove my way through the desks, Ian came in. He flashed me his magnificent smile at the same time as he shook his head.

"That was a rough one this morning."

"I'll say. There is just no pleasing that woman."

"No. There sure isn't. She just wants all she can get out of everybody she can get it from."

I laughed, enjoying our shared frustration.

"She was actually back in this afternoon. She just left from a powwow with me." This didn't sound like good news. "I'm afraid she's really out to get you after that meeting." I sighed and plopped my plan book and papers down on the nearest desk with irritation.

"What now?" I asked.

"I think she's going to try to get you reevaluated, Hannah. I'm really afraid she's going to try to get you fired."

"Fired! There's no way." But at the back of my mind, a little bell was tinkling, saying to me, does my tenure really have any meaning? There's been a lot of stuff in the news about school districts getting around it when they want to get rid of a teacher. I mentally grabbed the clapper of that bell to silence it. "What grounds would they have to fire me?"

"Well, the district has put forth a philosophy of inclusion, and Gretchen thinks you don't have that as a priority. And of course, she plans to use your sentence that we added to the IEP as proof of that."

My little sentence that I had been so proud of.

I so wanted to throw a temper tantrum, cuss, fume, and yell. But I couldn't do it in front of Ian. Much as we are friends, it's a professional friendship. This man has probably never cussed or thrown a fit in his life. I would save my fit for later. So instead, I sighed. "Okay. I really appreciate your telling me. At least if I get re-evaled, I'll know where it's coming from."

"No problem. And don't worry about it too much. She may have been just blowing off steam. But she did make a trip over here to share the happy news with me."

"Yeah, great. Thanks for letting me know."

"Okay. Take it easy, Hannah. I know this has been no fun for you."

"You, too. Not exactly a picnic for you, either."

"All in a day," he said, giving me another stunning smile as he turned to leave the room.

I knew it would be a waste for me to try to get anything done now. How quickly I get out of the mood to do the more tedious parts of my job. I scooped my stuff up and piled it haphazardly in my briefcase. I thought momentarily about grabbing a snack to eat on the way home, but decided ranting in the car would be more satisfying. And rant I did. I drove home, calling Gretchen Mitchell every name I could think of. I combined *bitch* with every curse word I had ever heard. When I ran out of curse words, I started being more inventive: scurvy bitch, vile bitch, repulsive bitch. I found myself smiling, calming down a bit as I pulled into my driveway. Waiting for the garage door to go up, I glanced up to see Stella out on her porch, waving at me. I gave her a little wave as I pulled in.

Upstairs, Rascal and I ventured outside. The combination of unconditional love and joy in seeing me that he gave, along with walking around the yard, helped me to calm down a little bit more. I didn't really think there was any use worrying about what Gretchen *might* do. I would just wait and see what happened. It was a gray, chilly day, and I snuck back up the stairs to my porch, leaving Rascal to sniff around. My phone was ringing as I came in. I tracked the sound back to my purse and picked up, smiling when I saw that it was Stella.

Chapter 7

The four-family that I live in looks very typical from the outside, like any other brown brick, two up, two down, built in the early fifties. But it has some inner novelty and an ideal setup for me, as well, I think, as for my three tenants. The driveway runs along the side of the house, then around to the back, where it expands to the width of the four single-car garages nestled under the building. The apartments are standard two bedrooms, except that each has a good-sized dining room because it was built in the fifties, when people were still civil enough to eat at the dining room table together. The best thing about the apartments is that each has a screened-in porch off the smaller bedroom. Since the garages are under the house, even the first-floor porches are up off the ground. One of the first-floor apartments has stairs from the porch down to the backyard, which is fenced in. This was what sold me on the place. One of the first things I did when I moved in was to replace the lowest portion of screen in my outer porch door with a screen-flap, a doggy door. Now all I have to do is open the door from my apartment to the porch, and Rascal can access the backyard. This lets him get out there quick to do his business when I get home. I usually have some business of my own to do when I first get in, but I like to join him and walk around the backyard, dodging the piles of dog poo like they're live mines.

When I bought the four-family, it came with three tenants who have all stayed. On the first floor is a quiet divorcee in his fifties. He is the ideal tenant, neat, quiet, and uncomplaining. Above him lives another divorcee, probably in her late forties. She is also undemanding, although she did complain last summer that her place needed painting. When I looked it over, I was embarrassed at how bad it looked and took a couple of days to paint the whole place. They both seem to lead pretty solitary lives, and I wonder sometimes if they wouldn't enjoy each other's company. Or maybe they do. Sometimes at night, I think I hear the stairs squeaking that separate the two floors. Is that Steve sneaking up to ravage Kathy? Or her sneaking down to hop in bed with him? This line of thinking always gives me the giggles. Remember, I work with adolescents. They tend to rub off on you.

Or is the squeak caused by Stella, returning from the neighborhood bar down the street after tipping a few too many? Stella is my third tenant. She lives directly above me and provides quite a contrast to Steve and Kathy. She's a unique one. Stella is proud to tell anyone that she is seventy-eight years old. She often acts like she's eighteen, a trait I sometimes admire and sometimes could throttle her for. She is constantly calling me upstairs to do things like knock down a spider web she can't reach; check for mice in the attic; or repair this, that, or the other thing. But she reciprocates by watching the building during the day while the rest of us are at work, by letting in people (such as the satellite guy) whom we'd normally wait all day for, and by occasionally being an ear for me to bend or a shoulder to cry on. And there's also the baked goods, but I'll get to those later.

Stella is, and I imagine always has been, a sight to behold. There are pictures in her apartment of her as a younger woman, startlingly pretty, in a creamy-skinned, fiery red-haired, beautiful smiley way that some young women have. She looks so full of life in those pictures, and she sure hasn't changed in that way. As an almost octogenarian, she still has the beautiful smile, keeps her hair a shocking shade of bright orange, and generally wears bright colors, mixed haphazardly. We're talking red sweaters with purple pants. Green shirt with orange shorts. You can always see Stella coming from a long way off. She would make a great cartoon character, Startling Stella. She has a cadre of old lady friends whom she refers to as the Blue-Haired Babes. She lunches, golfs, and plays pinochle with them (a game she has chastised me repeatedly for never learning to play).

She also has no reservations about taking herself down to the neighborhood dive just two short blocks away and sitting on a barstool all evening, drinking Manhattans. I tried to do this one night with her and discovered that Manhattans are really strong and really awful. I opted for beer after the first one, but she sat there and drank three of the things. The two of us toddled home with me wondering if she could have made it on her own. But as I chatted with the bartender a week later while picking up a carryout dinner (the place has great fried chicken,) he told me Stella comes in there fairly regularly to sit on her barstool at the end of the bar and drink her three Manhattans. What a woman.

But in her own little apartment, Stella has only ever offered me tea to drink. I confess I've spent more than a few hours up in her place, leisurely killing time, chatting when I should have been working.

Now I grabbed my phone in time to catch her call. "Hey, Stella. What's up?"

"Hello, Hannah. I hope I'm not bothering you, but I have three light bulbs burned out in my chandelier, and I can't move that big table by myself to change them."

"Do you have light bulbs?"

"Yes, I got them on sale at Wally World last week." I now got a long-winded description of the sale, which I won't bore you with.

"Okay, Stella. I'll be right up."

She was waiting for me at the door, adorned all in black that day except for her hot-pink shoes and a pink-and-turquoise scarf.

"Stella, you look hot!" I teased.

"You like? I'm going down to Charlie's Chicken Joint for dinner with the Babes. They have a live band after dinner, and there may be dancing." She smiled coyly at me as she shuffled a few steps.

I chuckled as I entered her apartment and went through to the dining room. With three bulbs burned out, her chandelier had only two left burning.

"Jeez, it's dark in here. You should have called me sooner. How can you even see?"

"Well, I never eat in here, so I didn't really notice it until I tried to do something at the table. Then I realized another bulb or two had burned out."

I quickly changed the bulbs, which didn't even require moving the table. I just stood on a chair, leaning maybe a bit precariously over the huge table as I unscrewed the dead bulbs and put new ones in.

"Oh, thank you so much. That's much better," Stella said as she moved into the kitchen. I knew the best part was coming now. Yes! She returned from the kitchen with a plate of cookies.

"I baked these chocolate chip pecan cookies today. Will you have one?"

Of course I would have one, or two, or five. Stella is a wonderful baker, and she knows I am an appreciative recipient. She had probably baked today, knowing full well that she'd call me and I'd come up. And that was fine with me. We chatted a bit as I wolfed down cookies.

"What's with the cutting board and the belt, Stella?" I said, noticing a huge leather belt lying across a cutting board on her dining room table.

"I was trying to put another hole in that belt because it's too big for me. Isn't it glorious?" she added, picking it up and putting it around her waist to show off the buckle, a large brass eagle in flight, complete with a rhinestone eye. "I got it for two bucks at a garage sale over on Woodford."

"It's something else, all right. How were you going to put a new hole in the leather?"

"With this," she said, brandishing a steak knife that I hadn't seen. "But it wasn't working. I guess the knife isn't sharp enough."

"I think it's just the wrong tool," I said with a laugh, knowing it would have been the first thing I tried, too. "I've got just the thing for that. I'll run down and get it." As I went down the two flights of steps to the garage, I chuckled at the thought of Stella decked out in that horrid belt. So her.

My huge old Craftsman tool chest is a prized possession that I inherited from my father when he passed away a few years back. It's the type with the lift-up lid that locks the whole box when you put the lid down. My father would not be proud of the fact that I never close that lid. Leaving it open gives me access to the screwdrivers, pliers, and other stuff in the lower drawers without having to open the top of the box. I scrounged through the open top for the awl, an ancient tool I had probably only ever used once or twice, but the sight of which always made me think of my dad. He used it often to create tiny holes to start wood screws in, but I don't know what else you'd ever use an awl for except poking holes in leather. So here was my big chance to use it again. The awl has always lived in that top miscellaneous part of the chest, but I couldn't lay my hands on it right now as I sifted through the metal tape measures, carpet knife, tire gauge, pencils, etc. I paused in mid-search and thought for a minute. Maybe I had moved it? I went quickly through the drawers of the chest but found no awl.

"Weird," I said to the empty garage. "Oh, well." I ran back up to Stella's apartment and told her I couldn't find it right now, but to hold off on further efforts with the steak knife. I was afraid she'd cut herself instead of the belt. I promised her I'd put a hole in the belt if she'd let me take it with me. She gave it to me grudgingly, as if I might not give it back. Fat chance. I gave her a quick hug and left with the belt in one hand and a couple of cookies for the road in the other.

Chapter 8

Thursday, March 14th

I hadn't heard anything else about the previous day's IEP meeting and was glad to forget about it. It had been a blissfully uneventful morning. The kids were being their more charming selves, being nice to each other, working up to their abilities, making me feel like just maybe I wasn't the shitty teacher I sometimes feel like. I celebrated by treating myself to a full lunch instead of my usual fifteen-minute gobble followed by errand running or scrambling to put the afternoon together.

Stopping in the office on the way back to my room, I pulled the usual pile of junk out of my mailbox and dumped most of it in the handy trash can Sam had placed right under the mailboxes. I saved one lowly piece of paper that actually had some importance. Next, I stopped by Julia's desk to say hello and ask her a quick question.

In case you didn't know, the school secretary is the person who really runs any school building, and Julia does a damn fine job of it. Right then, she had a little posse of office helpers behind her desk, and she was doling out assignments to them like a drill sergeant, except that she thanked them and called these gawky eighth-grade boys sugar, sweetie, and darlin', smiling as she sent them off on their rounds. She sat down and twirled in her chair to face me with a gracious smile on her face.

"Hi, Hannah honey. What can I do for you today?"

"Hey, Julia. I was just wondering," I said as I kept a blank expression on my face, "if you've heard anything about another meeting with Gretchen Mitchell?"

Without replying, she looked sneakily to her right, at Andrew's office, where the door was closed. Then she got up and came around the desk, peeking down the hall to Ian's office. His door was also closed. She came conspiratorially close to me and waggled her eyebrows up and down comically.

I felt myself grinning. No doubt, she had a gem to bestow on me. "There's no meeting that I know of, but there sure were some raised voices in Ian's office yesterday," she semi-whispered.

On more than one occasion, I have seen Julia leaning an ear toward either Andrew or Ian's office doors with a finger to her lips. She is totally obvious when she does this, which makes it even funnier. I guess if you are in the business of running a building, you need to know what's going on in it.

"She was in there after your meeting, saying she was gonna do this and that and he couldn't stop her. He was the one who really surprised me because he was just about *barking* back at her. Ian! Mr. Cool, Calm, and Collected. I could hear how mad he was by his voice, and you know that's not like him. He said he didn't wanna hear any more about it and she didn't have that much power, this had gone on for too long, and he was tired of her threats." Julia mimicked Ian by putting a hand on her hip and looking very stern. She never fails to crack me up. "Then she got all huffy and I could tell she was gettin' ready to storm out of there, so I thought I best skedaddle back to my desk."

God, I love this woman. She is always such a wealth of information, shares it with delight, and yet is surprisingly discreet. That may sound like sarcasm, but I mean it. I knew Julia wouldn't share this tidbit with anyone but me because she knew it wasn't anyone else's business but mine. I took it all in, knowing exactly what the fight was about. I was touched to hear how angry Ian was with her. He was standing up for me. I wondered how far up the ladder she had already gone with this bullshit about getting me fired. I knew I was not in any real danger of losing my job, but Gretchen could undoubtedly brew up a huge amount of torment in my professional life. The thought of having my work put under someone's microscope wasn't my idea of fun.

"That bitch," I said, to Julia's delight. "God, she loves to stir up trouble."

"Oh, honey, you should have seen the look on Ian's face when he came out of his office a few minutes later. There was a storm a-brewin'." She shook her head. Done imparting her gem, she began straightening the piles of fliers and notices along the high counter that separates her desk from the traffic that moves through the office.

"Thanks, Julia. You're the best little spy I know," I said as I turned to head back to my room.

We had a planned lockdown seventh bell, the last bell of the day. It's a sad commentary on today's world that schoolkids have gotten used to drills of what we would do if some wacko comes into our school, but that's the reality of life in 2019. The lockdown was to take place in the last twenty minutes of the school day so the kids could go pretty much straight to their buses and home when it was over. The end-of-day timing would also cut down on student chatter about the whole thing.

Lockdowns are usually pretty uneventful and really only a minor pain in the butt. In this case, since it was scheduled at the end of the day, we were allowed to tell the kids in advance that it was going to happen, and they went to their lockers in the middle of the bell so that, as I said, they could leave immediately when it was done. As they came back from their lockers, I reminded them that the lockdown would start in a few minutes. Did anyone need to use the restroom? Josh said he had to go, and he headed up the hall. I was a little concerned about Chloe on account of her restroom reluctance. Some kids who have autism have a real hard time getting moving. That's Chloe. It just seems like once she's in a spot where she's comfortable, it's difficult to make that transition of getting on her feet again. I compare it to that point I sometimes get to in the evening when I feel like I'm too tired to get off the couch and go to bed. I guess it's all part of how her sensory systems are wired. It's hard to get inside the head of a child who has autism, but I try to do it every day.

So anyway, at this point, as the kids were settling back in their seats, I made sure I was within Chloe's earshot and said to Anne, "I think I'll go use the restroom real quick before we're locked in."

Sure enough, Chloe popped out of her seat and said, "I have to go pee, Ms. H," as if it were her idea. I caught Anne's eye and gave her a wink as Chloe and I left the room together.

During a lockdown, the teacher locks the classroom door and no one is allowed in or out of the room. We're supposed to carry on business as usual during the fifteen or twenty minutes we're locked in. While we are doing that, the administrators go around the building, checking to make sure all the doors are locked and nobody is in the halls, and I suppose doing other administrative stuff that I don't know (or care) about. The whole point is that this is what we'd do if, as I said, some wacko came into the building.

Down in the bathroom, I hustled through my routine, wanting to get back to the room quickly and hoping Chloe would do the same. But as I was drying my hands, she was still in her stall.

"I'm heading back to the room," I called out, hoping that would get her going.

"Uh-huh," she said.

Rats. Apparently she was going to sit for a spell, and I had learned long ago (the hard way, as is my custom) that there is no use trying to rush Chloe. She'd wander down to the room shortly on her own, I hoped.

I had only been back in the room for about two minutes when the announcement came that we were to lock our doors. I did so, knowing that obviously I would cheat and let Chloe in when I heard her at the door. The door has a window in it, for heaven's sake. I would know it was her and not some wacko.

The other eight kids were all in their seats, and I began explaining a project we were going to start tomorrow. Each of them was going to make a model of a castle. I went into some detail, showing them the materials they'd be using and explaining that their castle had to have turrets, a moat, a keep, etc. I knew this would catch their interest and keep their minds off the lockdown, and I was right. My only concern was that a good ten minutes had gone by, and Chloe wasn't back from the bathroom yet. Finally, we heard her at the door, and Anne went to let her in.

As she went to her seat, Basil started in on her.

"You're in trouble. Nobody is supposed to be in the hall when it's a lockdown."

Wham! Chloe pushed her desk over and stood, looking defiantly at him. This was not a good omen.

When Chloe goes off the deep end, we try to react calmly and keep the other kids away from her. Anne went immediately into action.

"Chloe, why don't you come sit over here by me?" she said, indicating an empty desk across the room. Chloe did not budge.

"But she wasn't allowed out in the hall," insisted Basil, as if *he* is one to follow rules all the time.

I crooked my finger at him in a "come here" gesture, and he pouted his way up to the front of the room and sat at an empty desk next to me. I quietly told him that all was well, that I would talk to Chloe about her behavior and not to worry about it, hoping it was the truth.

Basil nodded his head and managed a pretty good downcast look. He has a beautiful lower lip, just built for pouting, and right before my eyes, it grew into a fat sausage. And I didn't blame him a bit, because of course he was right. Life really isn't fair. Meanwhile, Chloe stood by her tipped-over desk with a little black cloud over her head and a scowl on her face.

The other kids were only mildly fazed by this. Tony quickly got out of his seat and headed for the rocking chair, where he began rocking at a pretty high rate. He, too, is autistic, and he is not a lover of raised voices. But they had seen it all before and weren't very impressed by the hubbub. I went back to my explanation of the upcoming project and started letting the kids come up to the front of the room to choose the materials they wanted. Anne and I helped them to get what they needed, keeping an eye on Chloe, who finally sat down, looking a bit forlornly, I thought, at her tipped-over desk. As April returned to her seat, Chloe got up and made a move to tip over her desk as well.

"Chloe," I said sharply, startling her into inaction. I walked back and righted her desk, and that seemed to end it all. She and I would talk about the behavior after class. A moment later, she, too, came to the front of the room for supplies as if nothing had ever happened. Each of the kids did their best to put their name on a box, pile in their supplies, and put it on the long shelf under the windowed wall of the room, to be started tomorrow. As we were finishing, there was a knock at the door and the sound of a key in the lock. The door opened. Ian stepped in.

"You're bad! You're not allowed in the halls," chimed Chloe as she jumped out of her seat and approached him, shaking a finger in his face. I could see she was ready to shove over another desk.

Ian, of course, was taken aback by her behavior and sent a questioning look my way as he stepped back. I have always suspected that he is just a little bit afraid of my kiddos and their often unpredictable behavior.

"We're just having a little fallout from the lockdown," I commented. And to Chloe, "It's okay now, Chloe. The lockdown is over."

"No, he's bad, and I've had all of this I can take." She was a dog with a bone, shaking her finger at him again. But I had a hard time suppressing a smile.

Many kids who have autism exhibit a habit known as echolalia. This simply means they repeat what other people say, especially the last thing they say. In fact, they can't *help* but repeat it at times. A wise teacher can use this to her advantage if she chooses. For example, Chloe doesn't like to work on writing skills because they are difficult for her. So I can say to her, "Do you want to go for a walk first or practice writing?"

She will probably answer "practice writing" simply because it was the last thing I said. I know this is not her *real* choice. So am I just a mean teacher? No. (Well, maybe sometimes, yes, but not right here.) I'll let her go for the walk after she does her writing, but I want the writing practice done, and I also want her to think about what she says before she answers a question like this. I've seen this work with her over time, especially if I show her pictures of the two activities she's choosing between. So where she is the queen of repeating phrases she hears from adults, without maybe really knowing what she's saying, I've seen that in time she will begin to use a phrase more and more appropriately. Right then, for a kid whose testable IQ is somewhere south of forty, I thought this was a very good time to comment that she'd "had all she could take." I was getting pretty close to that point, too.

Glancing up at the clock, I saw that the bell would ring in one minute. "You all did a great job during the lockdown, so I'm going to let you get a head start for the buses. See you tomorrow." They all grabbed their backpacks and made a beeline for the door, calling out goodbyes and waving as they left. I knew this wouldn't get Chloe moving, but I thought that getting a few people out of the room might calm her down. Anne and Ava went along to make sure everyone found their bus. Chloe stood her ground. She glared at Ian with a dark look on her face, displacing her anger at the situation onto him. He was simply doing a room-to-room check of how the lockdown had gone. I told him we had had no problems—no reason to bore him with Chloe's late return from the restroom. It really made no difference in the long run. As Ian nodded and turned to leave the room, Chloe got one last jab in.

"You're in big trouble, buster!"

He slipped out of the room without acknowledging her. I shook my head, wondering where she had heard that one.

"Chloe," I scolded gently, "I think everyone has heard enough from you. That's not the way you should talk to adults. It's all over with, and we won't have any more lockdowns for a while. I also don't expect to see you pushing over any more desks. That is not acceptable behavior." (Mental note to self: make a plan for Chloe before we have another lockdown.) "Would you like me to go to your locker with you?" She looked away from me but took the reproof calmly. Dropping her head, she went out to her locker without comment.

I followed her out into the hall. She stood at her locker, but didn't make any move to open it. Again with the difficult transitions. Changing classes, going to and from the bus, getting things out, putting them away—all of these present challenges that most of us don't even see as change. We had been using a picture schedule for Chloe throughout the afternoon, but the change of routine caused by the lockdown, I guessed, was just too much for her. I opened her locker and helped her into her coat. Helped her get her backpack on, all the time acting calm and making conversation about what she might do when she got home, all the time hoping we wouldn't hold up the string of buses from leaving on time. I turned to walk out with her, as I did most every day, and thankfully she followed me.

I sighed as I returned to my classroom. Sometimes kids like Chloe are such a challenge to figure out that I just have to tuck them into the back of my brain to puzzle over later. My workday was done, and my troubles were at least temporarily over. Little did I know what was awaiting me in the girls' restroom.

Chapter 9

Friday, March 15th

When the clock finally showed five thirty, I dragged myself out of bed and went through my usual rituals: shower, makeup, clothes, short walk with Rascal, grab what I thought of as breakfast to eat on the road, and get out of the house by a quarter to seven. I did pretty well on the way to work, focusing on the day ahead of me, as I usually do (instead of on my nightlong vision of a dead body in a pool of blood).

I was having a real problem in the mornings with the kids at their lockers. Lockers are such a prime place for fallout. Kids are jammed together, in a hurry, trying to put in or pull out giant backpacks from skinny lockers. It's a setup rife with opportunities for altercations. I needed to figure out who was the instigator in what too often turned out to be a locker-door-slamming, book-throwing, voice-raising melee outside my classroom. I suspected April and, taking a professional attitude, thought maybe she needed some help in the mornings that she wasn't getting. I would be in the hall to greet her this morning and help her get a successful start on the day.

As I unlocked my classroom door, I noticed that Pen, my neighbor down the hall, was already there with her classroom door ajar, a sure sign that she was open to company. Of course, she had probably been up the hall to the office. Seen the crime scene tape. Heard the story.

Penelope Warren is a gem. She is my role model of a teacher. Well into her sixties, she still has the energy and enthusiasm of a young teacher. She works her ass off—well, not literally. She is actually pretty broad in the beam. But she toils tirelessly for her kids. Pen is the ESL (English as a second language) teacher in our building. Kids come to her classroom from all over the world, often knowing little or no English. She gives them a place that is safe and comfortable in the confusing world of their school day. Each of them is with her for only two bells a day. The rest of the day, they are in regular classes, where they may or may not have any understanding of what is being said. She has way too many kids on her caseload and in her classes, too many teachers to deal with, and she does it all with a shrug and a smile on her face. Pen would be an excellent person for me to tell my little story to. To practice on.

I put my purse away in my desk drawer, pulled my lesson plan book out of my briefcase (which I had carted home last night but not delved into,) opened the plan book for that week, and laid it on my desk. Some teachers hardly use their plan books, but since I teach so many subjects, I have to use mine or I'll forget where we are. Ava and Anne use it frequently too. So even though my desk usually looks like where havoc struck, my plan book is always open atop the mess.

I headed down to Pen's room.

"Good morning, Hannah," Pen greeted me as I walked in.

"Hi, Pen," I said as I sat on top of a student desk with my feet on the seat in front of it. She was busy stapling student work to a bulletin board in symmetrical rows. Pen's room is a busy place, but always neat as a pin. The walls aren't plastered with stuff, like in some classrooms, because she knows that would overwhelm her kids. But there are always a few interesting things on display to attract attention. This morning there was a bowl of about ten different kinds of fruit on the table where she often works with small groups, from the ordinary banana, orange, and apple to a few I wasn't sure of. Mango? Guava? Ugli? Her students would leave that day with new vocabulary that some US citizens don't know.

"How are you today?" she asked as she picked up another paper, held it up to the board, eyeballed it for placement, then hammered it in with the stapler. So like Pen to act like this was just another day. Always calm.

"Um, not so good. Have you been up to the office yet this morning?"

"Yes," she said, turning to face me. "There's yellow tape down the hall by the girls' room, and several police officers are standing around, apparently waiting . . . I don't know what or whom for."

Oh, shit. Not for me, I hoped.

She continued. "I heard on the news this morning that a woman was found dead in our building yesterday, sometime after school." She said all of this matter-of-factly as she turned back to staple up the next paper, again making sure it was perfectly in line with those before it.

"Yeah," I said. "Well, I'm the one who found her, and she wasn't just dead. She was murdered."

This stopped her in her tracks, the bottom half of the stapler dangling from her hand as she turned to look at me. "Oh, my goodness, Hannah. How awful for you."

I told her the whole tale, which I found I was getting good at. She oohed and ahhed appropriately and then interjected her wisdom into the situation. "How dreadful for you. But you're such a strong person, and I'm sure you handled it well." If she only knew. "Just think how horrible it would have been for one of our young girls if they had been the one to discover her."

56

Selfish me. I hadn't even thought of that. Can you imagine some twelve- or fourteen-year-old girl seeing what I had seen? The sight would be with me for a long time, but hopefully it wasn't going to change my life. For an adolescent girl, it could cause enough angst to put a shrink's kid through college. And that made me mad. The nerve of someone to do something like that where a kid might be the first to happen on it. But I put my ire on the back burner for now. Pen's faith in me was bolstering.

"You're absolutely right," I said, feeling a little better. "Thanks, Pen. You're always such a source of sanity."

"Oh, Hannah, it's scary that you'd think of *me* that way. I always feel like I have such a tenuous grasp on it."

"Ha! You're saner than most." I bid her thanks and goodbye and hustled down the hall to my room to get ready for the kiddos.

As I left Pen's room and headed down the hall, I saw Sam coming my way, pushing his huge, wide hall mop. He stopped, leaning on the mop as I had seen him do a hundred times.

"So how's the star witness this morning?"

"Okay, I guess," I said with a shrug.

"What time did you finally get home last night?" he asked with a sympathetic tone.

"I think it was around seven thirty," I said and shrugged. I had slowed my pace, but didn't really want to stop and talk. I had stuff to do and wanted to get out of the hall before I ran into any other staff.

Sam leaned in confidentially and said in a low voice, "Have they figured out who it was yet?"

"No, not that I know of," I said, surprised that he would ask that. "Gotta go." I gave him a little wave and headed on.

"Have a good one, Hannah," he said in parting. He really is a sweetie.

Not five minutes later, like wildfire, the news of my discovery the day before hit. I was inundated with teachers in and out of my room, asking questions, getting details, providing sympathy, and showing morbid curiosity. Don't get me wrong, the people I work with are my social group. My friends. My extended family. Their intentions were good, but I needed to get through the morning more than I needed sympathy, and they were taking up my prep time. It was like a dark little party was going on in my classroom, and it went on until I heard the first students starting down the hall. My peers dispersed quickly, knowing that if they didn't get to their rooms, there would be adolescent anarchy, always a bad way to start the day.

I could hear Anne out in the hall, helping the kids at their lockers, so I stayed in the room, greeting them as they came in. (How quickly I had abandoned my good intentions to help April at her locker.) As they drifted in one by one, each of the kiddos approached me; in fact, they crowded around me, with bits of news, questions, and complaints about other kids.

"Billy is throwing rocks at me at the bus stop again, Ms. H. I'm gonna beat his ass," from Josh. And then a quick change of subject: "I got a new Xbox game last night." Of course, I had to ask him to repeat this the usual three times before I caught on to what he was saying. His pantomime of the game helped. Josh wears two hearing aids, but what he gets from them is pretty distorted due to his severe hearing loss, so his speech is also distorted. "It's really cool," I caught on the first try.

"I had chicken for dinner last night." This from April, who must have had her usual uneventful evening.

The bell sounded and they all took their seats like the angels they only seldom are. I noted that Ava had not come in, yet Chloe had made it to class. That usually didn't happen without a bit of prodding from Ava. Oh well, I thought. She probably went for an extra cup of coffee. No biggie. I noticed that Rosie was absent and sent up a quick prayer for her on account of her leaky heart issues. For a moment, the kids had made me forget the horrors of the day before. But as I heard Ian's voice starting the morning announcements over the PA system with his brief remark about the front girls' restroom being closed until further notice, it all came sickeningly back to me. Amazing how the mention of something, or even just a sound, a smell, or a taste, can conjure up visual memories. The human mind is quite an amazing thing. Now my stomach literally turned over, and a millisecond later, the mental image of the woman propped up in the bathroom stall came to me. I was astounded at the sudden feeling that I might vomit.

As I fought that impulse, Chloe popped up out of her seat, hands over her ears, and started pacing around the back of the room, as far from the intercom as she could get. I glanced at Tony, who also hated loud noise, but it wasn't bothering him any more than usual. He just sat, rocking and glaring at the intercom. Every now and then, someone turns up the volume on the office sound system (probably at the request of teachers whose kids can't hear announcements over the chaos in their homeroom) and I then go ask them to lower the volume a notch so it won't drive my autistic kids crazy. Others might not even notice the change in volume, but some of my kiddos do. Anne went to Chloe to make sure she got back to her seat as the announcements ended. Chloe got in the last word as she pointed to the intercom and said, "I hate him."

Anne looked up at me with a smirk over Chloe's comment (since we *all* hate the morning announcements), but when she made eye contact with me, she said, "Are you all right? You're white as a ghost."

59

"I'm fine," I lied as I repeatedly swallowed the saliva pooling in my mouth in an effort to keep my breakfast down. Good Lord! I had never realized what a wimp I am.

I proceeded through the first part of the morning as usual, or as close to usual as I could muster. As the bell rang to signal the end of the twenty-minute homeroom, Ava came in and spoke quietly to Anne, who then left the room. I gave Ava a questioning look from across the room, and she signaled me with a raised finger, a flaring of her nostrils, tight lips, and a tilt of her head. I love her expressions. From all that, I knew she was aggravated and she'd tell me all about it in a minute.

The kids are well trained to get up and get a book at the beginning of reading class. They have five minutes of silent reading each day. For some, this means just looking at a picture book quietly, and for others, there are real attempts to read. This little pause in time allows us to set up for group work, which we pull the kids into one at a time. It sets the mood for quiet work. But this morning Ava and I met at the back of the room as the kids obediently opened their books.

"There are two cops up in the front office," Ava whispered a bit frantically. "Ian grabbed me as I came in with Chloe and made me go up and talk to them. He wouldn't even let me come in and tell you where I was going."

"That's okay. I knew you'd come back sooner or later." I smiled, trying to calm her down.

"They asked me a bunch of questions, then said I had to send Anne up next," she added.

"Was it Tweedledee and Tweedledum?"

"Huh? Who?"

"I mean, um . . ." I had to think a minute to come up with the two detectives' real names. "Kennedy and Appledom?"

"Maybe. I don't know. They wanted to know all about you. How long I've known you, what you're like to work with, stuff like that." She stopped rather suddenly and pursed her lips inward as if to stop the flow of words. I tried not to be taken aback, but it looked like such an obvious gesture to keep from saying more. Who would not want to work with me? Wasn't I delightful—most of the time?

"Don't worry," I said, patting her on the arm. "They're just doing their job. We'll talk about it later. Let's get going before the natives get restless." We modified our plans quickly, assuming Anne would be gone for a while, got the kids into two groups, and got to work. I tried to get involved with the kids, but my heart just wasn't in it. My mind was reeling just a bit over the idea that the police were asking questions about me. Anne returned to the room about halfway through the fifty-minute bell, and we actually got some work done. Tony was starting to make real progress with his iPad, and it was so gratifying to see him concentrating on things productively and able to show, at least somewhat, how much he knew. It was he who got me focused that morning.

I was relieved when the kids left for their art, music, and PE classes. I dug around in the pen tray of my middle desk drawer until I found a handful of loose change. Then I headed straight for the junk-food machine in the teachers' lounge, where I purchased peanut M&Ms, a regular part of my diet because of their protein content. I added a diet cola and a bag of barbecue chips (veggies to go with the protein) and returned to my desk, where I quickly inhaled it all before remembering that I had planned to start eating right today. Oh, well. Today was a day for comfort, not willpower. I had just started getting productive again when Ian appeared in the doorway of my room.

"You okay?" he asked without any preliminaries.

"Yeah, I'm fine," I fibbed through a smile. But I could feel my eyes filling with tears. What a sissy, I thought. I've got to get over these stupid physical reactions. He perched his tiny right butt cheek on the corner of my desk. Seeing that helped me feel a little better.

"Anyone would be upset after what you saw yesterday."

"I know. But I just wish I could get it out of my mind," I whined as I jerked a tissue out of the box on my desk and began dabbing at my tears. "It was just so horrible."

"I know it must have been. And I'm sorry to dredge it up again, but those two detectives are in my office. They've just asked me a few more questions, and now they want to talk to you one more time."

"Right this minute?" I asked stupidly, grabbing another tissue to blow my nose, which was now running like a faucet on account of the copious number of tears I was producing. So attractive. I bet Ian never gets a runny nose.

He was obviously waiting for me, so I dragged myself out of the chair, out the door, and up toward the office. He tried small talk on the way down the green mile, but it fell dead on my emotionally overloaded ears.

He escorted me into the conference room, where Kennedy and Appledom were waiting for me. They each had their little notepads on the table in front of them. They had taken the far side of the table. As Ian started to leave the room, I stopped him, putting a hand on his arm.

"Hold on a sec, Ian." I turned toward the two detectives. "Can he sit in on this meeting as my advocate?" They looked at me blankly, so I hurried on. "Yesterday, when I was downtown, a woman came into that little cell and offered to be an advocate for me. I told her no, but now I want an advocate. I want Ian. I know him. I'm comfortable with him."

The two of them conferred quietly for a moment, with Kennedy doing the talking and Appledom nodding, then giving a one-shouldered shrug.

"I guess that would be okay, although it's unusual," said Kennedy. "Are you agreeable to that, sir?"

"Sure," said Ian, giving me a tiny smile and taking a seat at the end of the table. The conference room we were in is the typical airless, windowless area that we've all been in, a small room that somehow, someone has magically squeezed a huge conference table into, complemented by huge cushioned chairs on wheels. The chairs, also too big for the room, run into each other and into the wall every time they are moved. The cops had a view of the door, but I had a view of the room's only redeeming quality; a print of Van Gogh's *Undergrowth with Two Figures*, probably put there by a guidance counselor. If things got dicey, I could just escape into Van Gogh's woods, and I felt a little better with Ian in the room.

Chapter 10

"Ms. Hutchinson, we have a few more questions for you about the events of yesterday," Kennedy began very soberly. (Really? Oh, gee, I thought this was just a social visit. Boy, did I feel antagonistic.)

"You told us you found the victim at 4:02. Is that correct?"

"Um, yes," I said, offering no more.

"But your call came into the 911 center at 4:17. Why did you wait so long to call?"

"I didn't wait. I called right away," I said without even thinking.

"That's fifteen minutes, Ms. Hutchinson. That's a significant amount of time."

Why *had* it taken me so long? "Are you sure about the time I called?" I asked.

"Yes. That's recorded by our computers. Are you sure about the time you found the victim?"

"Well, I checked my watch." And I did it again as I said it—a subconscious gesture.

"Is that the watch you had on yesterday?"

"Yes," I said. Appledom, who sat directly across from me, peeked at my wrist as I edged it toward him so he could see. He took a gander, then consulted his phone, laying it on the table.

"Time's accurate," he commented.

"So, Ms. Hutchinson, it took you fifteen minutes to call 911. What were you doing in all that time?"

"Well, I took her pulse, and I tried to rouse her." Okay, that last part was an out-and-out lie. I knew darn well she was dead when I first saw her. "Then I tried to get into the office, but it was locked. So then I had to come down to my room." I was *not* going to tell them that I puked, had a good cry, and cleaned myself up before I called 911. They would think I was nuts. They would think I was a weepy, weak woman. "I couldn't find my phone, and I had to hunt around for it for a few minutes before I called." Another lie. What was I thinking? You're *never* supposed to lie to the cops. I watch lots of crime shows. I know the cops always figure it out.

"Did you call 911 on your cell phone?"

Oops. Bad lie. "No. I was flustered. It didn't occur to me to call on the landline until I couldn't find my cell phone." They looked at me blankly. Then their heads turned simultaneously toward each other. And into my head again popped Tweedledee and Tweedledum. I managed to control a smirk, but just barely.

Kennedy looked down at his notes. "You told us yesterday that you don't know the victim. Is that correct?"

"No. I mean, yes. I don't know her."

"Are you sure about that?"

"Well, I don't think I do. She didn't look familiar to me."

"The victim is Gretchen Mitchell."

I was dumbfounded and actually felt my mouth drop open. I said nothing for a few seconds, then, "What? Who?"

"Gretchen Mitchell is the victim."

"Th-that can't be. I know Gretchen," I stammered.

"We're aware of that. That's why we're wondering why you told us you didn't know her."

My mind went back to those horrible moments of the day before, pushing the stall door open, peeking in, squeezing in to try to take her pulse, her stare, the blood, her lips. "She looked so awful. Her color. She was so gray. Her lips were purple. Half of her face was covered in blood." Now I was so close to tears, I could hear the quiver in my voice. They waited. "I guess I didn't really look at her very closely. But she was in a sweatsuit. Gretchen would never wear a sweatsuit to the school." Kennedy made a note on his tiny notepad. Then he sat and looked at me. Appledom made no notes. He also sat looking at me.

The silence in the room made my ears ring.

"Hannah, it's okay." This was the first time Ian had spoken. "I'm sure the detectives can understand and have some sympathy for how seeing Gretchen like that must have been quite a shock to you." He said this pointedly and looked from one of them to the other. They both shifted in their seats. Never mess with an assistant principal. They are the disciplinarians in schools, and they know how to make anyone squirm.

"How well did you know Mrs. Mitchell?" Kennedy asked.

"Well, her daughter Rosie has been in my class this year," I began. "I've had numerous meetings with Gretchen over that time. I only know her professionally. Knew her," I corrected myself.

"And did you get along with her?"

"We got along in a professional way. I can't say I was close to her. Gretchen was a pretty demanding parent." I paused for a tick, trying to think before I blabbed too quickly. "She could be a bit difficult to deal with at times."

"In what way?"

"She wanted the best for her daughter, and she wasn't shy about asking for it. Sometimes the things she asked for were difficult for us to provide. Sometimes she and I had different opinions about what Rosie needed." I felt that maybe I was starting to bore them. Yay. Maybe they'd go away soon.

"What were you doing in the girls' restroom yesterday afternoon?" asked Appledom.

"Peeing. What do you think?"

"But there is a restroom in the teacher's lounge, which is closer to your room. Why go farther down the hall than you needed to?"

Okay, maybe this guy wasn't so Tweedledum after all. Now I was honest. "I didn't want to do any socializing. It was late, and I didn't want to run into anyone. I just wanted to get on the road and get home." They did the symmetrical look thing again, and they were magically transported back into their roles from *Alice in Wonderland*. They might as well have said "Likely story."

Pregnant pause. I tried not to shift in my seat. I looked up at Van Gogh's woods.

"You had a meeting with Mr. and Mrs. Mitchell on Wednesday morning. Is that correct?" asked Kennedy.

"Yes, that's right," I said, thinking I didn't want to go there at all.

"How did that meeting go?"

"Well, it was an IEP meeting, so that's sort of a creative, problem-solving meeting where we plan what the student should learn in the coming year," I began.

They looked at me blankly for such a long enough time that I wanted to squirm.

"So that's what we did." I went on. "It was productive, but we had some problems agreeing on the best plan for Rosie, their daughter." I looked over at Ian, who was now studying his nails intently.

"Is it true that you had an altercation with Mrs. Mitchell at that meeting?"

"An altercation? I don't know that I'd call it that. We disagreed pretty strongly about part of Rosie's educational plan, but we got it ironed out," I said, hoping I sounded professional.

"Were you angry after that meeting?"

I paused but then fessed up. "Yes, I was angry. But really, more frustrated than anything."

"Did you, after that meeting, tell Ava Westerly and Anne Johnson that you'd like to kill Gretchen Mitchell?"

Holy shit! As I sat stunned by this, I saw Ian's head jerk up in my peripheral vision. I focused on breathing, as it seemed to no longer be involuntary. They had ratted me out! Ava and Anne, my supposed great friends, my right-hand women, had told these two boobs what I had said.

"That's not what I said!"

"Oh? What did you say?"

I could feel my ears on fire. I tried to collect my thoughts. "I said something like, 'If I could ever kill someone, I might think about killing Gretchen right now.' But I didn't mean it. I was just blowing off steam. I could never kill anyone."

Now they were not looking at me. They were too busy writing—both of them. "I don't even kill bugs," I added.

They were still busy writing. I turned my head slowly, just a tad, to look at Ian, my eyes wide to show him how freaked out I was. He raised his hands out to me in a silent "hold on" gesture. I half-smiled at him, but it was all for show. Inside, I was losing it. That comment was so incriminating. But on the other hand, I reasoned with myself, they couldn't really arrest me for making a malicious comment. Could they?

Thank goodness for the timeliness of the bell. Both detectives looked up and glanced at the big clock on the wall behind me. Amazingly, they dismissed me (probably now wanting to discuss me as a murder suspect), leaving me with the promise that they'd contact me if they needed anything else. Oh, goody.

Chapter 11

I hurried back to my room, trying to dismiss the shock of the interview I had just had, trying to get my head ready for science. I love teaching science, and my kiddos love learning about it. Two days a week, I'm alone with the kids for this class because Anne and Ava are needed elsewhere. This keeps me dancing as fast as I can, but it's still fun. And right then, I didn't feel particularly like being with Anne and Ava anyway.

That day we were working on magnetism, which is always fascinating to all of us. I had gotten a bit of prep help from one of the eighth-grade science teachers, a guy with the unfortunate last name of Shaft. He had long ago been dubbed "Crankshaft" by his students in honor not just of his name, but also of his notorious moodiness. Hey, it could have been worse. Think of how inventive eighth graders might be with a name like Shaft. He had fixed me up with metal shavings, horseshoe magnets, and fun stuff to do with them. I don't have many science materials in my room, which has to function in so many subject areas, so I'm constantly borrowing from the science department.

Everybody was into it that day, all having fun, and maybe even learning. Zak and Basil repeatedly called me to their desks to show me how they could make the iron filings move without even touching them. Only April seemed unhappy. This was the norm. She was concerned about the mess we were making, about iron filings in the carpet. I had to rein her in a couple of times as she started in on Chloe to quit losing filings off her desk. But the others were so engaged that it was gratifying for me.

Basil was the one who really seemed to take it all in. "Ms. H, watch this. These little things are like the earth. My magnet is the sun. If I get it too close, the earth crashes into it and is destroyed!" He demonstrated the end of the earth with glee, looking up at me and smiling. I smiled back in appreciation of him understanding the concept. Hallelujah!

My students are, to me, a constant fascination. Here is a kid who can't read at kindergarten level by today's standards. He is thirteen years old, so he has been working on reading for about eight years and getting nowhere. Yet he has decent speech, in fact, is a good communicator, and can grasp the abstract idea of the sun holding the earth in place by gravity. He has horrible ADHD and is a terror when not on his medication, but that is not all that keeps him from learning to read, write, and do math. He appears to have a severe learning disability for all things written. So, take one guess how he scores on a standardized test. That's right: really low, in what used to be called the "moderately mentally retarded" range. We don't call it that anymore, because of course, it's not politically correct. Mental retardation has been renamed "developmentally delayed," even on IQ tests, where things are not as blunt as they used to be. Basil is also PC (a term of my own making): Parent-Challenged, with a not-so-good home life led by one disorganized parent just trying to keep her head above the water.

Before I go any further, let me digress, just to make my work life a little clearer.

My official caseload list comes out each school year early in August. I take great delight in looking it over and thinking about how balanced or unbalanced it is, how overwhelmed I'm going to be, or how lucky I am that year to have the students I have, and the number I have. When I say balanced, I mean a balance of kids with given disabilities. Please take the following as tongue-in-cheek, sort of. For example, if you have lots of kids with Down syndrome, they may form a little gang to connive against you, to make you have fun but not get much done that is productive. If you have more than two kids with cerebral palsy, you won't be able to get in the door of your room because of all the equipment. If you have too many kids with autism, you will be totally exhausted by the end of first bell. So I was happy to look over my list in August for that school year. I made myself a cheat sheet so I could look at what and whom I had. You would *never* see an official list like this in this day and age since it's not PC to list disabilities like I've done, but hey, the list was for my eyes only. (The "unknowns" refer to kids who have no specific diagnosis other than developmental delay. This is very common.)

Student	Grade	Disability
Megan	6	Down syndrome
Josh	6	Deaf, unknown
Rosemary	6	Down syndrome
April	7	Unknown
Tony	7	Autism
Zak	7	Down syndrome
Basil	8	Unknown
Freddie	8	Unknown
Christie	8	Cerebral Palsy
Chloe	8	Autism

So this would be a nicely balanced year. Fairly even numbers of kids in each grade. Not too many new kids. Hopefully, not too wild and crazy of a crew.

Rosie was one extreme in the spectrum of how my kids participated in inclusion. She was in my room for only those twenty minutes at the beginning of the day (and Gretchen had never liked that, but agreed to it on a basis of practicality). At the opposite end of that spectrum were Freddie, Josh, Megan, and Chloe. These kiddos spent five out of seven bells a day in my classroom. My other students were with me for varying amounts of time, based on their needs.

Anyway, back to science class, which thankfully made me forget about the day before for about five whole minutes. The kids left for lunch and I cleaned up the fairly substantial mess that had been left behind.

I ate quickly at my desk, tired of people's questions and their pity. It's interesting for what a *short* time pity feels good. I tried to get a few things done but mostly just shuffled papers around. I moved a huge pile of stuff that needed filed from my desk over to Anne and Ava's. This made me smile, even if just for a moment. Every now and then, I surreptitiously shove some of my endless piles onto their territory. This is my way of fessing up that I'm overwhelmed. When they ask what I want done with it, I act innocent, like I have no idea where it came from or what they are talking about. They always grin and get it quickly taken care of. They are really quite wonderful. But I had my nose a little out of joint about them ratting me out to the po-po, so giving them the filing pile felt good. Ava had talked to them first, and I knew she had spilled. She's young and was taken by surprise, undoubtedly scared. I knew the cops wouldn't really consider me a suspect, but it was still unnerving.

I was startled as a voice interrupted the quiet.

"What the fuck, Hutchinson? What is going on with you? Fill me in." Dana plopped herself down in Tony's rocking chair and leaned toward me. "I heard you were up in the office talking to the cops this morning."

Never doubt the power and speed of the McKinley grapevine, I thought. I filled her in, including the part about Ava and Anne ratting me out on the "I could kill Gretchen" comment. She made me feel better by getting all self-righteous on my behalf, but finally agreed with me that under pressure from the cops, it would've been hard not to spill that gem.

Dana was the first friend had I made at McKinley. When I got hired, I went in early one day, a few weeks before school started, to set up my classroom. I hadn't met but a few of the staff, really only those who had interviewed me. As I shoved desks around, trying to decide how I wanted them arranged, a pretty auburn-haired woman came in and introduced herself. She was very welcoming and explained that we'd be seeing a lot of each other because she, too, was a special ed teacher.

She quickly became one of my best friends on the McKinley staff. The friendship is partly based just on who she is, but it's probably also partly due to how similar our jobs are in many ways. Dana teaches kids who are emotionally disturbed. Her students are not developmentally delayed, as mine are, but have so much baggage that they sometimes can't even get through a school day in regular ed. They are the kids with PTSD, bipolar disorder, and all such heavy burdens. So Dana, like me, is sort of an odd woman out in the special ed department. There are seven of us all together. The other five mainly serve kids with learning disabilities, although they have a few of our kids in their classes here and there. She is an inventive, energetic, creative teacher, but that's only part of why I love her. She's also just plain fun, and we sort of function on the same wavelength, but her most endearing characteristic is that she's a smartass.

Now she and I theorized a bit together about who might have offed Gretchen and why.

"Anyone who knew her might have killed her at some point in time," Dana commented. "Geez, she was such a self-serving, power-hungry bitch. I think she just brought out the worst in everyone. That woman could sow the wind like no one I've ever met. No wonder she finally reaped the whirlwind."

"Huh? Are you going all biblical on me? What are you talking about?" I asked.

She giggled. "Yeah, I guess that's Old Testament stuff. You know, like she finally got back all the bad stuff she gave out."

We heard the outside door open and the voices of kids as they started coming in from lunch and their daily run around the pavement. Dana greeted them, high-fiving each one as they came in the door. She turned and gave me a little wave before she left for her classroom.

We settled into our book.One of the things I love to do as a teacher is to read aloud to my kiddos. I do it nearly every day. I'm so grateful to authors, or editors, or whoever it is that takes great literature and abridges it ("dumbs it down," as they say) so it can be enjoyed by readers who aren't so literate. Thus, I can read easier versions of classics like *Tom Sawyer* and *Treasure Island* that are only slightly above my students' reading level and even show them a few pictures to help with their comprehension. Over the years, one of their favorites has been an abridged version of *Alice in Wonderland*. My copy includes a picture of Tweedledee and Tweedledum with huge, round bellies and wearing identical striped shirts. This was what kept popping into my head at inopportune times, as it did again when I talked to the detectives, making me smirk.

Basil quickly got me on track by asking what I thought Brian (the character in our current book) would do next. He is always the one most wrapped up in whatever we are reading. April commented that she hoped he would get rescued soon, actually wringing her hands as if she were genuinely worried about him. I opened the book and tried to get as involved in it as the kids were.

Chapter 12

One of the wonderful things that has happened for special ed teachers in the fairly recent past is that they have been let out of the rooms at the end of the hall or under the stairs. They've been invited into the world of regular education. Of course, it's even more wonderful for their students because the teachers have followed their kiddos there. So for a student with, say, a severe learning disability, a bright kid who just can't gain any meaning from what he reads, or maybe can't read at all, this means the difference of being in classes with "typical" peers all day. With special ed services in place (like a teacher's aide in the room or a special ed teacher co-teaching the class), this kid can have a normal school life, whatever that may be. Compare that to 1980, when that same kid might have been stuck in a special ed class all day long. Inclusion was first called "mainstreaming" in the world of education. But when educators screwed that up pretty badly, they renamed it and have done a lot better with it over time. Change is tough stuff, as we all know.

When I first took the job at McKinley eight years ago, I was thrilled to find out that I would be team-teaching seventh-grade social studies one bell a day with a regular ed teacher. (One of the reasons I had left my first job was that they provided no such inclusive practices.) I met Jamie McEntire two days before the kids started school. I knew he was younger than me but wasn't sure by how much—six years, as it turned out. Jamie is from a small town in eastern Kentucky, and man oh man, you can take the boy out of Kentucky, but you sure can't take the Kentucky out of the boy.

"Hey, there," he had said as I entered his room. "You Hannah?"

"Yes. Jamie?" I'd asked.

"Yes, ma'am," he had said, shaking my hand. "Pleased to meet ya. I guess we're a-gonna be workin' together second bell."

Holy shit, I had thought. Is this guy for real? What a corn pone. But I was so wrong. Yes, he has a down-homey accent, but behind it is a sharp guy who knows tons of history and imparts it to kids with a sense of humor, a flair for storytelling, and a casual, laid-back way of making sure everyone is included. He and I felt our way along slowly at first, with him leading all of the lessons and me acting more like a teacher's assistant, keeping order, moving around the room helping kids, and hanging out at the back of the room. But Jamie was willing to plan weekly with me, and over time his classroom became more hands-on. Our roles became more blurred. We were both having fun teaching collaboratively, and we could see the kids benefiting from it. There were some kids in that class who really struggled, and not necessarily just the special ed kids, but we saw them thriving. Jamie started doing some of the things we had dreamed up together in his other classes. I was complimented. He would report back to me on how things had worked in those bells with only one teacher in the room, and we'd hash out some adaptations that would make it easier for him during the bells when I wasn't around.

One of the things I love about Jamie is that he's the King of Easy. I always wish I could be like that. I probably spend about fifty hours a week on work. Jamie teaches, coaches soccer and basketball, gets to school at the last minute, leaves to go coach, and never takes any work home. Yet he is a truly good teacher. I think part of it is just the nature of the beast that is my chosen area. I have to make a lot of materials, teach to vastly different levels, adapt everything, blah, blah, blah. But still, I wish I were more like Jamie.

Over the first year we taught together, we developed a nice working friendship. I also developed a very secret crush on this corn pone, who spent his spare time hunting, helped his uncle on his farm, and made me taste things like deer jerky. (Good stuff, actually.) He was just so damn nice, so dedicated to kids. It made him sexy to me, although looking at him objectively, he is a very average guy. Average height and weight. Very lovely gray eyes. Dimples. I am such a sucker for dimples. I got into a habit of watching him closely when he taught, enjoying the way he moved around the room, checking out his ass when he was writing on the board, smiling at his soft accent.

Every now and then, he would do some little thing that would make me think maybe he was secretly lusting after me (yeah, maybe *wishful* thinking on my part). Once, on the rare occasion when I wore a dress to work, he told me I looked "real purty." No shit—he actually said it that way. And he gave me a look that made me turn red. Another time, as we sat close together, entering grades into the computer, he put a hand on my thigh as he made a joke. Little things like this got me going. Fed my little flame.

There's nothing like a little alcohol, or a huge dose of it, to turn a flame into a fire. One Friday afternoon toward the end of that first year we taught together, Jamie showed up for the usual happy hour that many of the McKinley teachers share. He wasn't a regular because of his coaching duties, but the end of basketball season signaled free time for him, so there he was. He entertained the dozen or so of us at the table with stories of drunken escapades involving moonshine and jumping out of haylofts in his younger years. The setting, so foreign to most of us, made us laugh at his adventures. As he told the stories, I noticed him slipping more into his accent, using words like *ain't* and *tarnation* that he would never have used in his classroom.

Our happy hours are usually well attended but short-lived since people have to pick up kids or get home to start dinner. So the crowd dwindles to just a few serious drinkers, of which I am one. Jamie was drinking shots, a celebration of his freedom from afternoon basketball practice.

After more beers under my belt than I should have been planning to drive on, I decided I'd better get home to let Rascal out. Jamie also said his goodbyes as I got up to leave and walked out with me. Parting at my car, I told him to drive carefully and waved, starting to get in.

"Hannah, hang on a sec," he said, walking over to me. He walked straight up to me as I stood with my car door open and paused for just a tick, looking me in the eye. Then, very slowly, he put his arms around my waist, maybe gauging what I thought of this by keeping eye contact with me. Then he kissed me full on the lips. "I've been wantin' to do that for a long while," he said.

Knock me over with a feather! I know I stood there like an idiot, saying nothing. Looking at him. "What ya say I come on over to your place and meet that ole dog of yours? Would that be okay?"

"Yeah," I said dumbly. "That'll be fine."

"I'll be right over. Y'all drive real careful."

I won't go into a lot of detail, but it was the first of numerous visits Jamie made to my apartment. He and Rascal became great friends, and his and my friendship changed hugely. It wasn't an out-and-out affair. First of all, neither of us is married. Secondly, it wasn't a regular thing. We'd go at it hot and heavy for a few weeks, then decide we should ease off. Neither of us took it too seriously.

It was a friends-with-benefits thing, and we didn't want anyone at school to know about it. This went on (and sometimes off) through that spring and much of the next school year, in which he and I continued to teach together for that one bell daily. At some point toward the end of that second year, it just sort of tapered off naturally. I had mixed emotions when I found this happening, partly relief at not having to worry about our teaching peers finding out, and partly regret at its ending.

For the next four years, I got paired up with other teachers in my team-teaching setups. Jamie and I stayed friendly, sometimes in our old way, just only ever so occasionally, and as coworkers too. When we finally got assigned to work together again this year, I wondered what might happen. The answer, apparently, was nothing. Jamie had done some dating and had a serious girlfriend for a while. The fires were cooled. He was now in his thirties and, I suspected, looking for a wife. (I guess guys do that. Right?)

Happily, he and I still enjoyed teaching together and were comfortable around each other. So going down the hall to his room for sixth bell daily was fun for me. It gave me a break from having to run the show all the time, and I always love watching other teachers in action. We were deeply into the development of Central America that week, specifically the building of the Panama Canal. The kids were very involved in practicing their roles for a skit we were putting on the next week for another class. Things that day went smoothly, even if a bit raucous. The bell surprised us all, and the kids scooped up their stuff and left quickly. I gave Jamie a casual wave as I left to head back up the hall to my room.

I had lucked out that year in my resource (special ed) social studies class. I never know from year to year whether I'll be teaching sixth-, seventh-, or eighth-grade social studies. Naturally, the curriculum is vastly different at each grade level. What I end up teaching is totally dependent on student needs. That year we had only seven kids in need of a self-contained sixth-grade social studies setup. That meant I switched from seventh grade with Jamie (mostly geography) to sixth (ancient civilizations), but I really liked that stuff and had taught it before, so that made it lots easier.

We were studying medieval times in my class and had booklets to finish making that day. Remembering Tony's horror at his rubber cemented fingers the previous day, I had him do the cutting, showing me where he wanted stuff stuck on, and I did the gluing. We got the booklets done quickly and pulled out our materials to start on our castles. Class went smoothly, and I even remembered to allow time for the kids to clean up so I wouldn't have to do it after school. As the kiddos loaded up their backpacks, the intercom came to life with afternoon announcements, which (thankfully) are much briefer than the morning version.

As reminders for afterschool clubs blared, Chloe repeated her behavior from that morning, hands over ears, pacing at the back of the room. And again, when they were over, Chloe threw out, "I hate him." Poor Ian. Probably best that he didn't know he was being bad-mouthed by Chloe.

When the buses pulled out, Anne and Ava came back to the room to gather up their belongings, and we had a little powwow about our talks with the cops. Ava was teary-eyed as she told about ratting me out to them. As I had assumed, she'd just been nervous, and she claimed they had tricked her into telling about my comments. Of course, once they had her, they had no trouble getting Anne to agree that yes, I had said that. I understood completely how this had happened, and I didn't blame them a bit, but some small part of me wondered if *I* might not have been able to keep my mouth *shut* to protect a friend.

Chapter 13

The people I work with are drinkers. Most of us take our jobs seriously. We're trying to change lives, to mold bratty kids into productive citizens. We have state tests, federal mandates, demanding parents, and the bureaucracy and bullshit that's involved in any organization. That's all just the backdrop to a room full of kids who, generally speaking, love to challenge the adult at the front of the room. So on a Friday afternoon, a decent percentage of the staff from McKinley Middle migrates to O'Connell's Pub.

That Friday, I was definitely up for tipping a few. I followed the buses full of kids out of the school parking lot, got home quickly, and let Rascal out to roam the yard for a few minutes. I fed him and dealt with his pitiful look by telling him I wouldn't be gone for long.

O'Connell's is a great little dive. It's dark and dingy and has that welcoming smell of old spilled beer. The ancient tile floor is sometimes still sticky, either from the night before or from a mop so old that it just spreads the spills around. The place has great old linoleum-topped round tables that easily seat eight. That day there were twelve or fourteen crammed around a table by the time I got there. Our server, Zeke, a college kid who knows us well, was running drinks as fast as he could. Ahh . . . nothing like a two-dollar longneck, some friends to unload on, and a hiding place where none of our students' upstanding parents would ever be seen. One of our reasons for hanging out at O'Connell's is the abovementioned bargain, but the other is that if we run into parents there, they are of the biker/trucker/blue-collar sort, unoffended by the thought of their kids' mentors sucking down a few cold ones.

As people scooched a little one way or another to make room for me, I became, unfortunately, the center of attention. Sympathy for me, questions about the murder, and hypotheses about who had done it flew around the table for a few minutes. I snickered demurely as I heard a few nasty comments about Gretchen and her aggressive bid to become the district's advocacy agency. Thankfully conversation returned shortly to the usual stories of crazy kids and overwhelming work. I settled in and enjoyed listening. Most of the teachers usually stay for only a couple of drinks and then are off to their other obligations. So after not much more than an hour, we were down to seven, then five. We were entertaining each other with stories about our students, trying to one-up each other with tales of terror. Ava was having fun recounting one at my expense, in which I had been stupid enough to reach in front of Tony to turn off the computer he had illicitly been playing a game on during social studies. I had given him fair warning that if he didn't quit the game and come back to his seat, I would turn it off. My error was that I reached across him to hit the power button. He chomped down so hard on my arm that I had a circle of purple teeth marks on my bicep for two weeks. Everyone got a good chuckle out of that. Why is it always so funny to us humans when others make fools of themselves?

By that time, I was in a bit of a beer-induced euphoria and giggled along with them as they laughed at my expense. When Zeke suggested another round, we were easily swayed, with me thinking, oh, I shouldn't, followed quickly by, oh, why not? We ordered fried pickles and nachos, burning our tongues on the fresh-from-the-fryer pickles when they arrived and scarfing down the nachos so fast that we needed another beer to wash them down. Now, Ava and Ellen (our hard-drinking cohort, disguised as a mild-mannered librarian Monday through Friday) took their leave, and it was down to me, Jake, and Jamie. They coach together, and this being their off-season, they were making the most of their freedom to drink on a Friday afternoon instead of getting ready for a big game. Returning from a trip to the ladies' room, I found that we each had a full shot glass in front of us. Shots are never a good idea for me, but it seems like whenever I get around to them, they appear so harmless.

"What have we here?" I asked.

"Patrón," said Jake, raising his glass in a toast.

"Yum!" I said, picking up the shot glass and toasting him and Jamie. So smooth. The next two were also smooth. I listened to a few soccer stories and a few drinking stories, enjoying the diversion. Finally we noticed that the place was filling up with evening patrons and figured that maybe the three of us should free up the large table we were hogging. As I stood up, the room took a little spin. Oops. I was feeling the tequila just a bit. But I was also feeling great, the best I had felt all week. As we wove our way out of O'Connell's, Jamie took my elbow, steadying me.

"Whoa there, partner," Jamie said. "I think you might be just a bit tipsy."

"Oh, no, I'm fine. I feel just peachy," I said, looking up and giving him a coy smile.

Jake bid us goodbye in the parking lot, with a fist bump for each of us. Mine nearly knocked me off balance.

"Where's your car?" Jamie asked.

"It's way back here," I gestured to the back of the lot, noting that for some reason, my arm sort of flopped around as I pointed.

"I'll just walk you on back there," Jamie said as he took my elbow, then put an arm around my waist. Halfway across the lot, he stopped me. "You know you can't drive home."

"Oh, no, I'm fine," I insisted, pulling away from him to demonstrate that I could stand up straight.

"Hannah, I know what you've had, and I'm not a-gonna let you drive."

I stood like a stubborn five-year-old, knowing he was right but still wanting to argue. It also passed through my mind that he might have an ulterior motive, but this was probably just wanton thinking on my part.

"I'll drive you home. Your car'll be fine here until the mornin'."

"All right," I said, feeling like I had given in too easily, as he helped me crawl up into the passenger seat of his truck. (It didn't occur to me that he'd had as much to drink as I had.)

When we went into my apartment, Rascal went wild in his enthusiasm at seeing Jamie. He always remembers fondly anyone willing to give him a belly rub. The two of them went down to the yard for some stick-throwing and fetching while I made myself a cup of tea, realizing that I was, in fact, quite drunk.

Damn that Jake and his Patrón.

I could hear Jamie talking to Rascal as they came in through the porch, crooning to him that he was a good ole boy. I turned around, leaning against the kitchen counter for support and sipping my tea. Jamie crossed the kitchen and removed the mug from my hand, setting it carefully on the counter. Then he kissed me forcefully, stopping just at the point where I was really buying into it. He pulled back, searching my eyes. I paused for two long seconds, then I leaned into him, putting my arms around his neck and kissing him back. He lifted me onto the counter, which in my Patrón-and-beer-induced state made me lose my balance and giggle as my butt fell into the sink. We spent a few minutes there, me wrapped around him, enjoying that which was familiar, but always seemed for some reason, forbidden. There was no conscious decision to head for the bedroom, but suddenly we were there, pulling off clothes and falling onto the bed. I found both familiar comfort and new excitement in this unexpected turn of events.

The early morning sun peeked through the blinds, giving the room a soft glow. I rolled over to find Jamie lying there, eyes open, looking at me.

"Well, that was a good ole roll in the hay, wasn't it?" he said.

"Yeah," I confessed with a titter.

"Wanna have another go at it?"

"Um, I don't think so," I said, feeling reason, or guilt, or doubt creep into my thick head. "Whoo!" I added, "I think maybe I could be a tad hungover."

"I know what'll fix that," Jamie said, hopping out of bed. He was, as he would have said, buck naked, and I admired his younger, lithe body as he pulled on pants and shirt.

"You sure were a-tossin' and a-turnin' during the night," he said over his shoulder.

"Yeah, I had my recurring dream a couple of times," I admitted.

"Should I ask what that is?"

"Let's just not go there," I said, closing the topic with a wry smile.

An hour later, we sat in Frisch's, finishing a carb-filled breakfast. I had downed two eggs, a couple of slices of goetta, toast, and hash browns.

"Damn, that's fine fare," I said as I wiped grease from my hands. "I feel better already."

"Good. Cause we're goin' to have some fun this mornin'," Jamie announced with a grin.

"Oh, shit. What am I in for?"

"You'll find out shortly," he said as he laid a tip on the table, picked up the bill, and slid out of the booth. I followed him up to the cashier, where he made nice with a young woman who was vastly overweight and very plain. He smiled and flirted and left her blushing, probably making her day.

"Why do you always do that?" I said as we got into his pickup.

"Do what?"

"You know. Flirt with every woman you meet, and yuk it up like you do."

"I'm just bein' friendly," he said defensively, looking directly at me before he pulled out of the parking lot. "I do believe you're jealous."

"I'm not jealous," I insisted, looking away.

"Oh, ho, ho! You don't like me flirtin' now, do ya?"

"I don't care one bit," I said, trying to sound serious.

"Damn, woman. It just figures the way I'd finally get to you'd be by flirtin' with some pimply-faced little porker." He was shaking his head and snickering, but I didn't like the direction the conversation was taking, so I changed the subject.

"Where we headed?"

"Down to AJ's Shooting Range," he said as if it was nothing. Jamie knew how I felt about guns, and he was of the philosophy that if I would just "get to know them better," I'd feel more comfortable around them. For some reason, I believed the opposite.

Chapter 14

The Columbine High School massacre took place on April 20, 1999. At that time, I was a naive twenty-two-year-old who was considering getting a master's in special ed as I finished my undergrad work. The world was horrified by the incident at Columbine, but I guess we were all naive. Although there were school shootings before this one, I think most of us believed nothing like that would ever happen again. Nonetheless, high schools in America started taking precautions, installing cameras and metal detectors, and having police presence in schools with greater frequency. Sadly, we didn't know then that school shootings would become part of our lives.

The school shooting at Sandy Hook that took place on December 14, 2012, was the one that put me over the edge. I know any shooting, any loss of life, is a tragedy, but the Sandy Hook slaughter of young, innocent children really got to me. I never in my life dreamed that I would even touch a gun. Now I found myself saying more than once that I knew I could kill someone who threatened my students with a gun.

It wasn't until 2016 (and many school shootings later) that my school district took the big step of allowing trained teachers to have guns locked away in their classrooms. When I first heard this news, I was ambivalent about it. But the issue was a huge one to us teachers. It got talked about a lot. Eventually, a group of us decided to take the district up on the offer of free training for a concealed carry permit. They also set us up with a combination-locking desk drawer that held a gun. We had a limited choice about what kind of gun that would be. I chose a Glock 42 on the recommendation of AJ, our instructor. According to him, it's small, easy to use, and lightweight. Its one drawback, he cautioned, is that the trigger can be a bit hard to pull. I thought that sounded just fine. The last thing I wanted was a trigger that was too easy to pull.

This was a big step for me and one that I almost chickened out on, but I felt strongly about the situation that was going on in our country, about what had happened to innocent children, teenagers, and teachers. So I swallowed my fears and went to the classes.

The gun shop and shooting range that AJ owns are a fascinating mix of the old and new. When you walk into the front of the building, you are in the gun shop. This is a place where guns are not only bought and sold but also repaired. There are guns on display, from small stuff like what I came to practice with up to stuff that frankly scares the crap out of me, guns that I didn't know people off the street could even buy. Most interesting are the guns in the showcases below the counter. There are old German Lugers from World War II and big shiny revolvers that look like they could have come out of the holster of some bandito. Some of these guns have price tags in the thousands of dollars.

Almost more interesting than the guns is AJ, an unusual guy, probably about my age, but also ageless behind the most hair I have ever seen on any human being. His beard would make Santa jealous, and the long ponytail down his back hangs below his belt. He even has thick, bushy eyebrows. Behind all that is a pretty ordinary guy, or so it seems, who loves repairing guns, teaching people about them, and, I'm sure, shooting them.

The first day we went to class, we spent a couple of hours in a small, unadorned room behind the gun shop that is as boring as the gun shop is interesting. This room is part of a huge addition that you'd never guess exists when you walk in the front door of AJ's. The class was actually very interesting once I got past the idea of touching, then holding, a gun. We learned about how to load, care for, handle, and operate a gun. And of course, a few weeks later, when we were done with our classroom instruction, we practiced shooting. This was done behind the meeting room in the huge, long shooting range that's built onto the back of the building.

Here's a little confession. I'm pretty good at a lot of things. I think I'm pretty handy, and I don't ordinarily shy away from doing things myself. But I am not at all good at sports, or, in fact, anything requiring any aim. As a kid, I was terrible at softball, volleyball, and even kickball. As an adult, I steer clear of tennis, golf, and especially cornhole. So you can imagine how I did with shooting. More than a few times, I pulled that paper target silhouette toward me to look at it, and it was completely clean, as if no one had shot at it at all. It would be an understatement to say that I was not the best shooter in that group. In fact, I was the worst by quite a bit. The broad side of a barn was brought up by everyone who watched me at target practice.

Fortunately, to get a concealed carry permit, you only have to take eight hours of class, then demonstrate your ability to load, unload, use the safety, not wave the gun around at people, and shoot . . . but not *hit*. So even though my accuracy improved very little over the limited number of hours of practice I put in, I still walked away with a permit, and I now have a gun locked in the bottom drawer of my desk at school.

Jamie grew up with guns. When the group of us took the shooting classes, he was a supporter. He came along to practice shooting with us even though he already had the concealed carry permit.

Now Jamie and I pulled into AJ's and went in. I protested mildly, saying that it was useless for me to practice when I didn't even have my gun. He countered that we could rent a gun of the same make and caliber.

I have to admit that once I got all set up and started shooting, it was sort of fun—just that thing of taking aim and trying to hit the target. But I had forgotten how bad I was at hitting the target. Jamie tried coaching me some, but ended up shaking his head, laughing at me, and saying that I might be just a tad hopeless. I laughed along with him, knowing that I'd probably never have to use a gun in a true emergency. We finally called it a day, with no noticeable improvement in my performance.

We pulled into O'Connell's parking lot, where my car sat looking lonely. Jamie pulled up to it, and as I started to get out, he pulled me by the elbow back toward him.

"Now, after the fine time I been showin' you, you're surely not a-gonna leave me without even a goodbye kiss, are ya?" he asked.

I grinned and gave him a lingering kiss.

"I'll be lookin' forward to seein' ya at the weddin' tonight," he added. I looked at him dumbly for a moment.

I had forgotten all about Jesse's wedding.

Chapter 15

Saturday, March 16th

I guess the events of the week had just overwhelmed me. With a gift bought and sent several months earlier and a dress found a few weeks before, the wedding had completely slipped my mind. I had been contemplating an evening alone with a book, but as I got dressed, I found myself looking forward to a more social gathering.

I had bought a sapphire-blue dress made of a fabric that begged to be touched. The dress was fitted but not too tight, and when I bought it, I thought it flattered me. But now, as I looked in the mirror, I looked a bit chunky in it and had a few bulges in places where I didn't want to bulge. And my hair! Could it never behave? I had blown it dry carefully, trying to get the curls under control, but it had its usual egg-beater-styled look. I sighed aloud, thinking I looked like a middle-aged frump. Never mind, I told myself. Just don't look in the mirror.

Anne called, offering me a ride, which sounded a lot more fun than going alone and would also allow me to not worry about how much I drank. Not that I was planning any sort of a repeat of last night. In fact, I thought to myself, I'd probably only have one drink tonight.

The wedding was lovely, the bride beautiful, and the service only twenty minutes long. Perfect. McKinley staff had been invited without spouses, but apparently no one was offended by that. We occupied four tables at the reception. At eight per table, this was about half of our staff, but we made up just a small gathering. I looked around and counted by multiples of the eight at each table. There were nearly two hundred people here. For me, it was nice to not be sitting at a table with three couples, the odd woman out. Ava had brought us each a cosmo to start things off. So much for my vow of alcoholic moderation. The dinner was served in courses: appetizer, salad, entree. This took some time since there were so many guests. To make the wait tolerable, our hosts had thoughtfully provided carafes of wine on each table. I found that my stemmed glass was magically staying full although I was certainly sipping it. And the event staff were making sure that the carafes got refilled as they were emptied. I'm not usually a wine drinker, but it was just so handy, and it went so well with the shrimp cocktail, the crusty French bread, and the Greek salad.

In the course of the chatter at my table, the subject of Gretchen finally came up, as I knew it would. I was spared having to repeat my little story by Ellen telling of Gretchen's presentation at our last school board meeting.

"She went on and on about how we have so many students in the district who need advocates. She was actually pushing for the district to hire her, or give her some official capacity."

"I didn't even know she had gone to the board meeting," I muttered.

"Well, you'd have to go to one of the meetings or read the minutes," Ellen offered. Ouch. Ellen is never one to beat around the bush. She is very active in school politics, which I run from as fast as I can. I sipped more wine to cover my wounded ego. There was general outrage over how nervy, tacky, and snooty Gretchen had been. I controlled my smile nicely, I thought, and sipped on.

After dinner and a few too many toasts to the lovely couple (Why do people always think the more they say, the better?), the music started. I am generally not much of a dancer until I've had some liquid courage. I tottered up to the bar, not realizing that I was already feeling pretty courageous. As the bartender fixed my drink, I turned to see Herm Shaft, my science teacher guru. He was also waiting for a libation.

"Well, don't you look pretty tonight," he commented as he looked me up and down.

"And you look very handsome," I told him.

"I hear that your murder victim turned out to be the parent of one of your students."

Wow, he sure got to the point quickly. And I didn't like the way he called her "my" murder victim.

"Yeah, it's sure a weird case, isn't it?" I didn't want to talk about this right now, but Herm went on.

"Murder is such an interesting thing. You have to wonder, was it for money? For power? Or did someone just reach their last straw? Ah, well," he added as he picked up his drink and prepared to move on, "time and police will find that out, I guess."

I was glad he had left me, but he did have a good point, and as I meandered through the maze of tables and people, I thought that Herm was right. Murder *is* interesting. Why do people kill each other? For all kinds of reasons, I'm sure, but it's certainly an act of desperation.

Deep in thought, I put my drink down on the table just as Ava grabbed me and dragged me onto the dance floor. Ava is one of those people with natural rhythm and great hips. She moves her 170 or so pounds around the dance floor like a pro and is fun to watch. I danced around with her, Dana, Anne, and others, whom I am so fortunate to call friends. I tried to put myself at ease and worked at not thinking about murder or even how I looked. This was surprisingly easy. Probably the liquid courage at work.

I found after a short time that I was dancing quite well. Why did I think I wasn't a good dancer? I had some good moves. I was all over that dance floor. I even stuck it out through a line dance, which I don't usually hang around for.

After a number of dances, and at a point when frankly I needed to catch my breath, I stopped to have another little drink and decided to use the ladies' room. I did my business, washed my hands, and, as I started to leave the restroom, glanced in a full-length mirror. I almost walked right past me, but something made me take a step back, another look. Alone for the moment, I paused, turning sideways to look at myself. I didn't look frumpy at all. In fact, I almost looked slender. I turned this way and that a bit and decided I looked rather sexy. My sapphire dress was gorgeous on me and I filled it out nicely. And my egg-beater hair was now falling into soft, pretty curls. I smiled at myself and rejoined the fray, ready for more.

Of course, Jamie and I crossed paths on the dance floor and danced a few together, but I opted out of a slow dance with him, whispering that we shouldn't, which made him snort and laugh at me. The evening passed in a whirl. Somehow I was no longer a middle-aged schoolteacher. I was young. I was beautiful. I was fun. I was the belle of the ball.

Thankfully Anne, having chauffeured me, had used more self-control with the wine than I had, and she got me home safely.

It was in the wee hours of the morning, for the umpteenth time in my dreams, that I pushed that stall door open, feeling the weight of her body against the door. I peeked in and saw her surprised expression. The blood. Her blue lips. But this time, the dream went a little further. I looked down past her face, and there it was, that odd little knife sticking out of Gretchen's chest. And I knew exactly what it was. It wasn't a knife at all. It was my missing awl.

I came up from a sound sleep to a sitting position like a bolt. "What the fuck? No, no, no, it can't be!" But I knew it was. I knew that old, round wooden handle. I just hadn't placed it because it was so incongruous. I threw the covers back and sprang out of bed. Or, rather, tried to spring. I guess I didn't throw the covers back all the way because my right foot got caught, throwing me forward in mid-leap. I landed facedown on the carpet, almost knocking the air out of myself. Good God. I couldn't even get out of bed dramatically without endangering myself. Rascal sat at the end of the bed, eyeing me sleepily but not coming to my rescue, I noted.

I pulled myself up off the floor, threw on my robe and slippers, and headed for the garage, turning on lights as I passed through the apartment, then down the stairs. I went straight to the tool chest. I searched the top compartment again with my eyes, then began taking things out one by one and laying them on the workbench. I emptied the top of the chest item by item, examining things as if they might magically be, or turn into, the awl: metal tape measures, permanent markers, a tiny level, a tire gauge, all manner of tool bric-a-brac. No awl. Next, I opened all the drawers, but the screwdriver drawer contained only screwdrivers. The pliers drawer, only pliers. The wrench drawer, only wrenches.

I knew it was true, but how could it be? How could the awl from my tool chest have come to be sticking out of Gretchen's midsection? I simply could not wrap my mind around it. I left the mess I had made all over the workbench and moved slowly back up the steps into my apartment, locking the door behind me. I sat on the edge of my bed in a daze. I just couldn't make sense of this. I felt as though my thoughts were moving like molasses. I wondered briefly if I was in shock, if this was what it felt like. But I reasoned that it was simply my mind's adjustment to something that couldn't be, but was, a paradigm shift of sorts. The whole thing was giving me a terrific headache. Or, oops, maybe all that wine I'd had at the wedding had something to do with the headache. I took a couple of ibuprofen and washed them down with a sports drink to fight the oncoming hangover. I started pacing around the apartment. I felt like a character in a sitcom in my old fuzzy slippers and huge belted robe, just storming around aimlessly. I actually caught myself wringing my hands and had to laugh at myself for a minute.

How could this be? I *knew* it was the truth, but how? I recalled thinking it was a funny sort of knife when I found her. Somewhere in my mind, I must have known it wasn't a knife at all. Then, finally, it clicked. It could be. It was, because someone had taken the awl out of my always-wide-open tool chest. Someone *intended* to use it on Gretchen. Someone meant it to look like I had done that to her. Someone was framing me.

I didn't want to accept this notion, but the more I thought about it, the more I believed I was right. But who? Who would do this to me? It had to be someone who really hated me. It was such a betrayal. Who would want to commit such treachery against little old me?

Or was I just a convenient patsy? So then, someone who hated Gretchen or had good cause to want to get rid of her. Really good cause. And the only person I could think of was Nathan. Herm Shaft's words at the wedding about someone reaching the last straw came back to me. There was the obvious discord in their marriage, reported to us on a number of occasions by Rosie, and there were the rumors about her fooling around, and there was just *her*. What must it have been like to be married to Gretchen? I couldn't imagine it had been pleasant. But Nathan didn't appear to be an unhappy guy. Yeah, right. He also didn't appear to be out to get me, but maybe I had that all wrong. Maybe Nathan Mitchell was just a really good actor. Of course, you'd have to be a good actor to murder your wife and then go around acting like you were devastated about it. I thought again for a minute or two about what makes someone commit murder: anger, fear, greed . . . revenge? I could check a couple of these boxes for Nathan.

Now my mind made a mental leap. I pictured myself in an orange jumpsuit. I've watched that show. I know how things are in women's prisons. And orange looks awful on me. Was I tough enough? Hell, no! I thought of the awl again. I closed my eyes for a minute. Maybe I was mistaken. Maybe I was just getting carried away with this whole murder thing. No, I knew my little recurring nightmare had been trying to nudge me toward the truth. And the awl was, after all, gone. How could I tell those awful detectives *this*? I couldn't. It was as simple as that.

I went into the bathroom and looked at myself in the mirror. Wow, I looked like crap. But I ignored that. I looked myself in the eye, practicing my shock and horror for when the cops told me that my dad's old awl was the murder weapon. (I didn't think saying "What the fuck?" as I actually had when I figured it out, would be a very good strategy.) I covered my mouth with my hands. I made my eyes bug out. I raised my eyebrows. No. No, I told myself. Don't do that.

As a teacher of middle school kids, I have been lied to a lot over the years, and I know all the classic signs. Raised eyebrows is one of them. Eye flutters, slow blinks, nose touching, mouth touching, too many details, repeating sentences, looking up to the right—all of these are symptoms of a lie being told. Maybe when they told me about the awl (as they surely would sooner or later), I would just cover my face with my hands and drop my head in feigned shock. This pantomiming in the mirror was sure getting me nowhere.

I knew there was no way I was going back to sleep with all ofthisstirring around in my head, so I finally did what I always do when I have a problem I can't figure out. I got out a spiral notebook and started making notes. I wrote several pages. I put down everything I could think of about the events of the last couple days. I tore the pages out and lined them up, reading over them and rewriting them into two columns, a column marked *Hannah* and one marked *Nathan*. And what I ended up with scared the crap out of me.

When I wrote it all down, I looked awfully suspicious, even to me. I felt a chill creeping up my spine and looked down at my arms, surprised to actually see goosebumps. But I didn't let my chickenshit ways stop me. I went on writing. This time I wrote down a list of questions. Most of them were questions about Nathan. I knew the police were working on these unknowns, but I had a "known" that they didn't: the murder weapon was mine. And I figured it wasn't going to take them very long to figure that out. I looked again at my list and it actually made me feel a little better. I'm pretty good at finding out and figuring out, and I thought maybe I could find some answers to these questions on my own. That was what I would do.

I celebrated my resolutions with a handful of cookies, then brushed my teeth, scolding myself for eating cookies in the middle of the night (such short-lived pleasure) and tucked myself back into bed, dreaming of plots to become the next Nancy Drew, or maybe Miss Marple.

Chapter 16

I woke up early Sunday morning with a splitting headache and a Saharan mouth. Two hangovers in one weekend. Was I trying to kill myself? I hydrated, re-medicated with more ibuprofen, fed myself a couple pieces of toast, and gave myself a good scolding. Then I decided to be a good girl. I would get papers graded and lesson plans done this morning rather than waiting until the eleventh hour, which I often do. I felt like shit anyway, I thought, so I might as well get all the bad stuff over with at once. I pulled the piles out of my crammed briefcase, arranged them, and started in. I made a determined effort to keep my mind off murder and sleuthing.

I actually enjoy lesson planning. It's somewhat of a creative exercise. And I like all that shuffling around of activities to make them fit in the week. But I have a particular hatred of grading papers, not at all uncommon among teachers. I had really let it pile up this week, but I started on the pile with determination. Somewhere about halfway through, I must have nodded off because I found myself back at the wedding reception, dancing, graceful, sensuous, laughing, enjoying the looks of envy from the other women and looks of desire from the men.

The jangle of my phone woke me with a start to the pile of papers my head was resting on. I wiped a little pool of my slobber off a spelling test as my lovely dream faded away. Belle of the ball, that's me.

The phone wouldn't quit. I picked it up, looked, and groaned. My mom.

This was not what I needed. I had toyed with the idea of telling her about the situation at school and decided it would only bring more grief into my life. I guess the best word for my relationship with my mom is *strained*.

This all started when I was about eleven and has never resolved itself. My mother is a bit on the high-and-mighty side. Always dignified. A lady. Her idea of how to raise me was piano lessons, ballet, and classical music. My idea was tree climbing, exploring the woods, and tooling around with Dad. This never sat well with her. I was told frequently during my childhood and teenage years that this or that was "not how a lady acts." I didn't care. I wasn't interested in being a lady. In addition, I've always felt like my mom doesn't approve of my chosen profession. She can't understand why I want to work with kids who, in her mind, have no future, kids who are so difficult, who sometimes physically hurt me, and who are so *messy*. (I swear, she has actually said that to me.)

When Dad died five years ago, it took her less than a year to sell the house I had grown up in and settle herself in Florida, near a group of her like-minded cronies. Her being in Florida is perfectly fine with me. The less I see of her, the better we get along. Because I have never had a desire to leave Cincinnati, she had always been near enough to interject herself in my life way too often. Since her departure to Florida, the conversations about me finding a husband and "moving up in the educational world" (a thing I have no desire to do) have tapered off greatly.

"Hi, Mom," I said as I picked up my cell.

"How did you know it was me?" she asked, as she always does.

"Caller ID, Mom. It's 2019."

"Now, Hannah, you don't have to get snide." Here we go, I thought. "I just called to say hello and hear what's new with you."

"Oh, nothing much." I lied easily. Lots of practice over the years. "What's new with you?"

"Well, I just finished helping out with the library book sale this week." She launched into a boring litany about all her charitable and societal doings. I listened politely, interjecting occasional comments with an eye on the clock, thinking I would end the conversation in a couple more minutes. And then she said something that more than took me by surprise.

"I heard from Marge Youst that a woman was found dead in your school."

Damn you, Marge. She was an old neighbor of ours whom my mom stayed in contact with, always the busybody. It was really no surprise she had bestowed this bit of gossip on my mom.

"Ahh, yeah. That's true," I said dumbly.

"Well," Mom plied, "tell me all about it."

I was paralyzed with raging emotions for a moment. The battle to not have to deal with her reaction to the whole situation waged itself against the childish desire to pour things out to a parent. The childish side won, and I somewhat tearfully told her most of the story, leaving out gory details like the tons of blood and me puking in reaction to it all. Of course, I regretted it within minutes as the conversation turned (how, I don't know) into the old one we have had time and again, about why I want to teach the kids I teach. In the end, I got short with her, told her I had work to do, and wished I had an old-fashioned landline to slam down as I hung up.

Three hours later, as I packed away my schoolwork with some satisfaction, I realized that I still felt like shit and was starving. I took a couple more ibuprofen and ate three granola bars and a banana. I grinned as I thought back to how much fun I had had at the wedding. I sort of grinned back over the whole weekend, but I backed up too far and got back to Gretchen.

Trying to take my mind off the unpleasant, I decided to do a little housework. I was already patting myself on the back for getting my schoolwork done, and now I was *cleaning*. I also thought some physical activity might help me get rid of the hangover. I made quick work of cleaning the flat, straightening up piles, dusting off surfaces (glancing guiltily at my weights and wiping them off a bit with my dust rag,) spraying a little Tilex in the bathroom. I found that it actually did make me feel better. I didn't get my mind completely off Gretchen, but I have to admit I indulged in a little pleasure at the thought of not having her in my life anymore. No more ridiculous emails about how we weren't meeting Rosie's needs. No more impossible demands. No more threats to my job. Not that I *really* wanted her dead, but there was no doubt that my life would be easier without her around. I found myself humming a little tune. What is that song? I thought to myself. I hummed a little more and suddenly stopped in mid-hum. I had been droning, "Ding Dong! The Witch is Dead." What an evil subconscious I have.

After a mere thirty minutes of cleaning, I decided things were sterile enough to meet my low standards. I put on tennies and a heavy hoodie. I could see hope in Rascal's eyes. When I got out his leash, he danced in circles, then sat statue-still while I put the leash on him. Grasping my end of the leash in his mouth, he pranced downstairs and hopped in the car.

I try to get to a park every weekend. That day we headed for Ault Park. For a park in the middle of the city, it has a fair number of trails in real woods and is pretty hilly, so it's not too easy of a hike. (There are so many hilly places in Cincinnati. It's because it's sitting right next to the Ohio River.) I love the entrance to Ault, where classy old homes give way to a wide, sweeping avenue. I'm not a big one for jealousy, but I have to honestly say that I drive slowly past those lovely old Tudors, wishing I lived in one. The road meanders left, then right, past mature woods, up to the manicured circle, complete with a pillared pavilion and stunning, orderly gardens.

I parked on the left side of the circle and we took off down a well-marked trail, through the woods toward a creek far below. "It's pretty effin' cold out here," I commented to no one in particular as my breath came out in visible wisps. Now, this may sound crazy, but honestly, Rascal hates it when I curse, which I do fairly often outside of school. There are many times throughout my school day when I'd *like* to curse, but being around the kids is like being around my mom in that way. There's a built-in, subconscious filter keeping the baddies at bay. I figure on my own time, though, what the hell? I'm all grown up. I can cuss if I want to. But right then, Rascal stopped in his tracks and looked back at me reproachfully.

"I didn't even say it. I just said effin'," I rationalized. "Don't be such a Goody Two-shoes." I walked past him and he hustled to retake the lead. We worked our way down the steep hill to the creek, where Rascal went in for a drink and a wade even though it was south of forty on a thermometer. We walked along the creek for a while, just enjoying the exercise, the fresh air, the beauty of the bare tree branches against the azure sky, and the wintry view that allows you to see the lay of the land. But eventually my mind shifted into murkier territory, and I started rehashing not just the past few days but the events leading up to them, and even Rosie's family.

The Mitchells sure are an enigma. Rosie is such a great kid. Down syndrome, of course, can come to any family. It doesn't care about brains, beauty, or money. And Rosie's parents have all that. But I could never figure out what Nathan saw in Gretchen. She was such an utter bitch, and he seemed like a pretty nice guy. Would a guy really kill off his wife just because she was a bitch? Why not just divorce her? And why do it at a school? But I had already figured this one out: to divert suspicion, of course. Going down another mental path, why did they keep putting Rosie's surgery off? Nathan had impressed on me months before how badly she needed the surgery and that we were not to let her exert herself too much at school. What kind of life is that for a kid? Yet they had postponed the surgery twice, never providing me with any reasons. But maybe they figured it was none of my business.

By now, I was hiking my way up a pretty steep grade. Rascal was giving me a bit of help by forging along, tugging me at a faster rate than I would have accomplished on my own. I almost tripped once and started watching for roots and loose stones. I tugged back a bit on his leash and called to him to halt, which he did, immediately putting his nose to the ground, sniffing around for entertainment. I paused to catch my breath, looking up the increasingly steeper grade that I had yet to climb. Just as I looked up, someone slipped over the top of the hill and out of my sight. I was a little surprised, as I hadn't seen anyone ahead of me on the trail until now. Irrationally, I felt a tiny twinge of fear creeping up on me. What was that all about? The paths at Ault are well used, and I often see other hikers here. Maybe it was all those murderous thoughts I had been thinking.

"Dope," I said aloud, shaking my head at my mental wanderings as I started up the steep path with Rascal climbing ahead of me. The only acceptable position to him is lead dog. A few minutes later, we came over the crest of the hill with me a bit winded and

Rascal showing that classic sign of dog fatigue, tongue hanging out the side of his mouth.

As we walked along the park's back path, my eyes were drawn to the pavilion above me. I thought of hiking up the little hill so I could take in the incredible view up there. On the one side was the Little Miami valley, and on the other, the formal gardens. From between two of the pillars, a young girl came out, looked down at me, and waved.

"Hi, Ms. H," came a familiar voice. She ran along the edge of the huge concrete base of the pavilion, then holding the rail, slowed down to descend the stairs carefully. I watched her in a state of mild shock. It was Rosie. What was she doing here? I walked over to the bottom of the stairs to greet her. Rascal was in full greeting mode, tail wagging, body gyrating. Rosie was unfazed. She patted him on the head, allowed him to kiss her, then turned and wrapped her arms around my waist, giving me a hug.

"What are you doing here?" I asked as she pulled away. I noticed a blue tinge to her lips. The short run and descent down the stairs had overtaxed her leaky heart.

"Dad and I came for a walk." She turned, looking up the stairs, and I saw Nathan, descending slowly, an unpleasant expression on his face.

"Rosemary, you know you're not supposed to run," he reminded her mildly. And then to me, "Hi, Hannah." I noticed a distinct frost in the air, and it wasn't on account of the temperature. Nathan stood there, glaring at me openly. This was the first time I had seen him since those awful events of Thursday.

"Nathan," I began, "I'm so sorry—" but he shook his head slightly and turned his eyes toward Rosie, stopping the words on my lips. The message was unmistakable. I nodded once and smiled at Rosie.

"I'm surprised you and Rosie are here, considering her condition," I said, realizing too late that it probably sounded like criticism.

"We were doing a few errands," he said, "and just thought we'd stop by for a few minutes. Rosie loves it here."

"We saw your car," Rosie chimed in.

"Come on, Rosemary. We need to get going," said Nathan. And he rather abruptly turned from me and started walking away. As she was being hustled off, she turned and waved to me, grinning.

I waved back but stood glued to the spot. What was that all about? They had seen my car? *Where* did they see my car? My mind wandered on. Had they followed me here? If so, why? Was it Nathan I had seen back in the woods? Now I was actually a little scared. But that was ridiculous.

Rascal was anxious to move on, so I picked up the pace and headed downhill to my car. While my four-legged friend filled his nose with aromas of dirt, squirrel, pollen, and poop, I filled my mind with meanderings. Why was I so shaken? Was Nathan really the nice guy he had always seemed to me to be? How much can a guy put up with before it actually changes him? I had seen Gretchen be kind and loving to Rosie, but had she been that way with Nathan? Or was he the recipient of the venomous vibes that she put out to so many others? My mind jumped back again to seeing Herm last night at the wedding and his comment about someone reaching the last straw. I allowed myself to muse on with ugly thoughts as I strolled past beautifully kept gardens just beginning to be touched by the colors of spring.

In the year that Rosie has been in my class, I have heard rumors about Gretchen. I try not to listen to nasty gossip. Well, maybe I listen, but at least I try not to advance it. In response to the rumors about Gretchen's infidelities, I had repeatedly responded that I didn't believe it. And maybe had even added, "Who would ever want to sleep with such a bitch?"

Reaching the car, I poured half a bottle of water into a bowl for Rascal, gulping down the other half myself. He took a couple of slurps, then hopped in the car, lying down across the backseat and heaving a big sigh—such a tough life this dog has. As I drove home, I remembered meeting Gretchen before Rosie was even in my class. I had gone to her IEP meeting at the elementary building, toward the end of her fifth-grade year, to meet her mom, and as it turned out, her dad. I recalled that I had thought Gretchen attractive, well dressed, intelligent, nicely done out, with hair, makeup, and nails just so. When had she become ugly to me? "Ha!" I said aloud, startling Rascal into sitting up and looking around. "When I got to know her, that's when."

Chapter 17

For nearly a month, I had been promising Stella that I would install a new garbage disposal for her. I had bought the damn thing immediately but had been finding what I told myself were good reasons not to install it. I didn't have time. I had more important stuff to do. I needed to sleep in, etc. I was finally sick of my own excuses. I went down to the garage and loaded a little tool bag, pulling what I needed from my dad's ancient dinosaur of a toolbox. My father loved his tools, took care of them, and kept them in exact order. Wrenches lined up by size, pliers in one drawer, screwdrivers in the next.

As a kid, I was allowed to use his tools as long as I put them back where they belonged when I was done. As the type of learner who always chose the hard way, I had once, at about the age of eight, left a hammer in our backyard and had hell to pay when Dad nearly mowed over it. My sore butt made me into a staunch follower of his organization ever after. And although Dad has been gone for a few years, all of his tools are still with me, and in their correct places. (If only I could apply this organization to the rest of my life.) I follow his example, except for the closing-the-top-compartment rule. When you close it, the whole toolbox locks. It just seems like a pain in the butt to open the top every time I want something out of a drawer.

While I was down there, I flipped the breaker for Stella's kitchen electricity. When I'd had a new breaker box put in a few years ago, the oh-so-patient electrician had helped me label all the new breakers, which has saved me a lot of trips up and down stairs when I have to do things electric.

I hiked up the two floors to Stella's apartment with tools and the garbage disposal, nearly dumping the tools twice during the climb. She heard me coming and was peeking out the door before I got to the second-floor landing, her orange hair aflame and her attire its usual entertainment, today a green muumuu adorned with pink flamingos. Where would a person even buy something like that? I felt a smile lift the corners of my mouth.

"Good afternoon, dear," she trilled. "Happy St. Patrick's Day."

"Hey, Stella. Same to you. How's life?"

"Glorious. I've been up since five thirty and have finished my baking."

Ah . . . the carrot had been presented. Stella knew very well that the way to my heart was through my stomach, via my sweet tooth. As she spoke, I detected the smell of cinnamon and sugar wafting my way. I stepped into her overheated apartment and spied a plate of cinnamon rolls appealingly placed on the little end table between her Queen Anne chairs.

"Tea, dear?"

"Sure. Why not?" This was part of our routine. The bigger the job, the more she plied me with sweet stuff. Stella is no dummy. She knew the garbage disposal was not a fun job (because I had whiningly told her as much). So I would get food both before and after the job. Fine with me. Today was Sunday. I make it a rule to eat whatever I want on Sundays.

I accepted the tea, inhaled a fat cinnamon roll, chatted for a few minutes, and finally got to work.

In case you've never installed a garbage disposal, it's a bitch. Getting the old one off isn't all that bad, provided that all the screws will come loose. I lucked out in that department today, managing not even to drop the thing on my hand as I lowered it and pulled it out from under the sink. Getting the new one in is the hard part. A garbage disposal weighs about ten pounds, which isn't so much until you try to hold that up with one hand while kneeling with your head under a cabinet and screwing screws in with your other hand. I gave it one try before I gave up and looked around Stella's kitchen for something to prop the disposal up on. We finally found a pot that, when placed upside down, was just the right height to hold the disposal in place. With a minimum of cursing (no F-bombs in front of Stella—it'd kill her), I finally got it in. She turned the water off and on a few times while I checked for leaks. Of course, it leaked. I tightened the screws twice and declared it installed, with a warning to Stella to check under the sink every few days to make sure it was dry. I turned the pot right side up and left it under the drain to catch any possible drips. We stood around the kitchen while I drank another cup of tea, demolished one more cinnamon roll, watched appreciatively as Stella wrapped up further confections for me, and listened to her litany of neighborhood gossip.

Sometimes I get a little impatient with her habit of reporting to me every tiny incident that happens around the building, but I'm not very observant about that kind of stuff, so I always figure there's no harm in listening. She bored me with tidbits: the across-the-street neighbor's dog had been barking all day yesterday. Steve (downstairs) had gotten UPS deliveries *twice* on Thursday. And then, something that caught my interest.

"I saw that handsome young man you work with. He came over last week in the middle of the day. That seemed odd because I knew you were at work."

I stopped in mid-chew. It seemed odd, indeed. What was Jamie doing over here during the day?

"Did he go to the front door?" I asked.

"No. He went into the garage through the side door."

I had mixed emotions over this; the first was to crack up over the thought of Stella peeping down at Jamie. The second was, what in the hell was going on? Or maybe she just had the day and time wrong.

"Are you sure it was the middle of the week? Could it have been late Friday afternoon?"

"Oh, no. In fact, I'm almost sure it was Tuesday. Or was it Wednesday? Anyway, it was right around noon. I know that for sure."

I made light of it to Stella. "Hmm. Can't think why he'd be here. Maybe he left something here last time he stopped in. I'll have to ask him." No doubt I'd be doing that.

Wanting suddenly to get out of there, I made excuses to leave, grabbed the goodies and my tools, and left. Back in my own apartment, I fussed and fumed around a little bit about Jamie being over here without me knowing it. Finally, I concluded that Stella had to have been confused. Maybe she saw someone she *thought* was Jamie, some delivery guy or cable TV dude.

I decided to retire early Sunday night. It had been a big weekend for me, and I was feeling the need for a good night's rest. Ha! That would prove to be a fantasy. But for now, I dove into bed and fell immediately and thankfully to sleep as my head touched the pillow.

It was one twenty in the morning by my lighted dial when Rascal set up a ruckus that would have awakened the dead. I started up with my heart pounding in my ears. I tried to shush Rascal and calm him down, but he would have none of it. He continued to run back and forth from me to the porch door, barking, whining, and pawing at the door as I struggled to get into my robe and grab the big old flashlight that I keep on the floor next to my bed. It's about fifteen inches long and I always figure it can double as a weapon if I ever have the need to conk somebody over the head.

I went to the porch door, now half-awake, and shined the light around the screened-in area, knowing that no one would be there. I always latch the screen door at night. But as I shone the light around, I caught a little bit of movement down low, on the floor. I flipped the light on, and what did I see? To my horror, Mr. O'Possum had been scrounging around on my porch. Of course, at the instant I flipped on the light, he "died" and was lying there, acting like the victim of a hit and run. Now I have a healthy respect and just a little bit of fear of all wild animals. They are *wild*, after all. And I know Mr. O'Possum has very sharp teeth, which, if playing dead fails, he will use. He also has the ugliest tail of any animal I know. I am disgusted by that giant rat tail. In fact, I have to admit that I hate possums. I knew immediately how he had gotten in: the doggy door. I had always feared this might happen one day, but I figured it would be a raccoon, way down the list from Mr. O on my fear scale. I knew I had to get this guy off my porch or Rascal would have me and all the neighbors up all night.

I grabbed a broom and shut Rascal out of the little bedroom. He continued to whine through the door at me, but at least he wasn't at full volume. I went out on the porch and, keeping the broom bristles aimed at the now "dead" possum, I sidled over to the doggy door. I lifted the flap and tucked it into the edge of the screen above it. It kept wanting to fall back down, but I kept at it, with one eye constantly on the critter, until on the fourth try, it stuck open. Now he would have a means of escape in sight. I stood there for a minute, looking at him and wondering what to do next. God, he was ugly. He had a little smirk on his face as he laid there playing dead, which frankly scared the shit out of me. I checked him out from ten feet away with my broom aimed at him just in case he decided to come back to life and attack. He was a well-fed, fat guy. Greasy looking fur and that hideous naked rat tail. I gave a little involuntary shiver as I estimated its length at eight inches.

Not even a tiny twitch came from him during this thirty-second eternity. I gathered up my nerve and approached him. I gave him a little nudge with the broom. Nothing. I nudged him a little harder. Still nothing. Now I gave him somewhat of a shove with the broom bristles, and finally, I got a little reaction. He still laid there playing dead, but his lips curled back so I could see the snarl of teeth they hid. That's all it took. I backpedaled full speed into the bedroom, slamming the door behind me, then turning to see him still laying there playing dead, but with those sharp teeth exposed. I sighed.

You win, I thought. I glanced over at the screen flap that I had tucked up. It was still up, so he'd see his means of escape. I propped my broom in a corner and slipped out of the room, closing the door behind me, much to Rascal's dismay, then wheedled him to come into my bedroom with me and shut that door too. He got up in bed with me and settled down with a few more whines of complaint.

I tossed and turned for a while, but sleep was elusive. I finally threw the covers back and grabbed the list I had made the night before. I added a few more details like meeting Nathan and Rosie at the park, which still had me freaked out. Could that really have been a coincidence? My notes were getting to be a jumbled mess. Deciding I needed a better display, I went into my office/second bedroom and pulled out a long-unused dry erase board. I had bought the thing a few years back to try to organize my time on. That lasted for about two days, and I had never used it since. I dug out three dry-erase markers and carted it all out to my dining room, where I propped it up on a chair. Rascal pouted after me, unhappy at the closed door denying him possible possum access.

I started columns of facts (green) and questions (red), a column for me, one for Nathan, and a new column for unknown suspects (woefully empty right then). I didn't even dare to write down the awl, referring to it as "weapon" under my column. Things did *not* look good for Nathan, especially considering that he had followed me to the park. *Maybe* he had followed me. But somehow, my column looked even worse.

I sat staring at the board, brooding. I was tempted to indulge in a major pity party for poor little me. But I really needed to get back to bed, and it just isn't my style anyway. I shook off the impulse. Instead, I roamed around the flat for a few minutes, resisting the urge to check out the situation on the porch, then had a bowl of cereal, my little gray cells in overdrive as I munched. Hercule Poirot would have been proud of me as I figured a few things out, made a few notes on the board, and hatched a little plot. I told myself again that I'm good at solving problems, at figuring things out. I could become an investigator on my own. Why not? I knew what I would do. It was a bit risky, but I could pull it off. Couldn't I? I felt like I needed somewhat of a miracle to get myself off the hook, and it seemed I was going to have to make it myself.

In the morning, as I opened the spare bedroom door, Rascal was by my side, curious, but quiet. A good sign. I shined the flashlight around the porch, twice for good measure, then went out onto the porch and shined it down the stairs and around the yard as well. Then I let Rascal loose. He wore out his nose sniffing around the porch, stairs, and yard, but Mr. O'Possum had vacated the premises. I know that possums are nocturnal and that he wouldn't come back while I was at work, but still, I grabbed a small bulletin board out of a corner of my little workroom and put it over the doggy door to prevent any entry.

Chapter 18

Monday, March 18th

I rolled into my classroom early Monday morning, as always, hoping to get organized before the kids arrived. I flipped on the lights and looked around the room, wishing I had picked up better on Friday. My classroom always has a lived-in look, with a few too many piles of papers lying around, half-finished projects lining the floor along the back wall, and a haphazard array of student work displayed here and there. But this morning, there were also pencils all over the floor and papers left lying on desks. The board hadn't been erased, and the row of plants that live along the windowed wall drooped in their pots, sadly in need of water. Oh well, I thought, I'll make the kids clean up. It's good for them to have some responsibilities, and besides, it's their mess. I'm such a good rationalizer.

Because I teach all subject areas, my room looks much like an elementary classroom, with a jumble of stuff on display. Science experiments live next to history projects, sharing space with writing journals and math materials. The room is overcrowded with therapy equipment, a big old rocking chair, and two teachers' desks. It's a good thing we don't have very many kids. There's a limited amount of room for people. But I prefer to think of it as cozy rather than crowded.

Ava and Anne's desk is always neat and orderly. Mine ranges from passably straightened up in the early part of the day to chaos by the end of the day. As the day goes on, I start simply throwing stuff on it because I'm too busy (I rationalize again) to put it away. It was in total chaos that morning. I hadn't even made an attempt to tidy it up when I had left on Friday. In truth, none of us ever sits at a desk when the kids are in the room. Some kiddo always needs help. Some adult always needs to run the show. I am usually the ringmaster, but not all the time. Both Anne and Ava also enjoy the role, and there are times when I gladly turn it over to one of them to enjoy the intimacy with the kids that working one-on-one brings.

I set my briefcase down under my desk and pulled out my lesson plans to remind myself of what we'd be doing that day. I slipped off my shoes to get comfy. As it turned out, this would be the last peaceful moment of my day. A steady parade of coworkers devoured my time. I was still a celebrity because of the whole "dead parent in the bathroom" thing. I didn't like all this early morning gossipy stuff, and I didn't want it to become the norm. To top it all off, people were starting to theorize about Gretchen's demise, which everyone now knew was, in fact, murder. Of course, the first suspect was Nathan, but more than one person jokingly commented along the lines of that I probably would have loved to kill her. While that may have been true, figuratively, I didn't want people to say it aloud for fear it would be taken literally. It made me squirm on account of my being pretty positive that the murder weapon was my missing awl. Of course, no one but me knew that, but I was worried it was only a matter of time before the police would somehow figure it out. I could feel myself getting a bit short of breath and my ears growing hot as my friends yukked it up, making me out as the murderer.

Finally, the last of my coworkers departed as she started hearing kid's voices in the hall. Alone at last, I took the time to look over the day I had envisioned. I knew the kids would be tumbling in shortly, but I would make the best of the few moments I had. I concentrated on my plan book.

After only a minute or two, rather than seeing or hearing something, I simply felt the presence of someone watching me. I looked up from my work to find Zelda planted in front of my desk. Zelda is Zak's older sister. The two of them are opposites on the continuum of what siblings might be. Zak is a wiry little guy, carrot-topped and freckled, happy-go-lucky, a sprite, sociable, the class clown. Zelda is serious and quiet, slow-moving, and a loner. She is tall and huge, probably weighing in at over three hundred pounds. She has long, silky hair that might be purple one week and deep red the next. She has a beautiful peaches-and-cream complexion and an infrequent, tight little smile. Sadly, her arms bear the scars of her discontent, in multiple marks where she has scratched herself until she bleeds. She has spent time in psychiatric hospitals, which she openly admits have not helped her. She is a shrink's nightmare, and I hear, often a hellion at home. To me, she is always polite, quietly friendly, and I believe, somewhat open.

"Good morning, Ms. H."

"Good morning, Zelda. How's life?"

"It sort of sucks, as always." This was said with a shrug and eyes cast downward. "I just stopped by to let you know that Zak will be late today. He has an orthodontist appointment." I already knew this since Zak's mom had emailed me. Zelda is a fairly frequent visitor to my classroom. I suspect it may be one of the few places at school where she feels accepted and safe. She also enjoys a bit of celebrity status here as the older sister of one of my students.

"Thanks, Zelda. I appreciate your stopping in. So what's making your life suck today?"

"Just the usual stuff; kids making fun of me cuz I'm fat. I can't concentrate in any of my classes. I've got an F in math." Now she locked her gaze on me, sober-faced.

"Why the F?" Zelda is a smart young lady, but she also truly has ADD, and medicinal attempts to control it haven't been very successful. But an F?

"I can't understand these algebraic equations, and Mr. Davis won't help me at all."

"Have you asked for help?"

"I raise my hand, but he never calls on me." I wondered about this. George Davis is a great guy, and, I've always thought, one who gives every kid in his classroom a chance.

"Do you want me to talk to him or check into what you could do to get your grade up?"

"It doesn't matter to me," she said with another little shrug, always the fatalist. But I had the feeling that it did matter, or she wouldn't have brought it up so readily.

"All right, my dear," I said, coming around my desk to give her a hug. "Try to have a good day. I think I'll have a little chat with Mr. Davis."

"Okay. You too, Ms. H." She plodded off to start her miserable day, tugging at my heartstrings as she went. This young lady had no idea how much more she haunted my musings than did my own students.

Rosie was heavily on my mind this morning. I knew there were people who would fault Nathan for planning to send her back to school only a few days after her mom had died, but I wasn't one of them. He and I had a fairly civil conversation about it by phone Sunday evening (with no mention *at all* of our unexpected meeting in the park), and I agreed with him that sending her in on Monday

121

was worth a try. What was she supposed to do, sit at home and cry all day?

The kids began trickling in, greeting me, acting excited to be back at school. (This always amazes me.) No Rosie yet. As the bell rang, I stepped out into the nearly empty hall, and there she was, holding hands with her dad and plodding along with her head down.

"Good morning, Rosie," I called out. She looked up and smiled, then let go of her dad's hand and came to me for a hug. I swallowed hard as I looked up at Nathan. "Why don't you go on into the room. I think there are a few more hugs waiting for you in there." She smiled again and went in without saying a word. Nathan looked gray. Without thinking, I reached out and hugged him. His arms went around me, and we just stood there for a minute, both of us trying to keep our composure.

"Thanks, Hannah," he said as he pulled away.

"She'll be fine. We'll take good care of her," I said. He nodded and turned to leave without another word. I pulled the classroom door shut behind me and turned to see Rosie hugging Anne, then Ava. Then every kid in the room lined up to hug her.

Few words were exchanged, although I heard Christie in her breathy, soft voice say, "Sorry about your mom."

Chloe was the last in line, patting Rosie on the back and intoning "Aww." Tears flowed among the adults, Rosie, and, to my surprise, Basil.

The kids took their seats and we started the day, but I could see things weren't going well for Rosie. She sat with her arms folded on her desk, head down. Anne took note of this, went to her, and whispered something in her ear. Then the two of them left the room.

When morning announcements came on, interrupting us as they did daily just as we were getting underway, Chloe jumped out of her seat, putting her hands over her ears and pacing back and forth across the back of the room. Ava tried briefly to get her to calm down and sit, but she would have none of it. Chloe is so volatile, and for her the balance is so tenuous that at times it's simply better to back off. Ava, realizing this was one of those times, withdrew, and when the announcements ended, Chloe stood for a few minutes at the back of the room, then eagerly passed out fliers when I asked her if she'd like to help me. Sometimes redirection is a teacher's best tool. I wondered what the deal was with Chloe's new hatred of the announcements. I hadn't checked on the volume as I had meant to do, so I made a quick note of it now. Having Chloe agitated was not a good way for any of us to start our day.

We worked our way through a very first-gradish routine that my students love: lunch menu for today, weather, calendar skills, and a little bit of social exchange that we call "News," which is really just a chance for them to share what's going on in their lives. Sometimes they're so newsy that I have to shut them down so their conversation doesn't cut too far into our reading work. On other days it lags and I have to canvas them on their lives. I have a repertoire of questions that I think are important for them to think about, which also help them to learn about how other people live. As it happens, these are also questions that give me significant peeks into their lives. Things like "Who do you have dinner with?" and "What do you do when you're home alone?" can garner for me, as someone who is responsible for helping them become more independent, valuable information.

At times these little talks are not only enlightening but also entertaining. I have learned that Basil's mom spends her spare time looking for dates online, that Josh's family always sits down to a home-cooked meal, that Zak can find a house key under one of the bricks by his back door, and that Rosie's garage entrance to the house is always unlocked.

Today we got through the pleasantries and down to business quickly. With Chloe listening to a book on CD and the rest of the kids in two groups that Ava and I led, we were all engaged when Anne and Rosie returned to the room. Rosie showed me a picture of her mom that Anne had pulled up on her phone (from social media, I assumed) and printed for Rosie. The two of them worked on getting it taped to Rosie's notebook, and I noticed that Rosie had visibly brightened. I mouthed a silent thank-you to Anne, and she gave me an it's-nothing gesture with a wave of her hand as she and Rosie left to get to Rosie's first class.

Close to the end of reading class, Megan's bus driver came to the door and whispered to Ava, who then came to me saying the driver wanted to talk to me. Ava took over at the front of the room and I went out in the hall with the driver.

This is a wonderful and kind driver, a lady who puts up with Megan's nonstop, often unintelligible chatter on the bus, and even loves her. She was not a happy camper at the moment.

"I'm sorry to bother you while you're teaching," she started, "but I had to write up Megan today." I was shocked.

"Oh, my God, what did she do?"

"She used her markers to draw all over the back of the seat in front of her on the way to school. She insisted on showing it to me before she got off the bus. She told me it needed decorating."

I rolled my eyes and sighed. I sort of wished the driver hadn't written her up for it, but I totally got it. The drivers have to clean those buses. The marker would have to be scrubbed off.

"Hmmm. How about this? What if we make her scrub off the marker? I could bring her out this afternoon a few minutes before dismissal to work on it until you're ready to leave."

"Well, I guess that'd be okay."

"That way, she gets a sort of punishment, and the other kids, getting on the bus, will see that she didn't just get away with it because she's one of my kids."

"Yeah, I think that's good," said the driver, "but I already turned in the write-up to Ian."

"No problem. I'll go and talk to him. He'll be glad he doesn't have to take any action." We parted ways, and I got back to the kids.

I tried presenting a new concept in math class, and the kiddos were lost and frustrated. So far, so bad. But during my planning bell, I actually got a lot done. No one bugged me and I felt better prepared for the rest of the day. Toward the end of the period, I moseyed on up to Ian's office to talk to him about Megan's write-up. He approved of the making-her-clean-up-her-mess plan but thought he ought to talk to her about the write-up. Fine with me. I sent her up to see him during fourth bell and had sort of a hard time keeping a straight face when she came back madder than a wet hen. Megan is a free spirit and a feisty little thing. She is full of creative ideas (thus the bus art) and proudly proclaims her Down syndrome to anyone who will listen. She talks very fast and has terrible articulation, so it's usually hard to understand her. The gist I caught was that she didn't appreciate it that Ian thought her artwork on the bus seat was scribbling. I deciphered the phrase "my decorations" several times and was actually a bit glad that Ian had been the bearer of the bad news instead of me.

Chapter 19

I have recess duty every Monday. Some teachers hate recess duty because you have to be outside, but I love it for the same reason. I like all the seasons. Summer gets a bit too hot and sticky for me, and yes, winter can be pretty flippin' cold. But I love the cold crispness of the air, and the sky always seems bluer on a cold day. Every teacher, counselor, and administrator in the building has to do a semester of recess duty, but it's just one day a week. Pretty hard to bitch about that, especially when the principal's out there doing it too. It takes two adults to police the large paved play area, which doubles as bus parking when the kids are arriving and leaving school. One adult usually stays at the top of the stairs overlooking the adolescent mass, with a whistle never far from his or her lips, while the other roams among the kids, keeping order. I am the roamer because I like to see what the kids are up to and enjoy eavesdropping on them a bit. Betsy the Bitch (not her real name, as you may have guessed, but what the kids appropriately call her behind her back) prefers the top of the steps, next to the building, removed from the kids.

I've never actually worked closely with Betsy, but when I was still fairly new at McKinley, she pulled a faux pas with me that I haven't forgiven. At the conclusion of a language arts curriculum meeting, she was telling me that she had heard such good things about me from two of the other language arts teachers. Just as I was basking in the praise, she threw in a comment that my mother has made to me several times. It went something like this: "You're

126

such a good teacher. Don't you think you're wasting your talents on those kids you teach?" I felt my ire boil up but gave her the same controlled response I have used on my mother.

"Don't you think the kids with the most challenges deserve to have the best teacher?" She backpedaled fast, but there is simply no good response to this. By design. Anyway, Betsy the Bitch seems like a fine nickname for her, especially when I see the way she deals with kids outside in the play area. For her, no one is good enough to avoid being tweeted at and railed on in front of their peers, no matter how small their infraction.

That Monday, the sun was out, and so were the kids. On cold days, many of them dawdle over lunch in order to stay in the cafeteria longer, but that day it was pushing sixty degrees and the play area was getting packed. Within five minutes after the first kids had burst through the cafeteria doors to get out into the sun, a fight was brewing at the far end of the paved area. (Naturally, as far from Betsy as the kids could be.) I heard the name-calling and saw kids creating a circle around the potential activity. A fight is always just too good to miss, even if you're not into the sight of two young dopes going at each other. I stepped into the open circle where, sure enough, two eighth-grade boys had their fists balled up, ready to duke it out. I stepped between them.

"Hey, hey, hey," I said, smiling at first one, then the other. They each danced a little to their own right, effectively circling me. They both kept their fists at the ready for the first jab. I really didn't think either of them would punch a teacher, but I was getting a little uneasy. "Chad, what's going on here?" I asked the one whose name I happened to know. I noticed that our crowd, rather than dispersing when I arrived, had gotten bigger.

"He called my mom a whore," said Chad, "and I'm sick of his shit. I'm gonna put his lights out."

"Go ahead and try," said the other kid, taking a step closer to Chad, and also, by the way, to me.

"Okay, this is over," I said in my loudest and strictest teacher voice. "Both of you. Get your fists down." I looked from one to the other, putting my hands on my hips to bring home my disgust with their behavior. And then I just waited, looking back and forth from one to the other. They each took a step first one way, then the other. I did the same, effectively putting myself between them. What an idiot. In desperation, I offered, "I guess I need to write you both up so you won't be out here to make trouble for a few weeks." Ah, the magic words. Fists went down. Fighting stances were abandoned. I waved a hand at the masses and told them to go find something else to do. I sent Chad to spend the remainder of his recess time next to Betsy and told his buddy he could walk the play area with me for the rest of his outside time. I learned his name during our little walking date, got treated to some righteous pouting over having to be my sidekick, and found out that he, of course, was completely innocent of any wrongdoing.

At one side of the paved area, there are two half basketball courts where several mostly male groups were playing pickup. I noticed Zak watching the action from the out-of-bounds area under the basket. I wandered a little closer and turned a bit away from the basketball court so it wouldn't look like I was spying. (I'm so damn sneaky.) Within a minute, the ball went out of bounds near Zak, and he chased it down, picking it up only to have it grabbed away from him by a tall, muscular eighth grader. I heard my new sidekick snicker, and I slid a sideways look his way that made him clam up. Will Dexley, grabber of the ball, is an athlete, a showoff, and a heartthrob of many an eighth-grade girl. I know Zak idolizes him because he talks about him in class all the time.

"I wanna play," said Zak.

Will ignored him. Then Zak ran around in front of him and positioned himself to guard Will as he started to toss the ball in bounds.

"Get out of the way," Will snarled. But Zak didn't get out of the way. He persisted in guarding Will and was actually doing a decent job of it, jumping around in front of him and waving his hands. Will put the ball under his arm and yelled at Zak, "Get out of the way, retard. We don't wanna play with you, cuz you suck!"

At that moment, The Bitch blew the whistle for the kids to line up. Zak turned and ran to get in line. Will bounced the ball hard once, then began sauntering across the playground. I stood with my arms crossed, glaring at him, willing him to notice me, which he did, but clearly couldn't have cared less. If anything, he increased his swagger a bit. Cocky little son of a bitch. I have a very short fuse for bullying, and I'd had my fill today. So much for my love of recess duty. I looked toward the sky, almost surprised that it was still blue.

The day plodded on, feeling very much like a Monday. The castle-building project in our social studies class was proving to be difficult for both kids and adults and made the classroom an even bigger mess. Days like that one make me feel like a bad teacher, although we still had those moments when the kids made us laugh, made each other laugh, and were their sweet, innocent selves. At a quarter to three, Megan and I left the classroom, leaving Ava to clean up the mess and get the kids headed for home. I knew I was the one getting off easy in going with Megan, but this one was the teacher's duty. We met up with Anne and Rosie in the hall. Anne reported that Rosie had done fairly well that day after Anne found the picture of her mom and took her under her wing. She is really good at that stuff. Rosie was excited about the plan to go over to her grandparents' house that evening for dinner, and I was sure it would be good for them all to be together.

As it turned out, Megan was still royally pissed off that she was being made to clean her decorations off the bus. As she scrubbed the seat back, she kept up a running commentary, which I didn't understand the words of, although the tone was perfectly clear. I watched, pointing out spots she had missed. Her driver (sitting in the driver's seat of the bus) and I made eye contact in the mirror, trying to keep straight faces. When other students started getting on the bus, Megan complained to them and even got some sympathy from a few. As the first bus started out of the parking lot, I told Megan she had done a good job and scampered off the bus with the bucket and scrub brush, not wanting to hold up the parade. Just as I stepped off the bus, I looked up to see Tweedledee and Tweedledum getting out of their car across the parking lot. I groaned aloud. Now it *really* felt like a Monday.

Dropping my cleaning stuff off in my room, I went up to the office quickly, hoping to be there and gone before the two portly cops had ambled that far. I pulled up Mr. William Dexley's file and took a look at his schedule. Study hall first bell. *Perrrfect*. This fit in *so* well with my little plan. I also had a peek at his grades while I was at it. C's in every class except PE, where he was sporting an A. He had a couple of recent write-ups in his record. I noted that his mom, Jessie, works at a neighborhood chili parlor. No dad listed. I hightailed it down to the classroom of Will's study hall teacher and asked her if he made good use of his study hall time.

She stopped shuffling papers into her briefcase and said, "Yeah, he makes good use of it. He flirts with the girls, yuks it up with his cronies, picks on kids, and gets on my last nerve." I refrained from asking her why she allowed all that. (I'm so damn self-righteous. Like I never let kids get away with stuff. Ha!)

"I'd like to borrow him as a helper in my reading class three days a week," I said. "Starting tomorrow."

"You can have him all five days if you want him," she said. "But I guarantee you'll regret messing with him. He's sort of a bully"— no shit, I thought—"and I don't think he's really a very good reader, anyway." She finished gathering her things up, making it clear she was ready to get out of there.

"That's okay. He won't have to be a great reader to help me. I'll stop by tomorrow at the beginning of first bell to recruit him."

"He won't want to help you," was her final warning. Oh yes, he will, I thought as I walked back to my room smiling, because I'll make his life hell if he doesn't.

Chapter 20

It was just getting dark when I headed for the neighborhood where the Mitchell family lives, an average upper-middle-class development of two-story homes on half-acre lots. It's an older development dotted with mature trees and semi-wooded lots. I thought about parking in the Mitchells' driveway. After all, I was coming over for a legitimate visit, right? Well, maybe not so legitimate since Rosie had told Anne that she and her dad were going "to Grandma and Grandpa's house for dinner." (I knew this was a Monday routine for them, one I was counting on. I figured that in the face of Gretchen's death, they'd surely not break this family tradition.) As I approached with their house on my right, I slowed down, deciding just to drive by and see if it looked like anyone was home. The house was dark. I drove past it and turned right on the first side street, three or four houses down from the Mitchells'. I pulled the car over and turned off the engine, sitting in the fast-fading light for a minute with my heart thudding a bit harder than usual. I was parked next to a row of pines in the side yard of the house on the corner. It was dark enough in the shadow of the trees to creep me out just a little. I grabbed my jacket and gloves, got out, and locked the car. I shrugged my way into my hoodie and pulled on the gloves. It was right chilly out that evening. I pulled my hood up, pausing on the sidewalk next to the pines for a moment. It was a clear night for March. I looked up at the sky. Half of a man in the moon looked down on me. Not a cloud in the sky. A few stars winked at me as if they were in on this crazy plan. A brisk breeze wafted the scent of pine toward me. Realizing that I was stalling, I put one foot in front of the other and walked in what I thought of as a businesslike manner down to the Mitchells' house.

I rang the doorbell, waited, then rang it again. No lights came on. No sounds emerged from inside. I knocked on the door. Still no signs of life. I turned and scoped out the neighborhood. Very quiet. Everyone was either not home yet or in for the night, probably parked in front of their televisions, watching *Big Bang Theory* reruns. As I should have been. I stood there for a few seconds, contemplating whether I really had the nerve to do what I had half-planned. Then I walked around to the back of the house and peeked into a set of French doors. The great room I was peering into was semi-lit by a light that had been left on over the stove at the kitchen end of the room. I cannot tell a lie. (At least not right here.) It was quite obvious that there was no one home. I tried the back door to the garage, and just as Rosie had told us months before, it was unlocked. I closed it behind me as I entered the garage and stood there in the darkness. My palms were sweating. My mouth was dry. My heart was trying to beat its way out of my chest. I reasoned with myself: I could walk out of here, and I would have done nothing wrong. Unless you count trespassing in someone's garage.

I put a hand on the knob of the door to the great room. It was, in fact, unlocked. I opened the door a crack. Were these people nuts? Who would go off and leave their house unlocked like this on a regular basis? Especially considering that a family member had been murdered less than a week before. (But, of course, if the murderer lived here, he would know that he and Rosie were in no danger.)

I called out, "Hello. Is anyone home?" I waited a few seconds, then stepped into the house, carefully closing the door behind me. The family room area yawned in front of me with the kitchen at the far end. It had been recently updated, all lovely modern furniture and beautiful granite, with stainless steel in the kitchen. I peeked through several doorways as I passed through the long room, seeing a dining room, entry hall, and small living room. At the end of the kitchen, I entered a laundry room. Crap! I had hoped this would be "Dad's office." I didn't like how far I was getting from the garage and a quick getaway. Of course, if they came home while I was here, wasn't I going to be trapped anyway? What the hell did I think I was doing? And yet I didn't turn back. Instead, I opened a door off the laundry and found myself in a small half bath. Trying the door on the far side, I was finally entering the hoped-for office. It was a small room with bookshelves along one wall and, to my relief, another set of French doors that opened onto a small side patio. An escape route. These doors were locked. (Gee, why bother when the garage is open to the world?) I unlocked the door, opened it, and peered out. A small stone patio on the side of the house was dimly lit by the clear sky and the half-moon.

I closed the door and turned to Nathan's desk. A laptop sat open on it. How convenient. I took a seat in his large, comfy chair and jiggled the mouse. The screen came to life, startling me a little with its brightness in the dark room. I couldn't believe my luck. Nathan had been checking email and left the account open. Guess he wasn't expecting me. I was really hoping to find some kind of evidence that would implicate him. Email seemed like a great place to start. I looked carefully at the open email, a notice from Duke Energy. Shit, I thought I paid a lot for heat! I made a mental note to make sure I left this email open when I was done with my browsing. I went to the inbox and perused what was there. Of course, I would only look at stuff he had already opened. Good God, did he ever delete anything? I worked my way backward in chronological time, as quickly as I could, and came to a notice dated the day before, from a life insurance company. This looked promising. I opened it and skimmed down.

Holy shit! Gretchen had been insured for half a million dollars. That seemed exorbitant to me, the owner of a tiny life insurance policy provided by the school district. Was that enough to make Nathan want to off his wife? I wasn't sure. It was certainly a fortune to me. Promising myself that I would consider that later, I went on, skimming through business stuff, a few social exchanges, and a couple of messages that went back and forth between Gretchen and Nathan. These were pretty businesslike as well. No lovey-dovey stuff. Just confirming dates of social engagements, some meetings, and a couple of doctor appointments regarding Rosie's surgery. But while they weren't exactly amorous, they also didn't display any animosity. Interesting. They just seemed like very ordinary messages between two married people. I was disappointed. But then, what had I expected? Maybe a threat to poison Gretchen? Or to stab her in the heart a few times in the girls' room?

I sighed as I noticed there were also a couple of messages sent by Rosie's doctor. I opened these just out of curiosity, but there was nothing special here; one had an attachment from a phlebotomist about blood tests for donor compatibility. This didn't quite sink in as I skimmed it. It had been years since I had studied heredity, blood compatibility, and all such complicated stuff. I made a half-hearted attempt to memorize a few of the details and then moved on. There was also one about postponing the date of surgery for another week. I already knew about the change of surgery date and wondered if it might even get postponed again due to Gretchen's death. I looked on, through paid bills and random messages from people I didn't know. I did some more sighing in frustration.

There was the insurance thing, which could be key or might be only a tiny clue, and possibly a red herring at that. Maybe I could afford just a little more time to snoop through the drawers of Nathan's desk. But I was feeling a bit skittish and thought I best not. What a waste of time this was. I had stupidly come here thinking I might find some big evidence and had found little or nothing. I had risked being discovered, embarrassed, possibly charged, with what? Criminal trespassing? That sounded horrible. I was possibly jeopardizing my career. What was I thinking?

Just as I clicked back to the Duke email that I had seen when I first sat down, I heard voices. Shit, shit, shit! They were home. Not just home, but in the house. I nearly screamed, making a little squeak as I clamped a hand over my mouth. I jumped out of the chair, had the wherewithal to open the French door quietly, and stepped out onto the little side patio. I carefully closed the door, forcing myself not to move too quickly. As I glanced back, I could see the computer screen, still lit up due to my activities, but there was nothing I could do about that.

A neighbor's dog started barking to beat the band. He had undoubtedly spotted me. I tip-toe-ran off the patio and threw myself on the ground behind a low hedge that ran along its border. Anyone looking out of the house would miss me, but the dog, I knew, could still see me. He continued with the ruckus. The hedge was barely high enough to shield me as I lay on the ground, so I crept along it on my belly, pulling myself commando style toward the rear of the house, which was now well lit. When I came to the end of the hedge, I realized I couldn't go back along the house without risk of being seen. Also, crawling through the grass like that was really strenuous for me. (Some commando I am.) I couldn't keep it up for long.

I looked around and decided my best flight route would be to head straight back and cut through the yards of the houses on the street that backed up to the Mitchells'. As I took off at a jog through the backyard, I heard a neighbor's door open. Heart in my throat, I had an urge to hit the dirt, but I kept running.

"Cujo, shut up!" said a loud voice. And then, "Hey, you!"

Cujo continued to bark, but I didn't wait around to see what his owner was doing. I poured on the speed, not looking back. I ran between two houses and didn't slow down until I hit the sidewalk on the next block over. Then I slowed to a businesslike walk, which I figured would look less conspicuous than running pell-mell. I was also totally winded from my hundred-yard sprint. Jeez, I need to start exercising. I walked down to the corner, turned, and fought the urge to run to my car. I was now walking along in the shadow of the pine trees, telling my heart to slow down, when there was a flurry of movement behind me. I actually felt pain in my chest, and it was about that time that I tripped. Over what? A crack in the sidewalk? My own feet? Whatever it was, it sent me flying forward, careening to keep my balance for a few wild paces. Recovering from the stumble (without falling on my face—yay, me), I realized the rustling had been only a flock of roosting birds that I had disturbed as I walked by the trees. I got into my car, locked the door quickly, put my head down on the steering wheel, and banged it a few times for good measure. Then I got out of Dodge as quickly as I could without leaving rubber behind.

I drove through the neighborhood, reciting a little ditty that went like this: "Fuck, that was close. Fuck, that was close. Fuck, that was close."

Once I was home, I gave myself a long, loud lecture about what a dumbass I was. Who did I think I was, Kinsey Millhone? What was I trying to do? I self-chastised with everything I could think of to throw at myself. And worst of all, it was all for naught. I hadn't learned a thing. Well, that wasn't quite true. Maybe half a million *was* enough for Nathan to want to do Gretchen in.

Rascal sat looking at me as if I had screws loose. Wise canine.

I wandered over to my dry erase board, still propped on a dining room chair. I gazed at my list of facts, questions, and suspects for a while, then picked up the green marker to add a few facts: "life insurance" and, just for good measure, "surgery postponed." I stood there and stared for a long moment, and another thing popped into my head. I wrote, "Rosie reported fight." I couldn't remember quite when that had happened. The week before? Seemed like longer ago than that, but time was somehow both rushing by and slogging slowly for me. Probably didn't matter anyway. But as I looked at my accumulated list, Nathan looked a bit better to me as a suspect.

I decided to celebrate that a little bit and maybe relieve some stress, too. I got myself a collection of snacks, which I grazed on while watching a stupid cop show on TV. I noted that the cop who illegally searched a house didn't get barked at, yelled at, or detected in any way. And he even got some actual evidence. Ha! TV is so unrealistic.

Chapter 21

I dragged myself out of sleep and out of bed, shutting off the alarm as it blared at me. I had finally slept well. But as I went through my usual morning routine, I found that I couldn't wake up. I slurped down a cup of tea and decided to make a second cup for the road, hoping the caffeine would give me a jolt. I try to get things ready each night before I go to bed—clothes out, school stuff put away in my briefcase, lunch packed. But I had been a lazy girl the previous night (or maybe a traumatized one, due to my narrow escape) and found myself scrambling that morning. I decided to buy lunch since I didn't have time to fix anything. I eyed a pair of corduroys lying on the floor of my bedroom, picked them up, and shook them out. Not too wrinkly. When had I worn them? Friday? Surely no one would notice. I pulled them on and threw on a baggy sweater, not bothering to look in the mirror. I just didn't want to see.

If I stop and think about it, I know I should pay more attention to how I look. I should take note of what's in style. I should wear things that flatter me. But the thing is, I really don't care. All that is just not who I am.

I managed to get myself to work by seven o'clock and had a productive hour before the kids arrived. I actually felt good that day, although when I thought of what I had done the night before, it left me a little aghast at my own behavior.

I told Ava and Anne my little story about Will Dexley and how he was going to become a "volunteer" in our classroom.

Anne gave me a conniving smile and nodded her head with a chuckle as I explained the plan.

Ava actually rubbed her hands together and said, "I can't *wait* to meet this kid."

After our short homeroom bell, I left Ava in charge of the beginnings of reading class since Anne would be leaving with Rosie. I hustled down to Will's study hall room, walked in, and gave the teacher a wink and a nod in Will's direction. She responded with a smile and a "you're welcome to him" hand gesture. I quietly whispered good morning to him and asked him to join me in the hall. Of course, he was surprised.

"Me?" was his only response. I smiled and said that yes, I meant him. Then I turned and walked toward the door, looking back to see him slinking along ten feet behind me. When we were both out in the hall, I got up close enough to his face to make him feel uncomfortable and spoke in a quiet voice.

"I need some help in my reading class first bell, three days a week, and I think you'd be a good person to do that." The look of shock and possibly horror on his face was priceless. I knew that he knew exactly who I was.

"No way. I don't wanna do that. Besides, I need my study hall to get my homework done."

"Your study hall teacher tells me that you don't do any work in study hall."

"Yes, I do. And I don't want to be a helper, especially not—"

"Especially not what?"

He thought for a moment, possibly changing what he was going to say. "Especially not in a reading class. I'm not a real good reader. I wouldn't be any help at all."

"You don't have to be a good reader. The students in my class are not as good at reading as you are. I promise you that."

"No. I'm not doin' it. There's no way." Now his voice was raised, but I kept mine very low.

"I think there is a way," I said. "You can choose to do this, or I'll write you up for bullying on the playground, which will get you a detention. That will mean you won't be running in the first track meet. I know you've had other write-ups, and mine will be the one that puts you over the limit."

He stood with his mouth hanging open and a look on his face that made me want to take a step back. If looks could only kill.

I smiled and said, "Go back into your study hall and get your stuff. You're starting today. You don't have to say anything to Mrs. Williams. She knows you'll be coming with me."

He sulked his way back into the classroom, slowly gathered his belongings, ignored the questions from his friends, and, at the pace of a snail, joined me in the hall.

You may disapprove of my methods here, but I don't really care. This was one of those times when I just think it's okay to do the wrong thing for the right reason.

"Okay, let's pick up the pace," I said, which may have made him move marginally faster, and we proceeded to my room at the far end of the building with him trailing thirty feet behind me.

I opened the door to my classroom and stood waiting as Will dragged himself the last few feet into the room. Everyone looked up.

"This is Will Dexley," I said. "Will is going to be joining us in reading class three days a week from now on." Again, if looks could kill. I could see the daggers coming my way from him, so I gave him my brightest smile.

Zak jumped out of his seat and nearly bowled Will over with a bear hug. "Will, my buddy!" he exclaimed. Will stood as if frozen. I took evil delight in his discomfiture. I know, I'm a bitch.

"Hey, Zak, would you like to read aloud to Will?" This came from Ava. God, I love her. Zak dragged Will over to our tiny reading corner and the two of them sat down. Ava and I exchanged satisfied smirks as Zak began enthusiastically showing Will his book.

I felt a tug at my sleeve. As I turned, I looked into the eyes of Josh, the master of "too close for comfort." He cupped a hand to his mouth and whispered something in my ear that I caught none of.

"What?"

He tried again with the animated whisper, and still I got nothing. "Josh, just tell me. You don't have to whisper."

"That's Billy," he said loudly as he pointed at Will. Billy, I thought. Billy of the rock-throwing at the bus stop.

Will had looked up when Josh spoke and now said, "My name's not Billy. He keeps calling me that, and it's not my name."

"Will," I said, "Josh has a hearing loss. Have you ever noticed that he wears hearing aids?"

"Yeah."

"He isn't *hearing* your name right." I went to the board and wrote Will's name on it. "Josh, his name is *Will*. He doesn't like it when you call him Billy." I wrote "Billy" and then put a big X through it.

"That's Billy," Josh stubbornly insisted.

"Is your name Billy?" I asked Will.

"No!"

"His name is Will." I repeated.

Josh looked from Will to the board, then back at me. Finally, he said, "Will."

"That's right. And you need to call him that at the bus stop," I said. I paused and gave Will a look. "And everywhere else you see him. Got it?" I said.

"Yeah. Okay. I got it. Will," he said as he looked over at Will.

"And Will," I added, "if Josh forgets, can you please *politely* remind him of your name?" I think Mr. Dexley had had about all he could take. He gave me no response other than a slow blink. Then he returned to Zak's book, feigning interest in it.

We got through first bell without further incident, and in fact, it was the start of a good morning. Everyone was there. Everyone was in a good mood, ready to work, cooperative. Math class (always my least favorite) was fun for everyone as I took the kids through a new activity. They had to use fake money to buy and sell supplies to and from each other in order to make a kite. I smiled at the kiddos as they played storekeeper, selling each other paper, dowel rods, string, rulers, etc. Josh, especially, took a very serious attitude, thanking his "customers" and telling them to "Come back again" as he looked up at me with a grin. Collecting their materials, they began (with varying degrees of help) measuring, marking, and cutting the paper to make their kites. I thought briefly of Rosemary sitting in her regular ed math class, trying to understand how to multiply fractions, but tucked the thought away. I didn't want to wreck my own good mood.

During my planning bell, I actually got things ready for the rest of the day and caught up on entering grades into the computerized grade book that has replaced the ledgers of yesteryear. Although I find myself somewhat tech-resistant, I have to admit the grade book program is a vast improvement over the old manually entered grades. It's fast and neat, and best of all, the math is all done by the computer.

Feeling proud of my productivity, I glanced at the clock. Seeing that I had fifteen minutes left before the kids would be back, I decided to check out the teacher's lounge for any freebies. Sometimes there's food down there in the morning: leftovers from a.m. meetings, sweets provided by the PTA, stuff like that. I hit the jackpot today. Glazed donuts. I scarfed one down in four bites, then bought a diet cola to wash it down. Herm Shaft came in and we exchanged good mornings, with him eyeing me up and down, as was his custom. He plopped down a huge pile of papers, spied the donuts, and sat down to have one. Just as I pulled out a chair to join him, George Davis came into the lounge and, spotting the donuts, headed our way.

"Good morning," he said, nodding first to me and then to Herm. He quickly shoved half of a glazed donut in his mouth and chewed contentedly.

Herm and I both said our good mornings.

"Hey, George, you have Zelda Myers in one of your classes, don't you?" I asked.

George nodded yes but said nothing, as his mouth was now full of the second half of his donut.

"I talked to her a day or two ago, and she seems to be having trouble catching on to whatever you're doing in class."

"Well, she hasn't been turning in homework lately, but that's not really a new habit for her," he said with a shrug, his eyes now back on the box of donuts.

"Is she asking any questions in class?"

"Never raises her hand. She sits and looks out the window. If I call on her, her standard answer is 'I don't know' or a shrug and no answer at all."

Wow. There sure are two sides to every story. I wondered if the truth lay somewhere between Zelda's story and George's.

"I'll tell you what I'll do," George went on. "I'll ask her if she'd like to stay for my afterschool help sessions on Tuesday and Thursdays." He said this as he picked up a second donut. "Ta-ta," he added as he turned to leave.

"Thanks, George," I said. I wondered for a moment if Zelda had been consciously lying to me. Or maybe she had raised her hand and George hadn't noticed. Who knew? I sat down with Herm, my mind leaving Zelda, now back on food. I helped myself to donut number two, which I nibbled on daintily as if it were my first. I eyed Herm's giant pile of papers to grade, feeling a bit sorry for him.

Chapter 22

Before I came to McKinley, I had worked at an intermediate school (grades four, five, and six) in another district. When I moved to McKinley Middle, which is grades six, seven, and eight, I found some real challenges. At my previous school, all of my kids had been in regular ed classes for science and social studies. At McKinley, the kids are placed on a more individualized basis. If it's appropriate for them to be in regular ed, off they go. If not, I teach them in my classroom. So I found myself in a new building, with new staff, kids, rules, and practices, and also having to teach sixth-, seventh-, or eighth-grade science and/or social studies every year. This was by far the biggest challenge. I think special ed teachers always feel a mile wide and an inch deep anyway (or like a jack of all trades, master of none, if you prefer to describe it that way). Still, all that new curriculum was really a challenge for me.

The social studies was okay. I brushed up on things like ancient Mesopotamia and the Civil War and felt my way along, developing activities and finding resources as I went. But science was a different story. I was sort of lost in trying to find both books the kids might be able to understand and activities that would be fun and actually educational for them. So one morning, during my planning bell, feeling desperate for help, I wandered up to the science wing to see if I could find a mentor. I walked along the hall, peeking into rooms where kids were attending raptly or goofing off, depending on their teacher, until I came to a room that was quiet. I peeked in. Ah, just what I needed: a science teacher who was on his planning bell too.

Never the wallflower, I walked in and introduced myself. Shaking hands with Herm Shaft, I saw a warm smile on the face of a fifty-something guy, heard a kind voice, and felt immediately comforted by his obvious delight at sharing his expertise with me. Never mind that he was blatantly checking out my figure while we talked. He was willing to help me, and the ogling seemed a small price to pay. I spent the remainder of the bell with him pulling out kid-friendly references that I was "welcome to borrow" and sharing ideas for experiments with me. He insisted I take the materials I needed to do an experiment with conductivity the next day, but by that time, I was already laden with the books he insisted I borrow. I was surprised as the bell rang and his classroom began to fill up with kids. Apologizing for taking so much of his time, I started on my way, but he stopped me.

"Hang on just a minute, and I'll have a couple of the kids carry the stuff down to your room for that experiment."

"Are you sure?"

"It's no problem at all. A couple of these boys will be glad to get out of class for a few minutes and walk a pretty teacher down the hall." (Gag me.) But he *was* kind and helpful.

"Okay," I said, moving aside as the kids filled the room.

"Strickler!" Shaft's voice boomed across the room, making me jump. A tall, gawky boy looked up.

"Yeah?"

"You better have your assignment book today." The glare that Shaft shot to the back of the room, where poor Strickler was now laying down his pile of junk, was a laser.

"I can't find it, Mr. Shaft. I told you that yesterday," the young man pleaded. At this, Shaft went from pink to purple and began a tirade aimed at this unfortunate kid, and it lasted for what seemed like an eternity. I froze as he lambasted Strickler for his lazy, irresponsible ways. The other kids, I noticed, went about their business as if they weren't even hearing the tongue-lashing, but I was sure they felt as I did: embarrassed to witness this abuse, not to mention shocked. Gone was the smiling, helpful, friendly guy I had just spent half an hour starting to like. And then abruptly, he was back again. He turned, greeting kids as they walked in, asking for "a couple of strapping young lads" to tote stuff down to my classroom. He was correct in that several of the boys jumped at the chance to help out. They carried the stuff down to my room on the first floor, laid it all out neatly on the shelves in front of my window, and went on their way.

From that day forward, I visited Herm regularly to pick his brain, borrow materials, and at times even get quick science lessons for my own edification. It's hard to teach something if you don't quite get the concept, and all this eighth-grade science stuff was in my very distant past. (Mind you, I give my students the quick-and-easy version because some of these concepts are difficult, and the only tests they will be given on the curriculum are tests that I write.) I found Herm always pleasant to me, even if he was a bit on the lascivious side. Or was that just my imagination? I just felt like he was always talking to my boobs. But I like to think that if you just ignore stuff like that, you give it no chance to develop further. I think guys like Herm feel the vibe, or maybe the lack of vibe—no fear and no concern on my part.

Anyway, he was and still is a great resource, and we have developed a decent working relationship. From other staff and kids, he gets very mixed reviews. Some teachers like and respect him. Others, not so much. The students feel the same. It had to have been tough for Herm as a kid growing up with the name of

Shaft. As I mentioned before, the kids at McKinley universally call him The Crank or Crankshaft behind his back. I know it's partly because of his demeanor, but of course, Crank goes so well with Shaft. I hate to be chauvinistic, but this must have originated with eighth-grade boys. Would the average eighth-grade girl have any idea what a crankshaft is?

"Are you recovering from your shock of last week?" Herm now asked as he munched on his donut.

"Yeah, I guess. The whole thing is still just so creepy to me. Why would anyone murder someone in a school? It's weird enough that I was the one who found her and that I didn't recognize her. Weirder still that she was in the girls' room."

"Yeah. Well, from what I hear, Gretchen Mitchell was always showing up in places she wasn't invited. She was kind of a weird one herself."

I snickered in appreciation of his speaking ill of the dead. "Well, she certainly made her presence known everywhere she went, that's for sure."

"I actually saw her not long ago over in my neck of the woods," Herm said as he helped himself to a second donut.

"Don't you live in northern Kentucky?" I asked.

"Yeah. That's why I thought it was odd to see her. But I'm sure it was her. She's the parent rep on the district science curriculum committee, and I've had a number of committee meetings with her this year. I'd recognize that witch anywhere and turn and go the other way. I saw her going into Shrout's Cafe," he said with a comically raised eyebrow.

"What's Shrout's Cafe?" I asked.

"A little dive of a bar, right there on Raglin Road. Right around the corner from my house."

Herm lived twenty or twenty-five minutes from the Mitchells. What would Gretchen have been doing over there?

"When was this?" I asked

"Hmmm . . ." He thought for a moment. "Just last week, I guess. In fact, it was last Tuesday. They have a trivia night on Tuesdays there. I thought maybe she was meeting a friend for that."

Trivia night at a dive bar? That didn't sound like Gretchen. She was all about power and control, not teamwork and fun.

"What time was this?"

"Let's see. Tuesday is a gym night for me. I must have been headed home from working out, so I guess it was around seven," he mused.

I tried not to show my surprise at the idea of him working out at a gym. "Huh," I grunted as I polished off donut number three. "I somehow can't imagine Gretchen drinking a draft."

The day rolled on through science, then lunch.

Freddie was the last to come in after lunch, and he was grumbling and gesticulating like crazy. This is a familiar scene with him. The world is apparently an unfair place to Freddie, and you just never know what will piss him off. He is a major mumbler, and I never understand about 75 percent of what he says. The one thing he says clear as a bell is "motherfucker," and he uses it often when he is ranting about the world's injustices. Freddie and Basil are best buddies, possibly partly because, for some weird reason, Basil can always understand Freddie. Basil went to work now, questioning Freddie, who ranted at him in his unintelligible way. Basil filled us in as he deciphered Freddie's grumbles. A couple of times, I understood Freddie as he nodded his head, saying, "Yeah, dat right."

Apparently, whoever had been on playground duty that day had blown their whistle at Freddie and berated him for wandering off the designated play area. I sort of agreed with him that this was bullshit. What, did they think he was trying to escape? The borders of the play area are somewhat nebulous and call for interpretation on the part of the kids, a difficult thing for Freddie. I got him calmed down and essentially told him to blow it off, that it was okay, not something to worry about.

Freddie is the youngest in a family of ten kids. He has older siblings who are grown and gone but apparently haven't gone very far. The population of black kids to white at McKinley is probably about one to four. Freddie sometimes walks the outdoor area with me when I have recess duty, and it seems like every black kid he sees, he says, "Dat my cousin." All these kids know him, high-five him, and go on to tell me that yes, they are cousins. Basil and Freddie have never claimed to be related, but from what I gather, their families know each other. Of course, the two boys have been in school together for years too. They both enjoy a certain amount of popularity at school. They're nice-looking kids and very social. But there is that thing about Freddie being so unintelligible. Guess it just goes to show how far a smile will get you.

With Freddie somewhat mollified, we dug into our book. They all seemed to be pretty into *Hatchet* (a popular classic survival story about a kid persevering alone in the wilds of Canada after a plane crash). I've read this book to past classes, and it has a lot to offer them. I've developed a whole unit around it, so I have good, easy resources to pull and use, which makes life easy for me. Just as we had finished our chapter and were getting out writing journals, the fire alarm sounded.

Sometimes staff are informed of fire drills and sometimes not. This one was a surprise to all of us. While I instructed the kids,

Anne went straight to the door and stood ready to lead them out. Basil ducked to the back of the room and brought me my shoes, bringing a smile to my lips. I thanked him as I slipped them on, and he darted over to file out of the room. Ava brought up the rear of the little parade that our class made. She gave a sideways look at Chloe, who was standing planted in the center of the room. I made a "go on" motion with my hand, indicating that I'd deal with Little Miss I'm Not Going Anywhere. I moved over to my desk and got my attendance book, a requirement for staff to bring outside during drills. I stood a few paces away from Chloe so she would be forced to move to get the book.

"Chloe, can you carry my book for me? It's really important that it go outside." Without a word, and with a look of determination on her face, she moved to take the book and walked out the door of the room. Hallelujah. I followed her out and closed the door behind me.

Middle school fire drills are never far from being a free-for-all. The average adolescent is so happy to be outside and getting out of work for a few minutes that they have a hard time controlling themselves. So while they are supposed to be standing in line by class while their teachers take attendance, they are often wandering off to visit with friends in other lines or just not paying attention when their teacher calls their name. This is when I have a huge advantage over other teachers. Right then, I had three adults watching only eight kids. My group was orderly and pretty quiet. Good PR for them. It was a bit nippy out, but not exactly frigid. Skinny girls were beginning to huddle up for warmth, while the boys, unbothered by the chill, were getting unruly. The bell rang for us to go in.

Back in the classroom, we quickly realized we had lost Freddie on the way in. Ava volunteered to backtrack and try to find him.

She was gone and back in about two minutes, and following right behind her was Freddie, walking arm-in-arm with two cute young ladies. They giggled as they bid him adieu. He flashed me the Freddie grin as he took his seat.

Naturally, the kids had lost their focus and we had a hard time getting down to work. Basil had to enumerate all the trifling sins he had witnessed out there. Kids were running, talking, tossing a tennis ball back and forth. Never mind that he had been jumping in and out of line and tapping people on the shoulder, then turning his back to them. Christie, giggling at him, raised her hand. When called on, she pointed this out to him, in a voice a bit bigger than her usual breathy whisper. This shut him down quickly. Ah, the power of peer condemnation.

To my surprise, Freddy piped up with "Dat right, Christie." Basil looked at him as if crushed that his best buddy would take sides against him. Freddie just grinned at him as Basil pouted and slouched lower in his chair.

As the kids left for their music and computer classes, Christie and I started off for social studies in Jamie's room. Christie needs no help getting there. She operates her motorized wheelchair with a joystick and can get herself up the hall, in and out of the elevator, and to class. We just usually travel together because it gives us a little one-on-one time that we both enjoy. But it was not in the cards that day. As we passed the office, I saw Detectives Kennedy and Appledom talking to Andrew in the outer office area. I groaned inwardly. Andrew happened to look up and out at me and came toward the door, signaling me to come in. I told Christie to go on without me and went through the door that Andrew now held open for me.

"Detectives," I said as I managed to plaster a fake smile on my face.

"We wonder if we might have a few minutes of your time," Appledom said as he looked down, over his paunch, toward me.

"I have a class to go to," I said flatly.

"I'll call up to Jamie and let him know you'll be a bit late," Andrew offered.

So helpful. Thanks a lot, I thought. Whose side are you on, anyway?

Chapter 23

I followed the two detectives down to the conference room, where Kennedy shut the door behind us before taking a seat. I sat down at the head of the table. This is a seat I never take, but today I wanted to feel a bit in power.

They sat next to each other with their backs to the door. They got the view of Van Gogh's woods that time. Kennedy spoke first. This seemed to be their routine. He asked questions and took notes. Appledom just listened. Maybe he was more of an auditory learner, mused the teacher in me.

"Ms. Hutchinson, do you know anyone who might have wanted to kill Gretchen Mitchell?" I was taken aback by the bluntness of this question. I felt myself react by pulling my head back, a little at what they were asking.

"Well . . . no," I said without much conviction.

"But you just hesitated before you answered. Maybe you should think about that for another minute." And there they sat, just looking at me. I wanted to squirm at the vacuum of unspoken words, but I managed to hold still. It popped into my head that this was an interrogation strategy they were using on me. And they had used it before. They wanted to make me uncomfortable with that long silence. Maybe they even wanted to make me confess something. And that is just what I did.

"Gretchen wasn't the most likable of people. She's made a lot of people around school dislike her over the year that Rosie has been here. But that doesn't mean anyone would have wanted to kill

155

her." Having spilled that much, I tried to clamp my jaw shut, but that's never easy for me.

"How did she do that, make people dislike her?" asked Kennedy.

"Well . . . she was very demanding. She didn't really ask for things nicely." I was walking on eggshells as I went on. "She would sort of insist on things and push people really hard to get what she wanted."

"Can you give us an example of this?"

I thought for a minute and then said, "In a meeting earlier this year, Rosie's language arts teacher was telling Gretchen that Rosie was doing fine in language arts. But Gretchen wanted Rosie to have an aide in that class, and by the time the meeting was over, that had been agreed on even though we knew Rosie didn't need it. So, of course, that aide had to be pulled from somewhere that she *was* needed to go help Rosie."

Kennedy wrote. Appledom stared at me.

"What was that teacher's name?"

"Dana Chenel," I said. I suddenly felt sorry for Ava and Anne. I had been a tad pissed off at them for ratting me out to these two, and here I was, giving them Dana's name. I tried to think of something to send them down another trail. I came up with a little gem. "And when I first met Gretchen and Nathan at the end of last school year, they had a huge disagreement about part of Rosie's IEP, and Gretchen wouldn't have it any way but her way. She just rolled right over Nathan as if what he thought didn't even count." Then I stopped. Yeah, go ahead and write down Nathan as a suspect if he's not already numero uno, I thought.

"How well do you know Nathan Mitchell?" he asked.

"Nathan? Pretty much the same as I knew Gretchen. Their daughter Rosie is an only child, and they're both pretty . . . devoted to her. So Nathan is more involved than a lot of dads. He sometimes drops Rosie off at school. He's dropped off her lunch to her a few times. He's at meetings about Rosie more often than not."

"And how do you get along with him?"

"Okay. Fine, I guess."

"Do you have a better relationship with him than you did with Mrs. Mitchell?"

"Well, I find him easier to get along with, if that's what you mean." I offered no more. I wasn't sure where this was going. I felt myself shift in my chair and hoped they didn't think they were making me squirm. Kennedy had that damn little notepad out again. He was scribbling away, but Appledom was maintaining eye contact with me. I desperately wanted to visit Van Gogh's woods, but they were over to my left since I was in my supposed chair of power. I could feel my palms beginning to sweat.

"Do you have a relationship with Nathan Mitchell beyond that of teacher and parent?"

"What do you mean?" I asked, confused.

"He means," jumped in Kennedy, "do you and Mr. Mitchell have a little something going on on the side?"

"Oh, my God, no! What would ever make you think that?"

"Well, for one thing," went on Kennedy, "you were seen giving Nathan Mitchell a big old hug yesterday, out in the hall outside your room, with nobody around."

"Well, obviously, there was somebody around," I replied a tad sarcastically, "since they told you I hugged Nathan. The man's wife just died. He brought his daughter to school and was unsure if it was the right thing to do. He was distraught. Yes, I hugged him because I'm a decent human being."

Well up on my high horse now, I refrained from huffing at them, but only just barely.

Now Appledom spoke up. "Ms. Hutchinson, let's revisit that day when you found Mrs. Mitchell in the bathroom."

Oh God, I thought, must we?

He pulled out his little yellow pad and glanced at it. "We've already gone over the times with you. According to what you told us, you found her at 4:02 but didn't call 911 until 4:17. We don't need to go back over all of this again, but we need you to think about it. In our minds"—he turned, glancing at Kennedy who, as usual, turned to meet his gaze, but this time I saw no humor in it—"something is wrong here. Something is missing. What were you really doing for those fifteen minutes?"

I looked him in the eye, and I knew I had to fess up. It sounded like they thought I might have been washing blood off my hands and wiping fingerprints off surfaces.

"I was losing it."

"You were losing what?"

"I was just totally freaking out." Now it all came pouring out.

"Losing my cool. I was throwing up. I was crying. I was acting like a child. I was bawling so hard that I *couldn't* call 911." I could feel myself redden in embarrassment, but I went on. "It took me that long to get my act together. I probably took longer than I should have, but she was so *clearly* dead. It was so obvious that no one could help her."

Kennedy slumped back in his chair and gave me a look that I thought might be filled with . . . disgust?

But Appledom kept his eyes on me and spoke again. "Why didn't you just tell us that in the beginning?" he asked, opening his hands, palms up.

"I don't know. It was really stupid of me. I'm sorry. I was embarrassed and pretty freaked out," I offered.

Now they were both jotting on their little yellow pads. I took my eyeballs to the left and visited those woods. I gazed at the trees, trying to let them calm me, but it was no good.

Appledom looked up and asked, "What else have you lied to us about?"

"Nothing. I swear, nothing." I was amazed at myself. Here I sat lying to these two about not lying to them! But at least I remembered to use my good lying strategies. I didn't raise my eyebrows, blink slowly, or flutter my eyelashes. I didn't gulp or touch my nose or mouth. I didn't look away from Appledom. This, I thought, was good practice for that point in the future when they found out the murder weapon had my fingerprints or DNA on it and confronted me with that.

Kennedy gave a pointed sigh. "Okay, let's move on." He must have seen my shoulders sag at the thought of more time spent with them. "Just one more question today." *Today?* How many times were they planning to talk to me? Maybe until they got a bigger confession out of me, I thought with a little wave of what I can only call fear.

"You told us the last time we talked that Mrs. Mitchell would never have come to school in a sweatsuit. What did you mean by that?" I couldn't even remember saying this, but it was certainly true.

"Well, Gretchen was always professionally dressed whenever I saw her. She wore suits and dresses and makeup. Always. I think maybe part of the reason I didn't recognize her that day was that she looked so plain. Almost . . . dowdy." I got more silence, but this felt different. It felt like they were digesting this. Thinking. As I thought about it, it seemed odd to me too.

"She apparently came the half-mile up to school on foot. I mean, it's not far from her home. Less than a mile," said Kennedy. "She had no purse. Brought nothing with her that we know of." He said this slowly and looked off into space.

I shook my head and gave a little shrug.

"Was there any kind of event going on at school that day that she would have come for dressed in a sweatsuit?"

Again I shrugged and opened my hands, palms up. "Nothing that I know of."

After comparing their notes for a couple of minutes, Tweedledee and Tweedledum decided they were done with me. As I got up to leave the office, Kennedy said, "Please make sure you keep yourself available to us."

"It seems to me that it doesn't matter if I'm available or not. You guys just round me up and bring me in here whenever you want to." I said, unable to stop myself from sounding a bit snide.

"Well, if you'd prefer, we can go back down to headquarters next time," Kennedy offered, matching my tone.

I gave him a smartassed smile and left the office without another word. My workday was almost over. I needed a drink, and I knew just where I was going to have it.

Chapter 24

Tuesday Evening

It was 7:05 when I pulled into the parking lot behind Shrout's Cafe. I went in through the back door, as I saw several others doing, and took a seat at the end of the bar. The place looked like it had the makings of a great dive: red vinyl booths, green linoleum floor, dim lighting, and, behind the bar, a heavyset, bearded bartender in overalls.

"What's your pleasure?" he asked as he meandered my way.

"I'll have a Bud Light longneck," I said as I took a seat at the bar.

He nodded and put the beer in front of me. He looked me over openly. I had spent some time trying to figure out what to wear. I wanted to look like I fit in, but I really had no idea what the bar would be like. I didn't want to stand out, but I didn't want to look like a wallflower either. I had settled on faded blue jeans, black boots, and a fitted, fairly low-cut black sweater. Maybe too low-cut, I thought as I tried not to squirm under the bartender's gaze.

"Haven't seen you in here before."

"No, it's my first time," I admitted as I spun on my barstool and looked around a bit.

"You here for the trivia?"

"Well, I'm not sure. How does it work?" I asked.

He grabbed a copied paper from a manila folder wedged into the bar behind him and started explaining points, rounds, questions, and categories. He had obviously gone over all this many times in the past. It seemed complicated to me, for something people do while they drink. He mentioned that teams could have four to eight players.

"Do teams ever pick up extra players?" I asked.

"Some teams do. Others are pretty set."

On an impulse, I pulled out my phone and brought up the picture that Anne had sent me of Gretchen. "My friend told me that she's played a couple of times with a team here and that they might let me play with them. She couldn't make it this evening." I said all this as I showed him the picture.

"Oh, yeah. I've seen her in here a few times. She plays with Clint and his buddies. Right there at that booth behind you." I turned to see an empty booth, but then the whole place was pretty much empty right then.

"Those guys like to pick up lady players. I mean, for the trivia," he said, smiling. "Women know different stuff than men, so it makes for a better team." He was apparently serious. "Your friend played with them four or five times, but I'm not sure she'll be back." I would have bet a million dollars he was right on that count.

"Why not?" I asked.

"She came in early last week and was sittin' with Clint. Looked to me like they had a little pre-trivia date set up."

Now he really had my attention. "A date?"

"Well, yeah. I kinda wondered if they had a little somethin' goin'. She always sat next to him. Close. And they usually left together, or at least at the same time."

I said nothing as I wrapped my mind around this.

"Anyway," my informative friend went on as he mopped the bar top with a questionable-looking dishcloth, "when she came in last week, they got into some kind of argument, all furious whispers and stuff, and she got up and left without even finishing her drink. She was gone before Trivia Night even started."

"Oh, she didn't tell me that," I managed to comment. I said no more as I tried to assimilate this info. Maybe all that gossip about Gretchen's fooling around was true.

"Hey, understand, I'm not one to stick my nose into people's business," he interjected into the silence, "but I couldn't help but notice them. They were right there by the bar. I try to just do my job and keep my mouth shut."

Really? I thought, as I mentally went over all he had just told me. "Do you think this guy Clint and his buddies will be in tonight?"

"Yeah. They come every week."

"Do you think they'd want a new player?"

"Oh, yeah. See, they're at a disadvantage. There's just the three of them now. Some of the teams have six or eight players. But Clint and them do okay. They win now and then, but more often if they got a lady with 'em."

"Win?" I asked. "What do they win?"

"Gift certificates to Shrout's Cafe, of course," he said with a grin, moving away to wait on a customer sitting down at the other end of the bar. I sat nursing my beer, pondering what he had told me.

Within minutes the place went from nearly empty to more than half full. And just as my bartender friend had predicted, the booth closest to my end of the bar was taken by three guys, probably in their early forties. They sat for a few minutes, chatting. I had a pretty good view of them on account of the mirror behind the bar, so it made for easy observation on my part. I could tell they were looking for a server, but the two on duty had their hands suddenly full. After a few minutes, the guy seated with his back to me, alone on one side of the booth, got up and came to the bar. He nodded to the bartender, who gave him a "be there in a sec" gesture. Then he turned to me.

"Hello there," he said as he openly checked me out. His eyes stopped at my cleavage and stayed there. Jeez. I had absolutely gone a little too fitted. A little too low-cut. I self-consciously lifted my beer to my chest so it would block the view a bit. His eyes came up to my face. "I haven't seen you in here before."

"It's my first time," I said. "I thought I'd come see what the trivia night's all about."

"It's going to start in a few minutes," he said. "Are you meeting someone?"

"No," I said. And found that I was actually a little embarrassed. At that point, it passed through my mind that I had probably never gone to a bar alone in my life. What the hell was I doing here? "I thought I'd just come and watch and see what it's all about," I added, feeling stupid.

"You should come and play with us. We need the mind of a woman to help us win." He smiled, and he was suddenly transformed from a nobody, just an average guy, to a personable, pleasant man. I hesitated. "Come on," he added. We don't bite." Now he stuck out a hand to shake mine. "I'm Clint Clayborn." Bingo. Could it really be this easy? This was surely the guy I was looking for, but there was also some little bell ringing at the back of my brain. He somehow looked familiar to me. Did I know this guy? I shook hands with him. "Hannah Hutchinson," I said. Too late, I wondered if I should have used an alias.

He got three beers from the bartender and I followed him over to the table, where he gestured for me to slide into the booth, then he slid in beside me. I was now essentially trapped. Introductions were made, but I instantly forgot the names of the two other guys at the table. Small talk ensued, which made me a little nervous. I hadn't thought ahead about a cover story. Some sleuth I am. I really didn't want these guys to know who I was.

Thankfully, we were interrupted by a very loud trivia emcee—the owner of Shrout's, my new friends informed me—and the game began. A trivia question was thrown out and five minutes were given for the teams to discuss the answer. After the first couple of questions, I got the gist of how this worked. This was, after all, a bar. The whole point was to get people to drink. So lots of time was given to answer the questions, but the patrons, who of course *were* drinking, were also taking the game seriously. As the evening progressed, there was a lot of talk at the table, but the guys only got far enough with me to learn that I lived in Cincinnati. Clint commented that he did too, and we compared parts of town we lived in. The other two guys lived in Villa Hills, near Shrout's, I assumed. As close as Northern Kentucky is to Cincinnati, I really don't know the many little burgs and towns that cluster along the Ohio River on that side. The guys quickly fell into sports conversation, and I was able to sit quietly to observe and ponder between questions.

At some point, one of Clint's buddies said something about the vampire business. This was so odd that it made my ears tune in more carefully. Clint commented that poking people all day long to get their blood got pretty boring. Now I knew why he looked familiar. A couple of years before, I had been briefly put on blood thinners and had been going to get blood levels checked weekly for about six weeks. As soon as I heard his comment, I knew he had taken my blood. I was tempted to fess up that I had been one of his victims but bit my tongue, thinking no real good would come out of him being reminded of this. I tucked this little bit of info (that I knew where he worked) at the back of my mind.

I was surprised to find that after a while, I was actually having a good time. These were nice guys, or at least they seemed nice right then. The time passed quickly and before I knew it, the game was ending. I glanced at my watch and was shocked to see that it was nine o'clock. Points were tallied and our team came in second. There was fist-pumping around the table, with me included.

"Do we win anything?" I asked.

"Five-dollar gift certificates to Shrout's," said buddy number one. And sure enough, our emcee appeared at the table shortly with four gift certificates and congrats to all. Clint gathered up his certificate, drained his beer quickly, and said he had to hit the road, he was working early mornings this week. Goodbyes were said, with him again offering to shake my hand. Very gentlemanly.

As Clint left, buddies number one and two were having a bit of a smirk. "What's so funny?" I ventured.

They hesitated for a moment, and then buddy number one said, "Clint's gonna be a good boy for a while. Get himself home early and stay outta trouble. He usually hangs around for a while, but not tonight."

"Why's that?"

Another hesitation, but only for a moment. Now buddy number two, John? Mike? I still wasn't sure, added, "Clint had a little somethin' goin' with some chick who started playin' trivia with us a few months ago. I think it got a little outta hand. Like maybe Clint got in a little deeper than he shoulda."

Now number one took over. "We're pretty sure Tessa found out about it and put a stop to things."

"Tessa?" I asked, feeling positively nosy, but what the heck? They seemed willing to tell all.

"Clint's wife. Tessa is . . . a force. She's an artist. Has a studio over in Oakley. She's pretty successful, I think. But she wears the pants in that family for sure. We think she found out something and put the kibosh on it, big time." He said this with a look at number two, who nodded in agreement. "Last week, this Gretchen chick never showed up here, and Clint left pronto after the trivia, just like he did tonight."

I grinned and shrugged, unable to think of anything to say to all this.

Number two added, "Clint's a really good guy. We were surprised at the way he was actin' with this chick. It's just not like him. He's got a great wife. Kids. It was like she had some kinda magic hold over him. If Tessa stepped in, I'm glad she did. Clint really seemed more like his old self tonight than he's been for weeks."

Number one nodded at this as he drained his beer. "And she really wasn't much fun to play trivia with. She didn't get into the game like you do." He said this with a smile, and I couldn't help but smile along. "You should come back and play with us again next week."

At this point, another customer stopped at the table. "Hey, Burt. John. How's life treatin' y'all?"

Oh, thank God. Names. I repeated them to myself a few times in my head while they exchanged guy talk. I noticed they didn't introduce me and wondered if *they* had forgotten *my* name. Just as well if they had. It seemed like a good time for me to hit the road, so I made my excuses, thanked them for letting me play, and shook hands with each of them, getting their names switched around, which they seemed unoffended at. They repeated their invitation to come back, and I told them I'd like to, finding, to my surprise, that it was true.

I left as I had come in, through the back door, exchanging a nod and a wave with the bartender on my way out. The parking lot was dimly lit, which always makes me a bit nervous, but I didn't feel unsafe as I punched the fob button to unlock my car. I have developed the habit of locking my car as soon as I get into it, just to be safe, which I would do now, I told myself. As I opened the door and got into the car, I caught movement out of the corner of my eye. Suddenly the passenger door opened and someone got in. I looked over, heard myself gasp, and saw a gun pointed at me.

Chapter 25

"Stay right where you are," said a voice that was somehow familiar to me.

I forced myself to move my gaze up from the barrel of the gun into the face of Nathan Mitchell.

"Close your door," he said.

I did so with the thought that you should *never* get into the car when confronted. But this was not fair. He had taken me by surprise. I didn't have a *chance* to not get in—no chance to lock the door. I sat looking not at him but at the barrel of his gun, aimed at me. I felt myself holding my breath, my heart racing, my body stiff with fear.

"What were you doing here?" he demanded, gesturing with the gun toward the bar. I gave a little start and tried to speak, but there was no saliva in my mouth, and only a little dry sound came out. "What were you doing here?" he repeated, louder this time.

"I was—" I whispered. I cleared my throat and tried to work up a little spit to wet my whistle. "I was playing trivia," I answered stupidly.

"Why? Why did you come here?" he asked. Again he gestured with the gun. He was scaring the pants off me. But his voice didn't sound as harsh. It sounded ragged and raspy. I looked up at his face again, and he really looked awful. Maybe it was just the light, but he looked ten years older than the last time I had seen him.

I took a few seconds to pull myself together, trying to relax my body, telling myself to breathe, turning toward him just a tiny bit.

"Nathan, you're scaring the shit out of me with that gun. I'm perfectly willing to talk to you, but it'll go a lot better if I don't have to look down the barrel of your gun."

"Why would I trust you?" he said, suddenly sounding angry again. "I know you had something to do with Gretchen's death. I'm just making sure you aren't going to pull a knife on *me*!"

This was so ludicrous that it made me snort in a quick guffaw of laughter in spite of my fear. "Me? I couldn't stab a stuffed animal. Why would you think I had anything to do with Gretchen's death?"

"Why?" he asked, his voice dripping with sarcasm. Now he used the gun to tick off points on his fingers. "Let's see: She got killed in an almost empty school. You just happened to go into that restroom and find her. You knew she was out to get you fired. And now you're here meeting with this guy she was fooling around with. So maybe he was in on this whole thing with you? Gee, why would I suspect you?"

He knew she was fooling around? So maybe that was the last straw for him, the thing that made him do it. But I still couldn't figure out why he would have done it at the school. And he knew she was trying to get me fired? Well, I supposed it made sense he'd know that. But then what was he doing here? Was this just a big charade? It sure didn't feel like one.

"I don't know anything about who Gretchen was fooling around with." I sounded like I was doing a bad acting job, even to myself.

Nathan drew his left hand down his jaw in that movement that people use when they're exhausted.

"Nathan, please. Put the gun down so we can talk."

And to my utter relief and surprise, he did. He actually laid it down on the floor of my car and leaned back, resting against the door. I released a huge breath.

"I'm not an idiot, Hannah. I knew she'd been seeing this Clint guy for a couple of months. I came here tonight to confront him, and who do I see as I walk in the front door? You. All cozied up to him, drinking beer with him and his buddies. Playing games and having a good old time. I watched you. You and he had quite a bit to say to each other, it seemed to me."

Good God, how could I have been so unobservant? I had been so wrapped up in getting in good with my little group that I had hardly even looked around the bar. And what did he mean by "confront him"? Confront him with that gun? Obviously, he hadn't brought the gun along because of me. He hadn't known I was going to be there. I hadn't even known I was going to be there until a couple of hours ago. Had he been planning to kill Clint, too? With the gun lying on the floor of the car, I was no longer paralyzed by fear, but I was still pretty darn scared. I thought I'd try being honest with him.

"Nathan, I came here on an impulse. One of the teachers at school told me they had seen Gretchen come in here last week. I came over here just trying to see what I could find out. I had never met this Clint guy until tonight. He asked me to play trivia with them, so I did. Gretchen's name never came up while I was there."

He looked at me, narrowing his eyes, and looked out the front of the car, then back at me. "Yeah, right. And of all the people in that bar, you just happened to hook up with this guy Clint."

"Okay. I admit the bartender mentioned to me that Gretchen had been in here before and sat with those guys." I paused for a moment, thinking about what I should or shouldn't say. "He mentioned that maybe she and Clint had some sort of a fight last week."

"A fight?"

171

"Yeah. He said that they seemed to be arguing, and she left after just a few minutes."

He looked at me, saying nothing, then looked again out the front of the car, in the direction of the bar's back door. "That must have been when it all went wrong," he finally said, as if thinking it over.

"All *what* went wrong?" I dared to ask. I felt like we had been sitting there for an eternity, but it was probably just the fear making every second stretch itself out. Yet I wanted to know what he was thinking, where his head was.

"Whatever they had," he said. "Then, when I saw you in there, I was sure that he was involved, involved with you in getting rid of her."

"Getting rid of her? Why would I want to get rid of her?" I could think of several reasons, as he had mentioned: She was working on getting me fired. She was making my life miserable. She was the biggest bitch I had ever met. He responded with two of the three I came up with.

"I know she gave you a hard way to go. We both know she was sort of out to get you. I know you had to have hated her." To my horror, he bent over and picked up the gun again.

"Nathan," I nearly begged, putting both my hands up in a pleading gesture, "those aren't things to kill someone over." Anyway, not nearly as good a reason as her being a cheating wife or him cashing in on all that insurance money, but I didn't think it was the time to mention those things to him.

"I swear to you," I went on, "I promise you, I never laid a hand on Gretchen. I could never have done anything like that. I would never have done that to Rosie. To you." I was pleading now. And maybe I got through to him. He suddenly slouched against the door, the gun still in his hand but now laying on his leg. A ragged sigh came from him.

"I just can't figure this all out. The police just keep asking the same questions. I feel like I'm their key suspect." Wow. I sure knew how he felt about that one. "I know Gretchen could be impossible, but she was really a good woman, a good mother. Why would someone want to kill her?"

I noticed he hadn't added "a good wife," but I let it go for now. "I don't have any idea, Nathan. But I'm sure the police are on top of this. They've made me feel like they suspect me too. I think it's just their way. And if you don't want to look guilty, I don't think you should go around carrying a gun and pointing it at people."

He looked down at the gun and then up at me. A sardonic grin crossed his face. "You may have a good point. Sorry. But you're the only person I know of who has anything to gain by Gretchen's death."

"You mean besides you?" This was pretty brazen of me considering that gun, but I just couldn't keep my trap shut.

"Me?" he said as if he might honestly be surprised.

"Well, you've sort of told me that you knew Gretchen was cheating on you, and I assume you guys have pretty good life insurance." Not much of an assumption, I thought as the email about the insurance payout appeared in my head.

"Yeah, we have insurance," he admitted. "And Gretchen cheating on me was nothing new. It wasn't really cheating—it's sort of hard to explain. I guess you could say we had a different kind of marriage than what most people have."

I tried to halt the raising of my eyebrows to the very top of my forehead, but it was uncontrollable. In fact, I could feel my eyes bugging out. Nathan and Gretchen wereswingers, or something akin to that.

173

"But I loved her. I would never have done anything to hurt her."

Somehow I believed him, at least for the moment. Maybe it was the ragged sound of his voice, the raw emotion I was hearing in it.

"And I wouldn't have done anything to hurt her, either," I said. "I have to admit Gretchen wasn't my favorite person, but nothing she could have done would have made me want to kill her." This was just a tiny little lie. That moment after Rosie's IEP meeting popped into my head, but I really hadn't meant it, even then.

"I guess I know that. I'm just desperate and frustrated."

"I get it. I feel the same way. Like I said, the cops seem to be all over this. And I think we just have to trust them and let them do their job." Gee, this sounded like good advice. Maybe I should consider doing this too. "You sure don't want to do anything rash like go threatening people, because that's just going to make them more suspicious of you."

"I didn't mean to threaten you," he said, looking first down at the gun, then up at me.

"It's okay," I said, although this had probably been the closest I had ever come to wetting my pants in my adult life. For a long moment, we just sat there, apparently with nothing more to say to each other. "Nathan, go home. Spend the rest of the evening with Rosie. She needs you right now, and I bet you need her too."

"Yeah, I guess you're right," he said. And without another word, he opened the car door, got out, and slammed it without a glance back in my direction. It took me less than one second to lock the door. I looked around to see where he had gone, but it was as if he had just disappeared. I had an impulse to sit and try to pull myself together, but the desire to get the hell out of there won. I started the car, jammed it into reverse, and pulled out of the parking lot with my tires squealing. I drove a block or two before I pulled over to the side of the neighborhood street I was on. I was shaking so hard that my hands were making the steering wheel vibrate. I took some deep breaths, which helped me calm down a bit. Then I had a little giggle at my own expense—what a wuss. The night before, I had thought I was all private eye, but that night, at the sight of a gun aimed my way, I was falling apart. I sat there for a few minutes, trying to put my thoughts in order, but seeing Nathan like that had thrown a big wrench into what I thought I knew. I finally gave up, put the car in gear, and drove home with more questions than I had answers for.

I don't know if it was the scary interlude with Nathan, the information I had gathered from Clint's buddies, the beer, or just the whole evening, but I sure couldn't get settled down once I got home. I wandered the yard with Rascal, went in and turned the TV on, sat for a few minutes, then turned it off, and finally got myself a box of Cheez-Its, which I munched on while I studied my dry erase board. It was starting to look like something out of a crime show, which I actually thought was sort of cool. (I know. What a dork.) I sat pondering what I could do next.

My mind went back to the email from Rosie's doctor to Nathan that I had scanned during my evening of playing private eye. I tried to scrounge out of my brain the essence of what that email said, something about donor compatibility not being an issue. It said parents no longer have to worry about being donors because there is plenty of donated blood, and there are other factors involved. Alleles and such. This was all Greek to me. The email had gone on to tell Nathan that they had tested his blood for eligibility, as he had requested, but that he was not an eligible donor. His blood type was AB. I knew that was rare. I remembered Gretchen's and Rosie's blood types because they're the same as mine, type O. I was confused. It seemed like a parent should always be able to be a blood donor for their own kid. But genetics is not my bailiwick. I decided to consult Dr. Google.

After some hunting around, I finally found a handy little chart of parents' blood types and possible offspring of those parents. So much for trusting Google. According to this chart, a parent with AB blood type and one with O blood type could only have kids with type A or B blood. This made no sense. I stopped to think about the info in the email again. I knew I had remembered the blood types correctly. I did some more googling and came up with two more sites that essentially told me the same thing. I sat back in confusion. I knew Rosie wasn't adopted. And then it hit me. Holy shit! Maybe Nathan was not Rosie's biological father.

Could that be right? I got up and started pacing. Rascal hopped up, catching my mood. Not wanting him underfoot, I opened the door to the porch for him. He happily hustled through his doggy door and down the steps. I stood there, closing my eyes for a minute, trying to recreate the sight of that email. I knew I was right. I turned to resume my pacing, and as I walked back and forth, I thought about Nathan and Gretchen's marriage, about all of that supposed infidelity, about the timing of that email, and even about the delays in Rosie's surgery. That stopped me in my tracks. Surely that couldn't have anything to do with this. No. But the more I thought about it, the more I considered this new revelation.

Had Nathan known this all along, or did that email shock him far more than it had shocked me? And could that information have been the thing that put him over the edge? It seemed to me like he had put up with a hell of a lot for a long, long time. Was that what had made him plunge a knife into his wife's heart? But why at school? Oh, yeah, I almost forgot: to implicate me, that's why. But why me? Maybe just because I was the easiest person to make look guilty. And, of course, my dislike of Gretchen wasn't any big secret.

Then there was that horrible IEP meeting and the rumor of her trying to get me fired. Maybe Nathan had just decided the time was ripe.

Then my mind made a little shift, and a new question popped into my head. If Nathan wasn't Rosie's biological dad, then who was? Of course, I had no idea. Rosie is thirteen years old. Who knew what went on thirteen years ago?

Chapter 26

Wednesday, March 20th

I got to work a bit late Wednesday morning. My events of the previous couple of evenings were catching up with me. I hadn't taken time to organize the night before, so I couldn't get out the door as quickly that morning. But as I walked down the hall, I still couldn't resist the welcoming light that poured out of Pen's classroom door. It had been a few days since we had touched base, and I felt the need for a dose of her sanity in my life.

I walked into her room and found her shoving desks around into the shape of an arc facing a rectangular table. As she pushed, her more-than-ample rear end powering the work made me think of an ox. Maybe it was also her work ethic that conjured up that image. Here was another person I worked with whom I wished I was more like. (Well, maybe not in the backside.)

"Good morning, Hannah," she said as she paused in her work.

"Hi, Pen. What's going on today?"

"Oh, I'm just setting up for a little panel discussion with a hopefully interested audience. What's going on with you is the question. Are the police becoming a daily part of your life?"

I gave a little guffaw. "Yeah, I'm afraid they are. I keep wondering if the next time I see them, they're going to have handcuffs waiting for me."

She paused from her desk-shoving to give me a serious look. "Hannah, the police are not your enemies. It may seem like they're out to get you, but you know they're just trying to get to the bottom of Mrs. Mitchell's death." She made ready to move another desk and I joined in, giving a shove to the next one most likely to join the curved line.

"I know you're right," I said, "but they're pretty intimidating."

Now Pen stopped again, putting her hands on her hips to address me. "Hannah Hutchinson, you are one of the most capable, well-spoken, sincere young women I know. Don't *let* them intimidate you. That's a choice you can make. I know you have nothing to hide from them. Just be yourself. For heaven's sake, you can offer to *help* them. That's what you do for everyone else."

This little pep talk was fraught with more assumptions than I even wanted to dwell on, but I still liked the sound of it.

"Ah, Pen, those are just the kind of words I came over here to get," I confessed. I could almost feel myself stand up a little straighter. To my surprise, she moved through the few feet that separated us and gave me a hug.

"You hang in there," she said. "This will all work itself out in just a few days." How prophetic that turned out to be.

The first couple of bells of the day went quickly. Zak and April were both absent that day. There are only eight kids in my first two classes, so having these two gone makes a huge difference. It's not that either of them is a particular problem or needs more than their fair share of help. But heck, that cut down the neediness for both Ava and me by 25 percent. I was glad when third bell came and the kids all headed out. I had an agenda for my planning bell.

I had been stewing over the Mitchell blood-type thing, not trusting Google's information to be completely correct, or maybe not trusting my ability to interpret it correctly. I knew someone who could clear up a few questions for me, and I set out to hunt him down. I zipped down to the teacher's lounge—no Herm. The junk food in the machines called to me, but for once I managed to ignore it. I was on a mission. I thought for a moment as I turned to leave the lounge. What was the quickest way up to the science wing?

McKinley Middle School is an old elephant of a building, huge and ugly with its dirty brick exterior and gabled roof, but nonetheless interesting. It lumbers along from add-on to add-on, with its parts not always seeming to go together. Built in the early 1900s, it has been added on to three times. The original building is ancient and terribly outdated, but alive with character, with detail that is no longer put into buildings today, things like alcoves for drinking fountains and decorated ceilings in stairwells. The newer parts of the building range from ugly 1940s to "modern" 1970s to only a few years old, techno-up-to-date. Because of all that adding on, the place is somewhat of a maze, with any number of ways to get from point A to point B. A couple of small courtyards serve as intersections and help with the traffic flow between classes. Now I cut through one of the courtyards and up a little-used back stairway, which brought me to the end of the science wing, where Herm Shaft's room is. I found him sipping on coffee as he tackled a pile of student work, red pen in hand. We exchanged pleasantries for a minute, but he knew this wasn't a social visit.

"To what do I owe the honor of this visit?" he asked.

"I need some help figuring something out," I said. He put down the paper he was looking at. I had captured his interest. I feel pretty certain that Herm is fine with sharing lesson plans and equipment with me, but what I think he actually enjoys is imparting knowledge to me. (He is a teacher, after all.)

"I have a question about blood types and heredity." This brought a puzzled look to his face as I knew it would. There is no study of genetics in the curriculum for middle school kids, so I figured it would seem like an odd topic. I was ready with a quick and detailed lie.

"I have a friend who is wondering if her dad is her *real* dad. As in, her birth dad." Now I really had his interest. "It's no one you know," I added quickly before he got his gossip antenna too tuned in. "It's a college friend of mine who recently had someone contact her on Facebook saying he thinks he's her father. She actually looks a lot like the guy, so now she's wondering, but doesn't want to confront her parents. She knows her dad's blood type, and of course, she knows her own as well. She is type O, and he's type AB. She did a little research, and now she thinks that doesn't make sense. So she asked me what I knew. I told her I didn't know *anything* but would check on it. I did an internet search, and I think she's right. But I didn't want to get back to her without being sure. That's why I came to you. I know you know all about this kind of stuff," I added, with what I hoped was an engaging smile. (One of the most important lessons my mom taught me in life is "flattery will get you everywhere.")

I swear I could see Herm puff up a little as he turned to reach toward a small bookshelf, hunted for only a few seconds, and pulled out a book. Turning back to his desk, he opened to the index and quickly found what he was looking for, then flipped to a page with a chart. "Let's see," he said as he ran an index finger down the chart. "You say she is type O and he's AB? But you'd have to know the mother's blood type, too. A father with AB blood could have a child with type O blood, depending on the blood type of the mother."

"Oh, I forgot that part. The mom's blood type is the same as my friend's, type O."

He gave me a look that made me want to squirm. Maybe my little made-up story wasn't holding up so well.

"Right," he said, looking back at the page. "Well, then, your friend is absolutely right. Look here," he said as he turned the book toward me and pointed. "It clearly shows that an AB parent and an O parent cannot produce a child with type O blood."

It took me a moment of studying the chart to realize what I was seeing, but as usual, Herm knew what he was talking about. This was what I had found in my internet search, but not quite believed. So that harmless email I had taken a peek at in Nathan Mitchell's study wasn't so harmless after all. Was the reading of that short little report the first time Nathan realized he wasn't Rosie's birth father? And was that news enough to make him take drastic action?

After my weird and scary meeting with Nathan outside Shrout's the night before, I had sort of felt like he was, like me, an innocent bystander to Gretchen's death. Now I rethought that, and he again looked pretty good as the person most likely to do her in.

I thanked Herm for his help and left him, vowing in my mind to leave him alone for a few weeks. I felt like I had been eating up too much of his planning time lately.

I was totally unproductive for the rest of the bell. I just couldn't get focused. I wandered down to the teachers' lounge, where I had a little feast as I yakked with a couple of coworkers.

When the kids came in for science, I wasn't really ready for them. I decided, spur of the moment, to abandon my lesson plan. I had a Bill Nye video I was planning to show them on Friday but used it that day instead, knowing full well I would regret it later in the week. I do believe Bill Nye is universally loved by all kids (and by their teachers, who appreciate someone else teaching their lesson for them).

I worked my way through the cafeteria line, greeting the wonderful ladies who cook and serve food to the kids every day. School lunch doesn't usually appeal to me, but I got lucky that day.

They had sauerkraut. I have no idea why anyone would put sauerkraut on a school lunch menu. Is there a kid on earth who likes it? I think not. But I love it. And cafeteria kraut is probably the sourest on earth. They may add a little sugar to what comes out of the can, but I wouldn't bet on it. I moved through the line, asking for only that and mashed potatoes. The hot dogs looked lethal. As I moved through the cafeteria with my tray, Rosie beckoned to me. She, April, Megan, and Christie were sitting together. (It passed through my mind that Gretchen would not have approved of Rosie's choice of who to sit with at lunch.)

"Eat with us," Rosie asked with a smile and a tilt of her head. Such a charmer. How could I refuse? I sat with the girls and we made small talk, which I enjoyed. Eating with my students is not something I do all that often. It was interesting for me to note how much work it is for Christie just to feed herself. Her movements are always a bit herky-jerky, but she is so much more fortunate than kids who have cerebral palsy were in years past.

In the first year I taught, 2000, I had a student named Calvin who had CP. Calvin was a very wiry and spastic thirteen-year-old. Sadly, I probably didn't do much for him other than treat him with respect, give him credit for having a brain, and make him comfortable. He was so spastic that he couldn't speak, although he did laugh and occasionally grunt or groan. So spastic that his arms and legs thrashed around uncontrollably. He took medication to relax those crazy muscles of his, but it was a delicate balance of drugging him enough to relax without putting him to sleep. He always seemed happiest when he was strapped down almost from head to toe in his wheelchair and able to just sit and listen to the gems I imparted. (Probably few and far between as a rookie teacher, I'm afraid.)

Fast-forward to 2019. Christie is also a wiry and spastic thirteen-year-old. She reminds me of Calvin because their CP is so similar. But Christie has the benefits of modern science and technology working for her. For years, she has had a baclofen pump that doses her spine directly and in appropriate amounts. Here's a quick and not very medical explanation of this wonderful thing: A hockey puck–shaped sort of bladder with a programmable battery is medically implanted into the abdomen. It's made of some magical material that they can inject medicine into without the medicine leaking out of the injection site. This is linked to the spine by a catheter, which slowly, over a period of months, feeds baclofen (a muscle relaxer) to the spine. It is a much better and more precise way of treating spasticity in many people who have CP. When the medicine runs out, Christie goes for another injection.

This means Christie can hold her head up, speak, hold a fat marker to write, control her head movement to read, use a joystick to move her wheelchair, feed herself, and a whole bunch of other stuff that Calvin could never do. She can also show how smart she is—very rewarding for her, I'm sure, and for her teachers as well. Christie is in my classroom for only two bells a day because she is capable of being in regular classes for all except reading and language arts.

It seems like teachers today have so little time to just enjoy their students. I lunched with the girls for about fifteen minutes, then excused myself, saying I needed to get back to work. Their trays were all empty (except for that pile of sauerkraut on each one), and they didn't seem to take offense at my leaving.

I had some time before the kids were due in from lunch and quasi-recess, so I stopped in the office, making a pretext of checking my mail. I dumped everything in the trash and turned to Julia. I wanted to tick one item off my list.

"Hi, Julia. How's life?"

"Life is just peachy. How're things with you, sweetie?"

"I'm hanging in there. I have a question for you." Julia is always busy, and I only had a few minutes, so I got to the point. I leaned over the high counter separating us and looked both ways. This was ridiculously dramatic on my part because there was no one else in the office, but I was starting to feel a little paranoid. "Remember last week when you told me about the argument between Gretchen and Ian?"

"Mm-hmm."

"Can you tell me that story again?"

She went through essentially the same version she had told me before, looking up at me from her desk as she spoke.

"Do you remember anything more specific? Anything in particular that they said? You said Ian was really mad, right?"

"Madder than I've ever heard him. Let me see . . ." She gazed up at the ceiling as if it would help her remember. "I think I've told you the whole story." Suddenly, she snapped her fingers. "I know. I heard him say, 'I've had all of this I can take. You've been holding this over my head for too long,' and I wondered what that was all about. I can't believe I forgot that part before. It was so weird."

Weird indeed. And what had she been holding over his head? Surely not making trouble for me. "Are you sure that's what he said, 'holding this over my head'?"

"Yes. 'For too long.' It was sort of strange. It almost sounded like she had been threatening him."

"Hmmm, interesting. That'll give me some food for thought. Thanks, Julia."

"Anytime, honey. I'm always here to help ya."

I turned to head back to class, ruminating over what she had told me.

As I opened the door to leave the office, I glanced down the long inner hall that led to the guidance counselors' domain. Sitting in a chair in the waiting area was the unmistakable form of Zelda. She gave me a little wave and I wandered on down to say a quick hello.

"What's up, Zelda?" It looked like she had been crying, her pretty complexion mottled and red.

"I'm just not having a very good day," she said, looking down at her knotted hands. I could see a few fresh scratches on her poor tormented arms.

"What's going on?" I asked as I sat down beside her.

"It all started this morning with Zak," she began. This, of course, got my antenna up.

"What did Zak do?"

"Sometimes he can just be such a brat, Ms. H. I know you think he's all good and sweet and cute. But he is sometimes so shitty to me, and my mom and dad always take his side." Now the words started rushing out. "So this morning, he was teasing me, and I had just had it. So I sort of had his head in a hold, and my dad started just yelling at me, all about how helpless Zak is, and how I need to be a good sister and stand up for him, not pick on him. And it was just so unfair." She was getting herself worked up and growing louder as she talked.

I spoke in a low voice that I hoped was comforting, trying to get her to calm down. "Well, that's not fair. You're right. And I know brothers can be annoying—"

She interrupted me, saying, "You know it's not easy having a cute little brother who has . . . needs like Zak has."

"No. I'm sure it's not easy at all, Zelda."

At this point, thankfully, the door to the guidance counselor's office opened, and a counselor stepped out, greeting Zelda. She got up, thanking me as she turned to go into the office. I hate to admit it, but I was relieved to have someone take over. I really like Zelda, but her problems are way beyond my ability to solve, and I needed to get back to my room. But that wasn't meant to be—not quite yet, anyway.

Chapter 27

As I walked down the hall to my room, I ran into Andrew Taylor.

"Ah, just the person I was looking for," he said.

"Oh, really?" I said with interest.

"Yeah. Let's head up to my office. I just need you for a few minutes."

"Okay. No problem. But, of course, the kids will be in from lunch in just a couple minutes."

"We'll be quick," he promised as he held the office door open for me.

Andrew sat behind his desk, and I took a chair in front of it. I was fairly comfortable there with him. Andrew is a nice guy, a good and fair principal. He is forward-thinking, and I like the changes he's made to McKinley in the five years he's been here. So I was taken aback at what he said next.

"Don't you think it would be a good idea for you to take a short leave of absence until the police have this whole situation about Gretchen Mitchell resolved?"

I took a breath and felt myself holding it, not even able to come up with a response to this. But of course, that lasted for about three seconds. "Oh, my God, Andrew. No! There's no need for me to do that. Why are you even suggesting that?"

"Well," he began slowly, "we've got police in the building almost daily, wanting to talk to you. I think that's sort of discomforting for all of us." He paused, seeming to have more to say. I looked at him blankly, wondering what was coming next.

"And, of course . . . you're, I guess, sort of a suspect to them."

Ah, there it was.

"Andrew, I really don't think they suspect me. It's just that I'm close to the family, to the situation." I didn't really know what else to say.

"Still, though, don't you think it would be easier for everyone if maybe you just took off tomorrow and Friday? This would be a paid leave. I've already okayed it with the district."

I put a hand to my left ear. Yes indeed, it was hot. I took a cleansing breath so I would speak calmly. Not a good time to blow a gasket.

"Andrew, please. I feel *sure* that the police are finished with me." This was an out-and-out lie. I was pretty sure they weren't done with me at all, but I was grasping at straws. The last thing I wanted was a couple of days to pace around my flat, worrying. I pulled out my trump card. "And you know how badly my kids do when their routine is upset. It's really hard on them."

We sat looking at each other in silence for a few ticks.

"Please—" I sat forward in my chair, giving him an imploring look.

He sighed deeply. "Okay. But if things don't get resolved by the end of the week, we'll need to revisit this."

"That's fine, thank you," I said quickly. And I popped out of the chair before he could change his mind. The bell saved me from any further groveling and I turned to leave, thanking him once again. But as I walked down the hall, I was doing a slow boil and trying to maintain my composure.

I walked into my classroom just as the kids were dribbling in from outside. I was feeling frazzled and was consciously trying to pull myself together so the kids wouldn't catch my mood. Reading aloud to them was the perfect activity for this. We dug into our book. I tried to read with extra enthusiasm, and it actually worked. When they are really engaged in things, it's always rewarding for me. We moved on through our routine of writing in our journals with varying amounts of help, and then on to a short lesson. Of all the students to make me feel better, I can't say that Tony has been the most likely over time, but thank God things are changing for him.

Tony is a seventh grader. He has pretty severe autism. He is nonverbal, but of course that doesn't mean he doesn't understand everything that is said to him, and sometimes said *about* him. He can be a wild man when he's upset. Ava, Anne, and I spent some time chasing him down halls and even outside at the beginning of last year. He has a tendency to bolt, and we used to never be able to predict when it would happen. But he finally got us trained a bit over the course of that school year, and we now know the things that are most likely to set him off and to calm him down. It's surprising sometimes how much you learn from your students and how it can help you deal with other kiddos later.

Tony is a big rocker, and if a kid loves to rock, I feel like there's no reason to fight it. He spends much of his time in the rocking chair in my room. Tony loves to flick the lights on and off. That's a pretty cool thing to control if you're a kid who can't talk and who doesn't have a lot of control over your life. So we've all learned to live with a light show going some of the time, although we can now tell him "just one more time, Tony" and he'll quit after that one last flick. In the past, Tony communicated with a few gestures, a few signs, by bringing things to us that he wanted and by freaking out, running around the room flapping his hands, jumping and moaning, or running away. Tony can follow lots of simple directions, loves music, loves to watch and observe, and has a winning smile. Also, he has a very funny sidelong look with a little grin when he knows he is doing something he's not supposed to be.

Although things improved for Tony over the course of that first year, I didn't think we were making much educational progress with him. He has wonderful, supportive parents who have tried many of the popular methods used currently for kids with autism. He was in an ABA (applied behavior analysis) program as a little guy and for a number of years. This is a well-respected program that in my mind is driven by common sense, and is pretty much what I did in my classroom for years before it became a thing. Toward the end of last year, Tony's parents got him an iPad. He's still learning to use it, but it has already started to make a big difference in his world. At first, it was just a better way for him to learn. He could give a voiced answer to people, something he had never been able to do before. But it is starting to truly become a communication system for him.

I now had a short little conversation with Tony about our book, with him telling me through the iPad that he liked it, that he thought the main character was smart, and that he thought the boy would be saved. This was so gratifying to me when I thought of how incapable of this Tony would have been last year.

I got up to Jamie's room for our shared social studies class a few minutes before the kids were all seated. We were going to have them work in groups today, and we needed a few organizational minutes just to make sure our plan didn't develop into chaos. We went through our strategy quickly and decided it would work. I hadn't really had much of a chance to talk with Jamie since our little interlude over the weekend. Monday's class time had been busy, and on Tuesday, I had missed half the class on account of my visit with Tweedledee and Tweedledum. Now we exchanged a look.

"I sure enjoyed our romp on Saturday night," Jamie said under his breath, with a grin.

"Yeah, me too." I looked away from him but couldn't help smiling as I watched the kids taking their seats.

"And I enjoyed bein' at your place, seein' that ole dog of yours."

Being at my place? Some thought was trying to work its way to the front of my brain. Why had Stella just popped into my head?

"Yeah. Right. Hey, you weren't over at my place earlier in the week for some reason, were you?"

"No. Why would I be?"

At this point, we realized the kids were all seated. They were quiet. Their eyes were on us. Jamie responded more quickly than I did. He explained the activity and got them moving into the groups we had planned, and we all got to work. About halfway through the bell, having made sure everyone was on task and making progress, we met at the back of the room.

"Why'd you think I was over at your place last week?" Jamie asked.

"My upstairs neighbor thought she saw you go in through the basement door." I couldn't help but jump to the thought of my toolbox sitting in the garage with the top wide open.

"Well, maybe somebody went in your place, but it sure wasn't me," he said.

I nodded without saying anything. But I couldn't help myself. I had to pursue a thought just a little bit.

"You went to school with Gretchen Mitchell. Right?"

"Yup. Thank the good Lord she never decided to use her teaching degree. That woman woulda been a dragon in the classroom." He said this as he looked out over the kids, acting as if we weren't having a private conversation.

I studied him for a moment until he looked back at me. "Did you know her very well?"

"I got to know her a little bit. Just about long enough to find out what a bitch she was." Although we were talking quietly, he lowered his voice even more when he came to the word *bitch*. "All uppity sorority girl, actin' like she could control all the folks around her." We looked at each other for a few long seconds. I could feel the corners of my mouth turned down. My brow knitted. Jamie caught my feeling of doubt.

"Hannah, you can't possibly think I had a *thing* to do with that woman's death."

I knew I was hesitating too long before answering him, but my mind was playing around with his words. He had "gotten to know her a little bit?" And then I saw the hurt on his face. He walked away from me without another word. When class was over, he walked out into the hall, saying goodbyes to the students and not looking my way as I left the room.

Chapter 28

Wednesday Evening

I looked in the fridge, knowing full well that the pickings were mighty slim. I couldn't think of anything to make with carrots, bread, Parmesan cheese, and yogurt. I also had two pruny apples and some grapes well on their way to becoming raisins. I pitched the fruit and chastised myself for acting like the grocery store was miles away when, in fact, it was less than one mile. I wanted real dinner, needed carbs and protein for my stressed-out soul. "I know what I want," I said out loud to Rascal, who always makes himself present when he hears the fridge door open. "I want a three-way."

I guess that in most places, a three-way is something for the sexually adventurous, but in Cincinnati it's dinner, or better yet, a 1:00 a.m. snack preceded by large quantities of alcohol. Maybe that's what makes the other kind of three-way appealing, too.

Every city has its idiosyncrasies, its oddities, its things that can only be experienced *there*. Cincinnati chili is rarely seen or tasted outside of Cincinnati, but it's part of our culture here. If you're a longtime Cincinnatian, you may refer to the restaurant that serves it as a "chili parlor." There are lots of these local sources of delectable cuisine around, and there happens to be one less than a mile from my home. Almost as close as the grocery store that I was too lazy to go to.

I have eaten at this particular chili parlor many times, but I've always sat in one of the booths that line the perimeter of the restaurant. I like a booth because it's private. I can sit there with my nose in a book and be in my own little world while I slurp down my dinner. There are tables for four scattered within that perimeter, but at the center of every chili parlor I know of is a huge U-shaped counter area that has the old-fashioned spinning, backless stools bolted down to the tile floor. This is the hub of the place. There are seats there for about twenty guests and in the middle of it is basically the kitchen.

I took a seat at the counter, noting that counter etiquette seemed to be to leave an empty stool between yourself and the next customer. As I looked around, I saw that all of the customers seated at the counter were lone diners. The place was busy, although it seemed the dinner rush was winding down. Most of my fellow dateless were finishing up and getting ready to leave. A waitress who I thought was a few years younger than me, but at the same time somehow looked older, hustled over. She wore the same uniform as the other employees: black slacks, white shirt, black full apron with only a few smears of chili on it, and a baseball cap. Unfortunately, no name tag. (Okay, now you know; I had a little bit of an ulterior motive in coming here this evening.) She brought hot sauce and a small dish of oyster crackers. These are the necessary accompaniments to the meal. "Hey there, sweetie. What can I get for you this evening?"

"I'll have a three-way and a large diet," I said.

"Comin' right up." And she meant it. I watched as she got my fountain soda and brought it to me immediately. Next, she turned to the center of the counter area, where a long peninsula was organized into a hot dog grilling area at the front end, six giant vats containing chili in some, spaghetti noodles in others. There were large stainless steel containers of chopped onions and beans (for those who opt for a four-way or a five-way) and, at the far end, a huge stainless steel receptacle containing the biggest pile of shredded cheddar I've ever seen. We're talking what looked to me like ten pounds of cheese. She grabbed an oval plate from the shelf below the peninsula and laid it on the large wooden cutting board that ran along both sides of the area. Then she deftly piled on spaghetti noodles, chili, and a mountain of shredded cheese. She turned and put the meal in front of me. I had walked in the door only two minutes before. You gotta love the service here.

"All set?" she asked.

"Yes. It looks great."

"Enjoy," she said as she moved on to the gentleman a polite stool away from me. "All finished, hon?" she asked him.

"Yup. That was great, Jessie. Thanks." Bingo! The name I was hoping for.

As I dug into my dinner, I watched her quickly write up a tab and lay it down in front of him. Cincinnati chili is, I believe, an acquired taste. I clearly remember walking into my first chili parlor when I was a freshman at the University of Cincinnati and thinking, What is that awful smell? This is not your mama's average chili. It is a thin, brownish chili that always has a little grease floating on the surface. It's a bit sweeter than regular chili and becomes heavenly when combined with spaghetti noodles and cheese or a hot dog and cheese. But you have to be daring enough to try it. Right then, I was trying to control my urge to inhale for two reasons, the first being that this is not a light dinner. Eating it too fast can lead to misery. The second reason? I wanted to talk to Jessie. As I nibbled politely at my meal, the place emptied out until only I and one other gentleman remained at the counter. Jessie returned to check on me, and I assured her that I was doing fine.

"Wow. You guys do quite a dinner business here, don't you?" I commented.

"Oh, yeah. We're this busy every night. Sometimes way later than this. And on weekends, we get it all evening long. More cola, sweetie?"

"Sure," I said as she whisked my glass away to refill it. "You do a great job at this. Have you been here for a while?"

"Almost ten years," she said as she moved dirty dishes into a hidden bus pan and wiped the counter on either side of me. "Let's see . . . I started when my youngest was three, so yeah, that's ten years. About a year after the hubby hit the road." I knew then that my new classroom helper, Will, must be the youngest in the Dexley family.

"How many kids do you have?" I asked as I continued to take very polite bites of my dinner, trying to make it last. I was feeling very pleased with myself. The conversation was going exactly where I wanted it to go.

"I got four boys," she said with a roll of her eyes. "And they'll like to be the death of me. They all still live at home even though two are growed up. Neither of them can keep a job, and one's on probation. My sixteen-year-old is talkin about droppin' out of school like one of his older brothers did. The four of them fight all the time. The older ones love to pick on the baby. You got kids?"

I shook my head, mouth too full to answer politely. "Smart girl," she said. "See that you don't." Now she came intimately close enough that I could smell the cigarette smoke on her breath. She paused her counter wiping and added, "If I got to do it all over again, I'd skip the marriage and the whole kids thing. They're all a pain in the ass, and now they're all too big to take a belt to."

I tried not to show my shock at this, but I'm sure I froze for a second and blinked at her, thinking I hadn't just heard what I did.

"Oh, well," she added as she resumed the cleanup around me, "what are ya gonna do?" She noticed that I was now finished eating. "You want a drink to go?"

"No, thanks. I'm nearly floating. Just the bill."

"Okay," she said as she pulled her little notepad from some inner pocket, wrote in a total, and laid it facedown next to my plate.

"Thanks," I said. "Have a good evening."

"You too, sweetie," she said as she removed my dishes and moved off down the counter. I laid two bucks down and went to the cashier to pay my $8.97 bill. What a deal: dinner in twenty minutes and a free peek into the home of Will Dexley. No wonder he was a bully.

Chapter 29

Thursday, March 21st

I woke up at 4:00 a.m. and knew there would be no more sleep for me. Rascal chose not to get out of bed that early. I wished I could sleep like a dog as I made myself a cup of tea and sat down to ponder my dry erase board. I had made a spot for Clint Clayborn on the board in that empty column for "other suspects" and even put his wife in with a question mark next to her name. Why not consider the wife of the guy who had an affair with Gretchen as a suspect? She probably hated Gretchen more than I did, and I was feeling like suspect number one.

Looking at the board didn't seem very helpful. It only served to raise more questions in my mind, but I had to admit I had added a fair amount of factual information to it. I sat staring at it and thinking about adding one more person. I finally put Jamie's name under suspects. He had known her in college. He actively disliked her. Did Stella really see him go into the garage just a day or two before Gretchen's murder? I gave up on the board, feeling a bit disgusted with it. Maybe a little disgusted with myself, too. I didn't like this feeling of distrust that I was developing.

I treated myself to a long shower and worked my way into my daily routine.

I got to work unusually early. I opened my door and decided to sneak in without turning on any lights. I was not feeling social and I wanted to get stuff done for a change. As I started to close the door, I heard a faint noise, turned and screamed. The silhouette of a man was not three feet away from me.

"Sorry, sorry, sorry," said a familiar voice. It was Sam. "I didn't mean to scare you. I just came back for a screwdriver that I realized I had left in here, and I didn't bother to turn the lights on."

I laughed in relief. "You scared the crap out of me," I said, giving him a light slap on the arm.

"I'm really sorry," he said. "I got your heating vent cleaned out." He indicated a small pile of junk sitting on top of the radiator.

"Thanks," I said. "I'll try to keep Tony from dropping stuff down there in the future. It's just so entertaining to him for some reason."

"That's okay. No problem," he added. "Have a good day, Hannah."

He left quickly and I went to work, picking the room up until it looked almost orderly, pulling dead leaves off the plants, and straightening all the piles on my desk. It still looked overloaded, but it was an improvement. As I worked, I wondered, was it weird that Sam was here in my room with the lights off? "Nah," I said aloud. "I'm just getting paranoid."

At 7:25, I was startled when the intercom system broke my solitude with the reminder that the special ed department meeting would start in five minutes. I groaned and did a little mild cursing under my breath. I had forgotten all about that meeting.

We have department meetings on a monthly basis. They are horrible. They are always scheduled before the kids come, first thing in the morning, so they can taint our whole day. They are mostly bitch sessions where nothing gets done, and we probably all leave more than a little frustrated. I generally try to keep my mouth shut in hopes that the meeting will end more quickly if there's one less voice adding to the milieu. I tend to watch the clock, wishing time would hurry up and pass so I can get to my real work.

Dana shares my feelings about these time-killing meetings, but she has a much better attitude than I do about how to get through them.

As we took our seats in the circle of desks, always arranged for us by the department head, I sat directly across from Dana. She was seated next to the department head, a seat she had been *assigned* several months ago. We used to sit next to each other, but it was decided that we had too much fun that way. All we were doing was passing a piece of paper back and forth on which we wrote notes and comments about what was going on in the meeting. I guess there may have been some giggling involved too. (Maybe this wasn't mature of us, but what fun is that?) Over time several of the teachers caught on to this, and I guess they didn't appreciate it. Okay, I admit they may have had good reason. Anyway, Dana now sits across the circle from me, and we communicate with a sort of code of eye rolls, tilts of the head, and other gestures mostly sent from Dana to me. As we got started and were told that this would be a short meeting, Dana briefly pinched her nostrils as if something smelled bad, code for bullshit. I smothered a smile. I kept my gaze focused pretty much on her, but her seat next to our supervisor made it look, I hoped, like I was hanging on our supervisor's every word. As the meeting progressed and we fell into the old habit of rehashing a longstanding problem, Dana, previously pretty quiet, spoke up.

"Is there any chance we could quit admiring the problem and move on to some real solutions, or are we all here just to bitch and moan?"

See why I love her? Our supervisor straightened her spine and took control back as Dana got shot a few glares from our coworkers, a group that Dana and I waste little love on. As the clock finally reached 7:55 and the warning bell rang, we were dismissed with, as usual, almost nothing accomplished and no prep time before the kiddos started piling in.

I stood at the door of my room, saying my good mornings. As April started past me, I remembered my little plan to help her at her locker. I put a note of cheer in my voice and said, "Hey, April, come on in the room for a minute."

She stopped and gave me a blank look for a tick, then turned and went past me into the room without saying a word.

"You know what?" I said conspiratorially, "I've been noticing that Basil always comes into the room to take his coat off and get stuff out of his backpack." She eyed me suspiciously, as is her way. April is not a trusting soul. "And Basil is usually the first one to be ready to work." I knew this would appeal to her. As if on cue, Basil walked in, said good morning, and started unloading his usual junk. April watched for a moment, then opened her backpack and took out a pencil and folder. Basil took off his coat. April followed suit. But as Basil gathered up his things and went out into the hall, April took a seat at her desk. I cued her to go put her stuff in her locker, which she did, I thought, somewhat sullenly. Change is hard. We all want to stick to our rituals, but I noted that there was no yelling or locker-door banging among my students that morning.

We started with our usual routine.

"Who has news?" I asked. Chloe's hand shot up. She stuck a foot out in the aisle. "Look at my new shoes," she crowed. All heads turned to look.

"Those aren't new," said April.

"They are!" said Chloe, sounding pissed. She looked up at me for confirmation.

"They sure are, Chloe. Look how clean and bright they look."

April crossed her arms over her chest, looking miffed.

"They look just like your old shoes, Chloe," said Christie with a giggle. And she was right. Chloe's mom and I once had a conversation about the red Converse tennies she always wears. Her mom had told me this had been going on for years. One pair after another, Chloe would only wear red Converse, no matter what her mom bought. My answer to this was "pick your battles." That day I hurried our conversation past the shoes and on to a play Christie had gone to the night before (her parents believe in making her world big). Then to a fight Basil had heard the night before between his mom and her current boyfriend (his mom doesn't seem to think about his world too often).

The day went quickly and smoothly. It was one of those days that restores my belief in myself as a teacher and my love of the job. The kids were at their best. They listened, caught on, and did well. I still had Clint Clayborn, Nathan Mitchell, Tweedledee, and Tweedledum at the back of my mind, but I was able to keep them at bay and be happy with life just a bit. As the kids left to catch buses at the end of social studies, I looked around and saw that the room wasn't even a mess. This made the day almost like a little miracle for me.

The Williams Gallery is close to, but not actually in, a large, popular shopping area in Cincinnati. I figure it gets an overflow of tired shoppers who need a little quiet and culture—not a bad marketing plan if you ask me. I knew from looking it up online that it was a co-op, a setup in which a group of artists come together to open a gallery, and they all work a shift or two a week to man the place. Also, good thinking on their part. Their website had helpfully provided something like office hours for each of the participating artists, a time during each week when they would generally be at the gallery. Tessa Clayborn's hours were on Thursdays from three to six. How convenient, I thought evilly.

I opened the heavy glass door and walked into a long, quiet room. My eyes went immediately up to the high ceiling, where light poured in through three skylights. This was a new building, all angles and white paint everywhere. The walls displayed paintings, drawings, and photographs. Small sculptures on chunky wooden stands dotted the middle of the room. The place smelled nice, sort of like lemongrass, and it had a very comfortable feel. Maybe it was just its warmth on the cold afternoon. I browsed, checking out paintings and price tags. Whoo! Too rich for my blood. Within a minute, I heard footsteps approaching, and an attractive woman with an abundance of long blond curls came around a corner. (It seemed like I knew those curls from somewhere.) I realized then that the room was actually L-shaped, with an area at the back hidden from view as you entered the gallery.

The woman gave me a nice welcome spiel, affable and interesting, with a few details about how the co-op worked and ending with the fact that she was one of the contributing artists, Tessa Clayborn. For all the bad luck I'd had the week before, I felt like I ought to buy a lottery ticket that week in the "finding people I was looking for" category.

I asked her where her work was, and she took me back to that out-of-sight area she had appeared from. I wondered if that meant she was a lesser artist in the co-op. I noticed that one corner at the back of the gallery was set up as an office with just a desk and a phone, and the other was a work area complete with several easels and a sort of artsy-looking mess: paints, brushes, spray bottles, rags, etc.

She indicated an area of the wall displaying a number of bright acrylic landscapes.

"These are beautiful," I said, meaning it. "I love them. They're so bright. So alive." I scanned several of the paintings and then glanced down at the corner of one where she had signed the work. Tessa Clayborn. Seeing that last name in *print* gave me a jolt. I had seen it somewhere. C. Clayborn, as in Clint Clayborn. Suddenly it came to me. It was that email to Nathan. The attachment had been signed by C. Clayborn.

"Thank you," she said with a smile. Then she surprised me by saying, "Aren't you a teacher at McKinley?"

Uh-oh. Caught.

"Yes," I said, smiling stupidly, at a loss for words.

"You gave a talk at a PTA meeting last year. About autism."

"Oh, right," I said. That must have been where I recognized her from. "Do you have kids at McKinley?"

"Yes. Our daughter Heather is an eighth-grader this year. Heather Clayborn. I'm sorry," she added, "I can't remember your name."

"Hannah Hutchinson," I said, giving up my anonymity completely.

"Nice to meet you," she said. "I enjoyed that talk you gave. You live over on Middleton, don't you?" Whoa! This freaked me out. She knew where I lived? Suddenly this visit seemed like a bad idea.

"I'm sorry. It sounds like I've been stalking you, doesn't it?" she said with a laugh and a toss of those curls. Yes, in fact, it did. "Nancy Reardon is a good friend of mine. We were over that way a few weeks after you gave that talk last year, and she pointed your place out to me. She was telling me about some big party you had there, and how much fun it was." She moved toward the easel, a few feet away. "Do you mind if I go on painting? Acrylics dry so fast. You can't leave them for very long."

"Oh, no. Go right ahead. I'll just look around," I said.

That would give me a minute to stop freaking out about what she had just said. Nancy Reardon is a teacher at McKinley. The party she was talking about was an end-of-year party that had been at my place last May. I had given that talk to the PTA just before the end of the school year, so I guess what she said could have been innocent, but it still made me a little uncomfortable.

"Please do," she said as she picked up a chunky brush and began slathering paint onto a large canvas. I made a pretense of looking at the works in the back area, but found myself more interested in watching her paint. Maybe I was just uneasy enough to not want to turn my back on her. She seemed to be just slapping color on and mixing it right on the canvas as she went. But out of the mess she made, trees started to appear.

"That's amazing how you do that," I commented.

"Oh, I'm just getting started. Not really much there yet," she said. She continued to work as she spoke, not looking away from the canvas nor pausing. "Do you mind if I ask you a question?"

Wow. This visit was full of surprises. It was exactly what I wanted to say to her. This lady was not a bit shy.

"No, go right ahead."

"Are you Rosemary Mitchell's teacher?"

"Yes," I said. I could feel my face sag, but Tessa didn't see my loss of composure. Her back was to me as she scrubbed at the canvas with globs of paint. I was fascinated at how quickly she moved across the large canvas.

"Did you know Gretchen well?" she continued. Now she turned to face me as she quickly added, "Are you terribly upset by her death?" If she only knew. "I mean, I don't want to ask if it's going to upset you." She seemed sincere as she stood, waiting for me to respond, her brush poised in mid-air. The expression on her face was completely blank—no clues for me there.

"I knew Gretchen only professionally," I said, thinking ahead and treading carefully. "Her death, of course, is upsetting. Someone murdered her in our school. But my biggest concern is Rosie, naturally, and how her mom's death will impact her."

"That sounds *so* professional," Tessa said with what looked like a smirk. She turned back to the canvas and started adding purple into the emerging treetops. Within a few seconds, she had made the color disappear, and the foliage suddenly started to have depth.

"So it sounds like she might have been as much of a bitch to you as she was to everybody else."

A giggle escaped my lips before I could stop it. This speaking ill of the dead thing was rampant. "She could be——" I was at a loss for a word that wouldn't sound too nasty. "Demanding," I finally came up with.

"Ha, I can imagine," snarled Tessa, now putting her brush down, wiping her hands, and taking a few steps back to eye her work. She turned to face me and put her hands on her hips.

"My husband got acquainted with her recently and says she was making demands of him." Her voice now had a snarky tone, and the word *demands* came out like a snarl. Suddenly she wasn't pretty at all. "The bitch!" she added.

I felt my eyebrows raise, but before I could respond, the doorbell sounded.

"I've got to go do my greeting bit. Please feel free to look around," she said, transforming back into the pleasant woman I had been chatting with.

"Thanks," I said, glad to end the exchange. She hustled around the corner and up to the front of the gallery, where I could faintly hear her talking to someone. I went closer to the painting she had been working on, looking at her brush strokes and admiring how she made her work look so easy. Glancing down at her work area, I saw a mess of paint tubes, brushes, little spatulas, rags—and there, among it all, her phone. Gee, a phone exactly like my own. I stood frozen. I could still hear her, far at the front of the gallery. Could I? My hand reached out slowly, paused, and then picked up the phone. I quickly turned the screen on, hit the icon for calls, and went to the call logs. As I paged down, I heard Tessa's voice grow a bit louder. I could hear slow footsteps of several people walking through the gallery. I looked down at her list of calls. Frantically I paged down, looking for just what, I wasn't sure. I knew I should put the phone down, but I just couldn't. And then I saw a call she had made to a number that rang a bell with me. An unsaved number. Whose number was that? I had no time to think. I turned the display off and nearly threw the phone down as if it were on fire. I took a couple of giant steps away from the work area and planted myself in front of a horrible painting so that as Tessa came around the corner two seconds later, I appeared to be studying the work. I hoped. I didn't trust myself to speak with my heart trying to crawl up my throat. I offered a weak smile instead.

"Awful, isn't it?" she commented as she joined me. I found myself giggling again, and surprisingly thought that I rather liked Tessa Clayborn.

"Well, it's not quite to my taste," I offered. She snorted at this and then laughed out loud. I made a pretense of looking at my watch and then said, "Oh, gosh, I've got to go. I really just had a few minutes, but I've wanted to stop in here for the longest time." Yeah, ever since Tuesday. "I'll have to come back when I have more time. Thanks so much for showing me around."

"My pleasure," she said and offered her hand. We shook and I made a quick exit, thinking I would actually like to visit the gallery again.

WHAT HAPPENED AT SCHOOL TODAY?

Back in my car, I scrounged in my purse and, finding a piece of scrap paper, wrote down the number I had seen in Tessa's phone, a number that for some odd reason I had been able to easily keep in my head.

Chapter 30

I forced myself to go to the grocery store on the way home. I was almost out of toilet paper. That's usually when I decide grocery shopping is critical. I ran through the store, gathering up food randomly: fruit, snacks, frozen dinners, pop, bread, cookies—life's essentials. And of course, the TP, which was what I had come in for.

Rascal and I spent quite some time nosing around the backyard when I got home. He is not a high-energy guy and has a tendency to put on the pounds. If I let him out the doggie door by himself, he goes down the steps, pees on the nearest bush, and lays down. But if I roam the yard, he runs around sniffing and chasing squirrels. I have worked hard to make my yard a place I like to be, so we both enjoy the roaming, and it's good for us. But my mind wasn't on the flora today. It was on Tessa Clayborn. I vowed to look at that phone number again when I went in, and then I spent some time mulling over the fact that Tessa knew where I lived. She had asked my name and if I was Rosemary's teacher, which she obviously knew the answer to.

I went inside and grabbed a bag of chips, a diet soda, cookies, and some grapes. I sat on the couch in a hurry to graze on my little feast and thought back to last May.

Our staff has an annual end-of-year party and its location changes from year to year. It's always at a staff person's home. I had thought about volunteering my house for a few years and finally decided last year that it was about my turn. It's an outdoor party, but you have to think about the possibility of rain. My little flat can maybe hold thirty close friends, but no more. So I had prayed for a nice day and figured some of the staff could hang out in the garage if we got a real downpour. I had feared it would be a lot of work for me, but in the end, I got tons of help. Ian brought over ice and got a drink area all set up before the party. Jamie brought cornhole games. A couple of the guys brought over grills, got them going, and did all the cooking. The weather was perfect. We had a great turnout, people stayed late, and most amazingly, a good number stayed to help with the cleanup at the end. I can remember teasing Sam that he didn't have to be the last one there helping with trash just because he's a custodian. I was glad I had volunteered. On top of the good time, I had gotten a lot of ego-pumping compliments on my yard, and best of all, I had taken my turn. I was off the hook for future parties.

But as I thought back, I realized that lots of people had learned the layout of my home that day. How many people had been in my garage? Had I closed the lid to my toolbox? No. I never close it. Could someone have taken the awl way back then? I knew I hadn't used it since then. When do you ever use an awl? Stella's belt might have been the only time I had ever wanted to use it. It's just one of those tools that gets shoved around as you scrounge for others. Or had someone just noticed it then and come back for it later? Surely no one had been plotting to kill Gretchen with my awl for almost a year. But how had they gotten in? The side door to the garage is always locked. Or nearly always. On an impulse, I hauled myself off the couch and went down to the garage. I checked the door and found, to my horror, that it was unlocked.

I stood there, staring at it. I couldn't believe, with all that had gone on in the previous week, that I had never checked this door. Never thought about the possibility of it being unlocked. The truth is that the four of us aren't diligent about locking it. We all have good locks on our apartment doors, and sometimes it gets left unlocked for the cable guy or a friend borrowing something. In my case, I had left it unlocked for Jamie to get in to let Rascal out a few times when I knew I was going to be gone all day on a Saturday. No. That wasn't right. I had just told him where the key was, under the rock, right there in the garden by the door. Had I told anyone else about the key? I tried to think back to the party and all the setting up that had gone on. I opened the door and looked at the rock sitting there, less than three feet from the door, thinking it might jog my memory. I snickered as I assessed the hiding place. If I were a burglar trying to get in through this door, where was the first place I would look for a key? I picked up the rock and pocketed the key.

I shut the door and twisted the lock with a vengeance, horrified at my own lack of security measures in a week when I had been frightened so many times. Never mind that some of those scares had been caused by a flock of birds leaving their roost and by a possum hunting for scraps.

As I came upstairs from the garage, I glanced out the front door and saw two familiar figures standing there. I stopped in my tracks and groaned aloud. Kennedy leaned toward the window and peeked in, seeing me. He gestured for me to come open the door. What choice did I have? I unlocked the deadbolt and stepped back to let them in.

"Detectives?" I said as I turned toward them, locking the door behind us.

"We need to have a conversation with you, Ms. Hutchinson," said Kennedy as Appledom walked down the entry hall, looking around.

"This your apartment?" he asked, looking back at me as he indicated the door to my place.

"Yes," I said flatly.

"Maybe we should go in and sit down for a few minutes while we talk," Kennedy said soberly.

Without a word, I slid past them, down the hall, and opened the door to my apartment. We got ourselves settled, me in my reading chair and them on the couch. The two detectives looked the same as always, suffering in their tight-collared white shirts and jackets. Competing with each other on who could pop a button first, with Tweedledum just a tad more likely to win. The button at the widest part of his belly was hanging on like a teenage girl who had just been jilted. They both wore somber expressions on their faces. Their notepads were at the ready.

Without exchanging any pleasantries, they got down to business.

"The DNA evidence on the murder weapon," Tweedledum started, pausing with a pointed look at me as he said this, "has come back. There are two sets of DNA on the awl, and one of them is yours."

"How do you know it's mine? How do you have my DNA?"

"We got it off the soda bottle you threw in the trash when you were down at the precinct last week," volunteered Kennedy.

"Can you do that?"

He smirked at me. "Yes, it's all quite legal."

And now I folded but somehow managed not to lose my composure.

"I have to tell you about something weird that's been happening to me."

I wouldn't have told them this a few short days ago, but I was getting so *tired* of talking to them. Gee, I wondered, did they feel the same about me? At this point, I wanted to get things out in the open. I hoped that if I fessed up about the awl, maybe they'd be done with me. And while I wasn't too happy that they had come hunting me down at home, I was also glad they hadn't shown up at school again. I didn't think Andrew was going to tolerate any more visits from them without putting real pressure on me to take a couple days off. I half expected to be led out of my own home in handcuffs that night anyway, so I figured, what the hell?

"I've been having this recurring dream. A dream where I find Gretchen again, in the stall, in the girls' room." They both stared at me, deadpan. "But I guess my psyche, or whatever," I said with an open gesture of my hands, not knowing if that was the correct term, "wouldn't let me see the weapon. But last night, I had the dream again, and it woke me up. I woke up thinking that maybe the weapon was my awl."

This was almost the truth. It had really happened that way. I was just telling a little white lie about *when* it had happened.

"Why didn't you call us when you realized that?" asked Kennedy.

"Well it *was* a dream. I wasn't really sure of it." Okay, that was another little whitey. I was *positive* about the awl. I went on to tell them my thoughts about last year's party and how people could have seen the awl way back then. I filled them in, right up to my going downstairs and checking the lock. To bringing the key in.

And there it was. They did the look again. Was this a telepathic thing or what? But somehow, it just looked so funny to me. Even now, with the thought that they might be here to arrest me, I almost cracked up as they turned their heads to make eye contact, then turned them back to look at me.

What followed was a barrage of questions from them about the party, who had been here, how much access they might have had.

And the question I couldn't answer: could the awl have been taken on that day? They even followed me down to the garage to see my tool chest, with its still-open top. I was tempted to close it after they had a look, just to show them I wasn't going to let anyone else help themselves to another murder weapon. But it was just such a foreign move to me that I couldn't do it.

As we went back up the steps, it was clear to me that they weren't ready to leave. Back in our same seats, we moved on to Nathan. I had hoped by that time I wasn't their prime suspect, and apparently I wasn't. We went over old ground on Nathan, and a few new things too. Was I aware that there was a hefty insurance policy on Gretchen? I tried to stay straight-faced as I answered this one, picturing myself in the darkness of Nathan's office, peeking at his email.

"Well, I figured they'd have life insurance. They're fairly well-off, I think." By then, I was used to the two of them just sitting and looking at me. Waiting for me to say more? But this time, I didn't. I just sat looking back at them. First at Tweedledee. Then at Tweedledum. I counted as I took four slow breaths. That's really a long time to not speak, for me anyway. I waited them out. Kennedy was the first to give. He looked down at his notepad.

"Has Nathan Mitchell ever threatened you in any way?"

"No." I didn't want to be pointing a finger where I really had no grounds. And I didn't think our little interlude on Tuesday evening in my car actually qualified. Did it?

"Is there anything else you can think of, about Nathan Mitchell, that you haven't told us?" I scrounged through my brain for a moment and came up with one little thing.

"Yeah. I almost forgot. One of the teachers, probably more than one really, saw Nathan Mitchell at school on the day of

Gretchen's murder." This little gem got their attention. "He was in the cafeteria. Apparently, he brought Rosie her lunch that day."

"What time would that have been?"

"Let's see . . ." I thought for a moment, raising my eyes to the ceiling as I computed the minutes in Rosie's fifth bell class and enough time for her to get to the lunchroom. "I guess around twelve fifteen. Maybe between then and twelve thirty." I gave them Dana's name again, making a mental note to let her know they might be talking to her.

"Ms. Hutchinson—"

"You know, you can call me Hannah," I said and then wondered why I had said it. I guess I was just tired of all the formality and politeness.

"Okay. Hannah. Here's where we are. We know you didn't kill Gretchen Mitchell. As it turns out, the wounds that were inflicted on her are much too high. The angle of entry is wrong for someone as short as you." I could feel myself sit up a little straighter, as if ready to argue my height, at the same time as a huge feeling of relief swept over me. I opened my mouth to say something, and Kennedy held up a hand to stop me.

"Of course, that means there is someone out there who has killed, and who might have reason to kill again." This really piqued my attention. Was this a warning?

Then Appledom jumped in. "We aren't trying to scare you, but you are awfully close to this whole thing. You do need to be careful. Keep your doors locked. Look around you before you get into and out of your car."

My mind jumped back to Tuesday night outside of Shrout's Cafe. Surely they couldn't know about that. I sat, nodding in agreement. "I will be careful. I'll be really careful."

"We don't think you're in any real danger. If we thought that, we'd be offering you protection."

"Oh, God, I don't need protection," I blurted, horrified at the thought of some cop hanging around, watching my every move.

"Okay," said Kennedy. "I think we're done here. Thank you for your time. If you think of anything else you want to tell us, please give us a call." Again I nodded my head enthusiastically. Yay—they were going to leave. I followed them down the hall to the front door, locking the deadbolt behind them as they left. Appledom turned and gave me a nod as he heard the click of the lock. I found myself softening toward the two of them a little bit. Maybe they weren't really such bad guys. Maybe they were actually pretty decent cops. But, still, I was glad they were leaving and hoped not to see them again.

I didn't know how to feel about this meeting with them. I was relieved at having the whole awl confession over with, but at the same time, I felt a bit apprehensive. I needed to be careful? Really? I hadn't, up until this point, given any real serious thought to the idea that someone out there could be dangerous to *me*! But as my thoughts backtracked through the past few days, I pictured Nathan pointing a gun at me as we sat in my car. I gave a little shiver and double-checked my deadbolt.

Chapter 31

I groaned as I checked the lighted dial on my clock. It was 12:23 a.m. and Rascal was having a fit. At least it wasn't my recurring nightmare, but I was pretty sure I knew what it was. That damn possum was back. I knew I should have left the board over Rascal's doggy door for a couple more days, but we were both so used to him going in and out that way. It just seemed so inconvenient for me to have to open the porch door to let him out. The King of Pitiful had also made me feel guilty for blocking his normal exit.

Now I grabbed my big old-fashioned flashlight, not even bothering to turn it on. As I headed for the smaller bedroom, I heard an un-possomlike scraping sound. I slowed down and peeked around the door frame through the small bedroom. It must have been cloudy, or maybe the moon was up, because it wasn't all that dark outside. In fact, it was plenty light enough for me to see the figure of a man using something like a knife or a screwdriver to try to lift the hook that held my screen door shut. And as I watched, maybe just a bit frozen with fear, he succeeded, swinging the door open and entering my porch. He paused as if waiting to see if he had been heard, then turned to close the door quietly behind him. I know I should have closed the bedroom door and dialed 911. But some inner part of me was more pissed off than scared. I crossed the small room on speedy tiptoe, unlocked the door quickly, threw it open, and in three steps had crossed the porch. I raised my flashlight high and bashed the back of his skull. And he went down, both hands holding the back of his head. He howled in pain, and then I began to distinguish words—a familiar voice.

"Good God, woman. Are you tryin' to kill me?"

It was Jamie. He wobbled his way up from knees to standing position, still clutching the back of his head.

"I come over to pay you a friendly little surprise visit, and what do I get? I get boshed on the head."

The waves of alcohol hit me in the face as he turned toward me. Bourbon, I believed.

"Jamie? Holy shit. You scared me half to death."

"My head. My head. What in tarnation did you hit me with?"

I held up the flashlight sheepishly. "I'm sorry. Come in, and let's have a look at it." I helped him into the apartment and got him seated on the couch. He was still wobbly, but I couldn't tell if it was from my bop on the head or from the booze. I examined his head while he moaned and groaned a bit. It's really quite incredible how fast a goose egg forms. I quickly fixed a bag of ice and tried holding it on his head. He yelped at me. It hurt. It was too cold. I wrapped a washcloth around it and tried again, more gently this time.

We sat for a few moments, neither of us saying anything. Him sitting, elbows on his thighs, forehead held up by his palms. Me holding the bag on his head, thinking that he would have had a headache in the morning anyway, but now it would hurt on the back side, too. I broke the silence, trying a gentle voice.

"Jamie, I'm really sorry I clobbered you, but I was pretty scared. You woke me up, and I wasn't expecting you. I thought you were a burglar."

"Yeah, I get it," he mumbled into his hands.

"Why did you want to come over at this time of night?"

"Well, in case you didn't notice, I been tippin' a few this evenin'." Now he sat up a little and looked at me with a lopsided grin.

"Yes, I *did* notice that," I said with a chuckle.

"And it's really your fault that I was doin' that, so it just seemed like I oughta come on over here and talk it out with you."

"My fault?"

"Yeah. Cause you made it real clear that you don't trust me. That you think I came over here to plant evidence or somethin', that maybe I had somethin' goin' on with that ole bitch." He looked so hurt.

I put the ice pack down on the table and looked at him, thinking about how long I had known him, how much I liked him, all the moments we had shared both in and out of the classroom.

"I'm sorry. I've just been so freaked out about this whole thing," I said. "I'm not myself. I feel like I'm suspecting everybody. But I know you'd never hurt anyone."

"That's right," he said. "And the last person I'd wanna hurt would be you, Hannah." He was slurring his speech and heavily into that boyhood accent. He took my hands in both of his, sort of sliding off the couch as he did it, and ending up down on one knee. I suppressed another giggle because he was being so serious.

"I love you, Hannah. I know that you and I could make a serious go of it. I want ya to know I really mean that."

This was about the last thing I would have expected him to say, and I wasn't a bit comfortable with it. "Oh, Jamie. You don't have to say that."

"No, I wanna say it. I mean it. I've been a-thinkin' it over and this is how I really feel."

I gave him a tiny smile and didn't resist the kiss that followed, but noticed that he was indeed *very* drunk. I didn't have to convince him that my couch would be a good place to sleep. After a few frisky minutes, he essentially passed out on it. I pulled off his boots, dragged his legs up onto the couch, covered him with a blanket, and stood there, shaking my head, my thoughts all over the place.

Chapter 32

Friday, March 22nd

I woke up Friday morning somewhat in a fog. I laid in bed for a moment, trying to get my brain in order, feeling like something was wrong. Oh, yeah, I had Jamie out on the couch. But when I got up to check on him, he was gone. The blanket had been neatly folded and placed on the arm of the couch. That had been an interesting visit. In fact, an interesting day.

My mind jumped back to Tessa Clayborn. I wanted to like her but was somehow suspicious of her at the same time. Could she have killed Gretchen? I couldn't picture it, but then I really didn't know her at all. And then I remembered the visit from Kennedy and Appledom. That had taken a surprising turn. I found myself liking them a lot better, respecting them a bit more even though they had sort of scared the crap out of me with the stuff about being careful. That was really the crux of it all. Detectives who had worked this case for a week now were telling me to be careful. Of who? Or would that be whom? They didn't seem to know or, rather, weren't willing to share it with me. But if they knew, surely they'd be making an arrest. And then there was the whole thing with Jamie. I promised myself I'd think about that later as I threw on sweats. I roamed the yard with Rascal for only a few minutes, stretching minimally here and there. While he was busy sniffing, I snuck up the back steps to get in the shower.

I stayed under the hot water for a long time, trying to sort out the new developments of the previous day. What more could I do? How else could I "chase the case," as Bill Hodges would have said and done? I smiled at my own corniness: Hannah Hutchinson, amateur sleuth. But there was one little idea that popped into my head. Clint Clayborn's buddies had mentioned that Tessa knew about what had gone on between Gretchen and Clint. And Tessa had certainly all but admitted to it when I visited her at the gallery. Could Tessa, or Clint, or maybe even both of them, really have had something to with Gretchen's death? I cooked up a little plan and started thinking about how I could squeeze it into my day.

Suddenly I realized I had never checked on the phone number I had seen on Tessa's phone the day before. I wrapped a towel around myself, scrounged through my purse until I found the scrap of paper I had written the number on, and sat down with my phone. I tapped in the number, and one guess who popped up: Gretchen Mitchell. So Tessa had called her at some point in the not very distant past. Interesting.

When I got to school, I could see Pen's light was on, and I went on past my room, stopping in to see her before even unlocking my classroom door. I spilled everything I knew to her as she stood staring at me, listening intently.

"Hannah, my goodness, you *do* need to be careful. I'm shocked the police would warn you like that and not offer you protection."

"Protection?" I had to snicker at this. "What, you think they're gonna put a bodyguard in my classroom?"

"Well, maybe they should. And you really need to stop this prying into other people's business. I'm worried for you."

"But, Pen, you're the one who encouraged me to try and figure things out in the first place."

"But I didn't mean for you to go poking around in other people's lives to a point where you're afraid someone may be out to get you. You need to do what the police say. Be very careful. I'm so sorry. I probably gave you bad advice. You need to back off and let those two detectives handle this."

"Why? Do you think I'm sowing the wind?" I asked, recalling Dana's words about Gretchen.

"Well, you just might be," said Pen with a little laugh. "And that's certainly not something you want to do," she added.

I felt a little pout developing on my lips, and Pen saw it.

"You're like a dog with a bone," she said, chuckling at me. "Do what you always tell me you *want* to do. Go into your room. Close the door. Forget everything else, and just teach."

I gave an exaggerated sigh and said, "I know you're right. It's just hard for me to do that. But I'll give it a try. Have a good one." I picked up my briefcase and left her.

That was *not* the advice I had wanted.

I got busy in my classroom and within ten minutes had things pretty well set up for the morning. On the bulletin board behind my desk, I have a little poster of Parkinson's law: *The work expands to fill the time allotted.* Amazing how much I can get done if I really need to. I should move that little poster to my desktop, but then it would get covered up so often.

I went in search of more encouraging words than what Pen had provided. I found Dana in her room, laying work assignments out on kids' desks, consulting her plan book as she went so she would put out the right work for each kiddo. Her students' needs might be as individualized as those of my kids even though they have completely different disabilities.

"Wow. Been a while since you've darkened my door," she offered as a greeting.

"Yeah, but I'm desperate for some advice," I confessed with a grin.

"Chloe again?"

"No, not Chloe this time, although she has been pretty wound up lately. It's this whole Gretchen Mitchell thing." Feeling like I was running a recording of what I had just told Pen, I went through an update of what I knew and suspected, and how Kennedy and Appledom had warned me. And from Dana, I got the reaction I was looking for.

"Holy shit! You can't just hide under a rock. If they aren't offering you protection, they can't really be that worried. What are they thinking, somebody is going to try to *off* you?" she asked with a note of sarcasm.

Ahh, this was more like it. I told her what I thought my next move should be and reveled in her response.

"Hell, *yes*, you should do that. And I'll come down to your room at the beginning of fourth bell and get things started if you're not back."

I had hoped she'd make this offer. Dana has fourth bell as her planning bell, and she knows I do my science class without an aide. But she was willing to stand in for me if needed. Now I had a plan.

What is it about Fridays that makes them more fun? In every place I've ever worked, people just come in on Friday with a different attitude. And I'm no exception. Of course, part of it is the TGIF thing, but somehow it always seems like there's more to it than just that. The kiddos came rolling in that morning with smiles on their faces and enthusiasm for the day—all except Zak.

Zak shlepped in, dropping his usual collection of odds and ends next to his desk and putting his head theatrically in his hands. Anne and I exchanged questioning looks, and she went to him, squatting down to be at his level. As I started the kids on their morning news, I watched a quiet little conversation unfold between Anne and Zak. Then the two of them got up and headed for the door. Anne turned and gave me a sober look, shaking her head as they left the room. She was back five minutes later, with no Zak.

"I took him up to guidance. He was just a mess. I guess Zelda is in the hospital. According to Zak, she tried to kill herself last night."

"Oh, my God. What did she do?"

"I couldn't get that out of him. I'm not really sure if he knew. But once he started talking, he couldn't quit. By the time we got to guidance, he was in tears."

"Poor little guy," I said as I thought of my conversation a few days before with Zelda. So much for Friday fun. Of course, the other kids were oblivious to all of this, so I got myself back on track as best I could.

The first two bells of the day passed blessedly well. As the kids, Anne, and Ava left for other classes, I grabbed my purse and was on the road within five minutes. Teachers aren't really supposed to leave the building during the day, but it's a rule that is often bent, and unless someone really abuses it, nobody seems to care. I knew the clinic was less than five minutes from school since a few years back, I had gone there five or six weeks in a row, straight from school. Weekly tests to get blood thinners just right are common to anyone who's ever been on them. Clint had been the person who took my blood on two or three of those occasions. I walked into the clinic, added my name to the list, seeing that there were only two people ahead of me, and had a seat.

I couldn't help but check my watch every minute or so. I was on a tight schedule. When the second name was called, I got a little panicky knowing I was next. What was I going to say to him? What did I really want to ask? What was I thinking, coming here? I should have planned things out better. I picked up my purse and stood up to leave. The door to the tiny lab opened, and goodbyes could be heard.

"See you next week," said a familiar voice, and then "Hannah Hutchinson." Clint looked out from the tiny room, smiling at me. "What a coincidence. Come on in here." He gestured with an arm for me to go through the door.

"I promise I won't hurt you," he said in his best bedside manner, mistaking my attempt at a smile for a grimace of fear. I sat down as he closed the door.

"Clint," I began, "I don't really need a blood test." He stopped with his rubber armband poised in the air.

"Then why are you here?" he asked, looking confused.

"I just really needed to talk to you," I said, knowing that I sounded like I was pleading. I was sure he could hear the quiver in my voice. He put the armband down and propped a hand on each thigh. I couldn't tell if that meant he was ready to listen or just pissed off. I plunged on.

"I know you were somehow . . . involved with Gretchen Mitchell. Her daughter Rosie is a student of mine. I'm really afraid the police are looking at me as a suspect in her murder." This wasn't exactly true, but up until the night before, I had thought it true.

As my words tumbled out, I watched his expression change slowly as he tilted his head to one side. At least I apparently had his interest.

"I didn't kill her. I swear!" I put a hand up, palm out, as if he was really asking me to take an oath. "I just wondered . . . is there anything you can tell me about her, about your . . . friendship with her, that might help me out?"

He sat staring at me, saying nothing. What in God's name was I doing here? This man had to think I was a crazy meddler at best. And at worst, *he* was Gretchen's killer, getting ready to stab me with one of his instruments, then leave me to bleed out. He would know how to do that. The silence stretched out for an eternal ten seconds.

He moved so suddenly that it startled me, but he was only reaching up to rub his hands through his hair, then down his face.

"I'll tell you something because you sound pretty desperate. It seems like Gretchen sort of had that effect on people." He said this with a slow shake of his head and a sardonic chuckle.

"But you can't tell anybody. It *has* to be confidential."

I made a cross-my-heart, zip-my-lip gesture.

"Yeah, we had a little friendship going, as you call it. But hindsight being what it is, I think she plotted the whole thing out. I think she sort of . . . targeted me."

I gave him a questioning look, hoping it would encourage him to continue.

"After we got to be friendly," he said with a mock smile, "she asked me to do something unethical, something I would never do." I waited, but he said no more.

"Please, Clint. I promise this will stay between you and me." I hoped he could hear the desperation in my voice.

"She wanted me to tamper with a file."

I waited, resisting the urge to look at my watch. It felt like this was taking forever. I wished he would just spill. "And did you?"

"No. Hell, no! I would never do something like that. I could get fired." He looked around as if he suddenly thought the walls had ears.

"What exactly did she want you to do?"

And finally, he caved. "She wanted me to go into Nathan's file and change what it said his blood type was. God, I couldn't do that! That could have life-threatening implications for him someday. *And* she wanted me to lie to him about his blood type. "

"Did she say why she wanted you to do that?" I asked, feeling pretty sure I already knew the answer.

"No. She just said it could save her marriage." He shook his head as he said this. "She didn't have much of a marriage anyway, if you ask me."

I sat for a moment, letting all the pieces slide into place in my brain, thinking she really and truly was a horrible woman.

Clint got up, opened the door, and stood waiting for me. "Confidential," he reminded me.

"Absolutely, and thank you so much," I said as I got up to leave. He gave a nod but said no more. Somehow I had a feeling I wouldn't be welcome at Trivia Night at Shrout's Cafe again.

Chapter 33

Chloe and I had gone to the girls' room together many times over the two years she had been in my class. It should have been old hat to both of us, but this was the first time we had gone together since the day I had found Gretchen. As we went through the door, a little frisson hit me and I stopped short. Chloe, no doubt catching my mood, also stopped. We both just stood there for a few seconds, staring at each other blankly. I recovered quickly, not wanting her to catch on to my discomfort.

"Gotta pee," I said with a smile and started into my regular stall.

"Gotta pee," echoed Chloe, but I could see that she was stuck. She wasn't budging. Shit. This was my fault.

On an impulse, I said, "Maybe I'll just use a different stall today," and I went down to the stall just past Chloe's, realizing as I pushed the door open that this was the stall where I had found Gretchen. I felt myself gag as I entered, but my movement had stirred Chloe, as I hoped it would. She went into the stall next to mine and I could hear her pulling her pants down. I looked at the toilet. There was no way I could pee in that toilet, or even sit on it for that matter. I turned around and just stood there, facing the door, trying to get my breathing under control, my heart rate down. I did this to a mental mantra of What a wimp, what a wimp.

Chloe did her business and flushed but didn't exit the stall. Meanwhile, I was having a little difficulty getting myself to move. Was this what it was like for Chloe when she got stuck? I was just standing there, trying to calm myself down. Why didn't I just open the door and get out of the stall?

I nearly jumped out of my skin as right next to me, I heard "I see you" in a sing-song voice. It was Chloe, of course, with her mouth, and no doubt her eye, at the huge crack where the metal wall separating the stalls meets the stall door. I leaned over, and sure enough, I could see her eye pressed to the crack.

The jolt got me moving and as I left the stall, moving to the sink to wash my hands (always the good role model), I said, "Chloe, you scared the bejesus out of me." I thought she had done the peeking as a sort of joke, but a glance at her face told me that she was in no joking mood. "Are you okay, Chloe?" I asked.

She exploded at me. "I told you I don't wanna hear any more about it!" she bellowed, and then turned and stomped out of the bathroom, leaving me stunned. I stood there, trying to dredge something out of my brain, but I couldn't put my finger on what it was. Was that a phrase Chloe used all the time, or was it one she had just picked up from somewhere? It seemed like I had heard someone else say that recently, but the who just wouldn't come to me right then.

I followed Chloe back toward the room, trying to sort through the fuzz in my brain. It seemed like I was having a lot of thoughts I couldn't quite chase down. But before I got back to the room, I stopped short in the middle of the hall. I had suddenly had a forehead-smacking realization.

I got through the rest of the school day without my head ever really being in the game. Jamie and I never actually spoke to each other during our shared teaching bell, instead giving each other meaningful looks from different spots around the room as we helped the groups of kids with their mapping projects. But what exactly did these looks mean? I wondered.

I stopped in the office on my way back to my room, as I sometimes do after sixth bell. I hadn't checked my mailbox yet that day. I pulled out the usual junk, going through it quickly and dumping all of it in the trash.

"Hannah, you have a good weekend," came a voice from behind me. I turned to see Julia pushing her chair in, getting her coat on, and shouldering her purse. "I'm outta here," she added with a grin.

"Where you goin'?" I asked.

"My hubby and I are gettin' outta town for the weekend," she said with a smirk and a little dance step. "And I'm leaving a couple hours early."

"Good for you. Have fun!"

"Oh, I intend to," she said as she headed for the door. "See you Monday."

"Right," I said, but without any feeling, because the sound of her voice had started some slow cog turning in my brain. I tried to grasp at something, and to my surprise, it fell into place. It was Julia. Julia had said something about "not wanting to hear any more about it." But when was Chloe ever around Julia? And what had Julia been talking about when she said that? It seemed like it wasn't very long ago that I had heard her say it. I tried to remember. I watched as Julia walked out of the office.

I stood there, glued to the spot. I could picture myself leaning on the high counter over Julia's desk, then her standing and leaning toward me as if what we were saying was private. And then it all clicked. She had said it when she was telling me about the argument between Ian and Gretchen. Those weren't Julia's words. They were Ian's. But how could Chloe have heard Ian say that? She never spent any time in the office, and I didn't think she would have picked up an expression like that through a closed door. But maybe he had said it again. Maybe he had said it when Chloe was very close by.

I thought back to the day I had found Gretchen. Back to the lockdown before the kids had left school. I now knew that my realization from earlier in the day was right. As it all came together for me, I became furious. Furious for poor, harmless Chloe, who has so many challenges. Furious at what I felt sure she had seen that day.

I muddled my way through seventh bell. The kids were pretty excited that the boxes and toilet paper tubes they had started out with were beginning to actually resemble little castles with turrets. The assembly and addition of things like windows and "cobblestoned" paper in the courtyard were messy, but they allowed me to work with just a couple of kids at a time, relieving me of actual teaching duties. Ava and Anne were also wrapped up with kids, so I spent the time quietly helping and wondering what in the hell I should do next.

Chapter 34

I peeked into Ian's office, knowing very well that he wasn't there since I had just heard him talking to Pen as I passed her room.

I walked down to the open office area that Julia rules, but of course she was already gone. No one was around—typical Friday afternoon. I moved slowly back down the short hall to Ian's office, looking in again. I walked in, noticing that he had been doing some rearranging. He does this periodically, always wanting the place manically neat. On the floor, just inside the door, sat a box with a few framed things sitting upright in it. I looked around the room, noticing that they had come off the wall. I pulled out the framed picture of his graduating class from UC Teacher's College that I had never gotten a good look at. This picture had always hung behind his desk in the far corner, where anyone wanting to really look at it would have had to go behind his desk, past his chair. I knew Jamie was probably somewhere in it. Or maybe not. Maybe he hadn't shown up for it. I scanned the picture for Ian, knowing he was there somewhere. There were hundreds of people in the rows, but I finally found him, standing at the end of the third row, second from the end. I looked closely because I could see that he had his arm around the girl next to him. It wasn't his wife. But it was someone I knew. It was Gretchen.

As I began to make sense of this, I heard the outer office door close. Footsteps approached, but I didn't move. Couldn't move. In a millisecond, the thought passed through my mind that Chloe's habits were rubbing off on me, and I felt myself smile in spite of the predicament I knew I was in. Ian stopped short as he came to the doorway. He looked at me, still holding the photograph. I put it back in the box.

"I—I'm sorry," I stammered. "That was very rude of me. I had no business looking at your things. I apologize."

"I think you should have a seat," he said, and he came into the room quietly, closing the door behind him. I backed away, feeling the back of my leg touch the visitor's chair, which I lowered myself into slowly. Ian walked around behind his desk and sat down. He folded his hands, a position I had seen him take so often, and looked at me for a few seconds.

"It seems like you and I have a problem," he said calmly. "You can't seem to mind your own business, and you can't seem to let the police be the ones to investigate Gretchen's death."

"I know," I said stupidly, with no real plan of what I was going to say to him. "But the police keep questioning me like they think I actually killed Gretchen, and I would no more do that than you would." Wow, nothing like digging myself in deeper. But suddenly, as I looked at Ian's face, I knew without any question what my stubborn mind had been trying all day not to accept. We sat for a long moment, gazing at each other in silence. I had never seen Ian look as he looked at that moment. His whole face was dark—not red, but gray. He looked made of stone. He let out a big sigh.

"How did you figure it all out?" he asked flatly. I said nothing. And then, with his face getting even darker, he raged at me, a surprise storm bursting suddenly. "Oh, come on, Hannah! I know you know. The least you can do is tell me how you figured it out." He half-rose out of his seat as if he might come across the desk at me.

"Easy, Ian," I said as I raised my open hands in a defensive gesture. I felt my back pressing harder against the chair I sat in.

"I think Chloe heard you and Gretchen in the bathroom. She was there in the stall next to you. I think she was actually peeking through the crack and saw . . . something." I knew I was right, but stopped to gauge his reaction. He put his elbows on his desk and rubbed his forehead with both hands.

"I knew she was there," he said. "Not until . . . afterward. But as I started to leave the restroom, I noticed the half-open door. Her feet in those stupid red shoes she always wears. And I knew who it was. But I also knew she couldn't tell you what she saw." And a little grin appeared at one corner of his mouth. "I got lucky there. Of all the kids who could have been there, it was one of your retards. One who can't even make sense when she *does* talk."

Now it was me, nearly jumping across the desk to throttle him, but I wasn't really in a position to be the aggressor here. I forced myself to be calm enough to ask in a quiet voice, "Why'd you do it, Ian?"

"Oh, I think you know that. After all, you've snooped through my private belongings, so you should know," he said with a nod of his head toward the box on the floor.

"So you're Rosemary's birth father."

"Yes." He nodded his head slowly, looking down, then met my eyes. "Gretchen and I were hot and heavy right before we graduated. She got pregnant, but neither of us wanted to get married, at least not to each other. She insisted she was going to have the baby, even though I pushed hard for an abortion. We ended up going our separate ways, and a few months later, we were both involved with somebody else."

"Imagine my surprise the day she walked in my office when I first started here and announced that I was going to help her land a job as the district advocate. I hadn't laid eyes on her in over nine years, and here she was, telling me in a very pushy way what I was going to do. When I asked her why she thought I'd help her, she had an answer all ready. I would help her, she said, because if I didn't, the truth would come out about me being Rosemary's father."

"Did she have any proof?" I asked quietly.

"She said she did," he nodded. "When she told me Rosemary's birth date, I knew it had to be true, and she said that, of course, it could be proven with DNA evidence. She told me she'd start with Shelley and go on to the school board from there. I told her it would never work. She sat and *smirked* at me. She said she'd be patient, but that I'd do what she wanted, or she'd destroy my marriage and career, all in one fell swoop.

The fell swoop of a true witch, I thought.

Ian's countenance had slowly changed. His whole face sagged. He sat with his eyes unfocused. I actually felt sorry for him for one tiny moment.

Then he looked up at me, and I saw something else in his eyes. Could it be a bit of menace? I inched forward in my chair a tad, thinking I might at some point want to get the hell out of there.

"This year with Rosemary in our building, she really amped it up. She had such easy access to me, and she was unrelenting. She finally gave me an ultimatum. If I didn't make it happen for her at the next board meeting, she was going straight to Shelley. I *love* my wife and my girls. Hell, I love my job. I didn't want to lose any of it. And it just wasn't something I could even make happen. It's not a power I have." He spread his upraised hands apart and shook his head.

"But why at school, Ian? God, why here?"

He folded his hands back into prayer position. "Because I needed a scapegoat," he said with a wry smile. "And you were such an easy one, Hannah. Everyone knew you couldn't stand Gretchen. Then you got in that huge blowup with her at Rosemary's IEP meeting. It was so easy to spread the rumor about her trying to get you fired. I think you even half-believed it."

"And you did that to me so easily?" I said in disbelief.

"Well, not all that easily. Don't get me wrong Hannah. I like you, but you know how it is—every man for himself," he said, spreading his hands apart again as if we were having a normal conversation. The storm I had thought was coming a minute earlier was now completely in check.

"I first got the idea way back last May, when I was helping set up for the end-of-the-year party at your place. Gretchen had just happened to pay me a visit that day, reminding me that her daughter, *our* daughter, would be in my building in the coming school year. She was there to tell me we would be moving forward with her plan faster. Then there I was in your garage, and your toolbox was wide open. You really should be neater, you know. It never pays to be sloppy."

Was he for real? Was he making a *joke* right now?

"I saw that awl lying there. I almost grabbed it and stuck it in my pocket right then. At first, it was sort of a little private fantasy. But the more I thought about it, the more it seemed like a real answer. Last week I just popped on over to your place, let myself in, and grabbed the awl. And, of course, the lockdown was the perfect opportunity." Oh, my God! This was who Stella had seen. Not Jamie. Ian. Ian was a handsome young man, and Stella had met him several times at McKinley events.

"How did she happen to be up at the school that afternoon?"

"That was so easy. I told her the school board had reversed their decision about not hiring a district advocate, that they would be accepting written applications for the position at that night's board meeting. I told her no one else had applied because they weren't aware of the reversal. She *believed* that I had to get the application to her on the sly. So we agreed that she would come to the side door during the lockdown. I simply unlocked the door and let her in. I told her I had left the application down the hall in a janitor's closet." He actually chuckled at this point. "The whole ruse was sort of ridiculous, but she was so greedy that she bought it. When she followed me down the hall, I just stopped and shoved her into the girls' bathroom. Of course, no one was supposed to be in there," he said with a glare at me.

I sat staring at this man whom I had thought I knew, whom I had thought was my friend. He stared back at me for a few seconds that lasted an eternity. We both jumped as the phone on his desk rang. He held me with his eyes as he picked up the phone, answering it with his usual greeting as if he had just been sitting at his desk, doing paperwork. As he looked out the window momentarily, listening, I quietly got up, and by the time he looked back, I was opening the door. I pulled it shut behind me and then ran for the main office door. By the time I was opening it, I could hear him coming.

Chapter 35

"Hannah, come back here. You and I are far from finished!"

Maybe so in his mind, but I was completely done. I ran down the hall to my room, locking the door behind me. I went straight to my desk. Opening the bottom drawer, I entered the four-digit code that made the safe spring open, and in a second, I had the gun that I had vowed never to use in my hand. I knew I was being ridiculous. Ian wouldn't hurt me. But a little voice in my head said, does he have a choice?

He was at my door now, banging, calling out my name. I quickly hid the gun under the mess of papers on my desk. I grabbed my purse and pulled out my phone, punching in 911.

I was trapped in my room with him at the door. I could hear his master key turning the lock. I quickly put my phone in my purse and stood behind my desk as if it could protect me from him.

As he opened the door, I could see anger in his face, or maybe it was just exertion from running down the hall. His voice told me it was the former.

"Did you really think you could get away from me?" he asked in a strange voice.

"Ian, you've got to turn yourself in," I said. He took several steps toward me but stopped just a few feet inside the door. He had nothing in his hands, but each was a fist.

"Ha! That's not going to happen. After all I've done? After all the time I've spent making you look guilty? No. I'm pretty sure the police are about ready to arrest you. So you'll just have to disappear." He made a little gesture with one hand as if something had gone up in smoke. He actually smiled at me now. Then he began moving across the room.

"Stop right there," I said as I pulled the gun out from underneath the pile of papers and aimed it at him.

And he did stop. His hands went halfway up in a defensive gesture, but then he began to lower them.

"Oh, come on, Hannah. Everyone knows how you really feel about the whole guns in the classroom thing. You're not going to use that on me."

He took a couple more steps. I raised the gun, steadied it with my left hand, aimed for his heart, and pulled the trigger. Just as the sound of the gun firing reached my ears, I saw a little explosion of carpet a few feet in front of Ian, and he went down, both hands holding his left knee.

I stood for only a second or two before I made the decision to run. I tried to take a wide berth around him as he lay writhing on the floor. Just as I got past him, a hand reached out, grabbing my ankle, and I was pulled down. The gun flew out of my hand, but it was safely out of Ian's reach, just outside the door of my room. I slapped at him and tried to pry his fingers away from my ankle, but he was stronger than me. As he sat up, he pulled me toward him.

"Shut up, you bitch," he growled. Blood was gushing from his knee, but he was focused on me now. He twisted my ankle, sending pain shooting up my leg.

"Give me that gun."

"No!" I screamed at him as he twisted harder.

I turned, reaching to get the gun. I could just touch it. With one finger, I pulled it toward me until I could wrap my hand around the barrel. I swung around, raising the butt, and got ready to smash at his hand where he held my ankle. But he anticipated the move, and as I began to bring it down, he quickly released me, grabbing the gun.

"Get me something to stop this bleeding," he ordered, now aiming the gun at me. I looked into the barrel and knew I should be far more frightened of my own gun than I had been of the one Nathan had aimed at me a few days before. "Get me something!" he roared. I looked around the room and got up slowly to get a roll of paper towels sitting on a counter. I held them up as if for his approval, and he nodded.

"Bring them over here. Tear some off and hold them on my knee."

"I'm not touching you," I said, tearing off a bunch of towels and tossing them within his easy reach, then backing away a few feet. He grabbed the towels, wadding them up with his left hand while he held the gun on me with his right. He cringed in pain as he held the wad of towels to his knee, and I felt a tiny little wave of happiness. Abandoning his attempts at first aid, he managed to get up and, brandishing the gun at me, indicated that it was time for us to go.

Go where I thought?

"Out the back," he answered, reading my mind. "Pull your classroom door shut," he said, speaking quietly. I did as he ordered. He waved the gun, indicating that I should get moving.

"Not too fast if you don't want to get shot," he said. "My aim is certainly better than yours. Get your car keys out," he added as we exited the building and moved toward my car, the only one remaining in the back parking lot.

I took the keys out. I didn't know whether to yell, run, or try to hit him with my purse. Not having much faith in my aim since my shot into the floor, I didn't think the purse was a good option. There was not a soul around, it being late on a Friday afternoon.

"Open the trunk," he said. "We're going for a little ride."

"Ian, you've got to be kidding."

"I'm not kidding at all. Get in there," he said, gesturing with the gun. Those little jerks of the gun were scaring the crap out of me. I had another quick flashback to Nathan doing the same thing outside of Shrout's Cafe. But I was vastly more frightened right then than I had been on that night. I didn't think there would be any talking Ian out of this.

"Get in," he growled.

As I climbed into the trunk, he wrenched my purse away from me. He slammed the lid down hard. I squeezed my eyes shut for a moment, sending up a prayer that I would live through this, and another that he wouldn't look in my purse. Then I tried to get my heart rate under control. I took a couple of deep breaths as the car started and we began to move. For a few seconds, the radio blared, and he turned it down, but not off. That's good, I thought. It gave me a little hope.

I opened my eyes and found myself looking inward, toward the back of the backseat. But how could I see it? There was a strange green glow inside the trunk. I wiggled around to see the little fluorescent green tag, the pull to open the trunk from inside. Thank God for modern car makers who think of things like kids stupidly shutting themselves in car trunks. At one time, I had known my car had this little perk, but I had long forgotten it. I reached up and almost pulled, but the car jerked suddenly to the left. I knew we were turning out onto the street from the parking lot. I pulled my hand back as Ian stepped on the gas and we started down the road. McKinley is in the middle of the city. He would surely have a number of lights to stop at, no matter where he was going.

I worked at getting myself positioned a bit better to get out of the trunk. It wasn't like I could sit up in there, but I had enough room to turn over and get ready to pull with one hand and push myself up with the other. Within a minute, we came to a complete stop. I reached up, but we quickly lurched forward again. I waited. An eternity that was probably two minutes crawled by with no more stops. I started thinking about opening the trunk and just jumping out while moving, but I didn't trust my ability to execute a move like that. With my luck, I'd get run over by a car behind us. And then my opportunity came. The car came to a full stop again. I held my breath for luck and pulled the green tag. The trunk popped open.

Sunlight blinded me, but I didn't hesitate. I pushed myself up and crawled out of the trunk. We were in the middle of stopped traffic. I looked up to see an elderly woman in the car behind us gaping at me with her mouth wide open. I ran to the passenger side of her car and pulled at the door handle, nearly pulling my arm out of the socket. The door was locked.

"Help me!" I pleaded. She sat staring at me with her hands firmly planted at ten and two, shaking her head slowly back and forth. "Please help me!" I yelled as I stupidly tried the door again.

"Hey, over here," came a voice from behind me. I turned to see a scrubby-looking young guy in a banged-up old van in the next lane. "Get in." He motioned for me to come around the front end of his car. At any other moment in my life, getting into that van would have probably been the last thing I'd do, but right now, I could clearly see a halo above this guy's head. With a glance back at my car that horrified me, I ran to get in the van.

Ian was getting out of the car with my gun in his hand. The light had turned green, and traffic ahead of my savior was starting to move. As I jumped into the passenger seat, my hippie hero hit the gas and pulled away, leaving Ian standing between two lanes of traffic, gun raised at the van as we pulled away. But we didn't get very far. I heard sirens approaching and saw two cop cars, lights flashing, pull into the intersection up ahead, blocking cars from going through it.

"Holy shit!" commented my young chauffeur under his breath. Then he looked over at me and said, "Is this all because of you?"

"I think so," I said. "I hope so."

As I looked ahead fifty yards, I saw four cops emerge from their cars with guns drawn. They ran between the lanes of cars, heading toward us. I had lost sight of Ian, but suddenly my car door was jerked open, and there he was, bringing the gun up toward me.

I didn't even hear the bullet hit him, but suddenly he jerked sideways and collapsed. He lay on the pavement next to the van, yelling in pain, blood staining the right side of his jacket. I stared, transfixed.

"Whoa," I heard from my driver. I glanced over at him and saw his hands raised as his door was pulled open by one of the cops. And then another was next to Ian, pulling him up off the ground, shoving him against the front fender of the van. He yelled in pain as the officer pulled his right arm behind him to put on handcuffs.

I still couldn't move. I sat staring as the cop talked into his radio while he kept a hand on Ian's back. Slowly Ian turned his head to look at me. I barely recognized the face of the man who stared at me with what I felt was hatred. It was enough to jar me into motion. I got out of the van and, staying as far away from Ian as I could get, I walked around the back of the old clunker to the driver's side. Traffic was completely stopped. People were out of their cars, gawking at the little circus we were putting on. The young man who had offered me a ride was talking to a cop.

"Thank you so much," I interrupted as my arms went around his neck in a hug. I clung to him for a moment, relishing the contact with this kind man.

"Are you Hannah Hutchinson?" asked the cop, surprising me.

"Yes. How did you know that?"

"From your phone. When you called 911, we tracked the phone. We heard what was going down. Knew where the car was. That's what brought us here."

I could hardly believe my little last-minute plan of throwing my phone in my purse without hanging up had actually worked.

The traffic jam got worse before it got better, but within ten or fifteen minutes, it was at least moving slowly again. I found myself sitting in a cop car for the second time in less than two weeks. Ofcourse, I was taken to CIS again. But I sure felt differently about this trip. The cop who drove me downtown was very concerned about me, asking me if I was hurt. Did I have any symptoms of shock? Did I need him to call anyone for me? His partner followed us, driving my car. This was actually somewhat of a comfort to me. Although I kept telling my kind young driver that I was fine, I was truly pretty shaken up and was trying to do some controlled breathing to feel more composed.

Arriving at CIS, I was politely escorted in and taken to one of the tiny rooms again. A young guy came into the room immediately, leaving the door behind him open. He had on a polo shirt embroidered with "Detective Raymond" on the left chest. He shook my hand and asked me if I'd like something to drink, which I declined. He invited me to sit down.

"Where are Kennedy and Appledom?" I asked, immediately wondering why I had inquired. Maybe I just wanted what had become familiar to me.

Detective Raymond held up both hands in a calming motion, making me realize that maybe I had sounded a little desperate. I tried to relax a bit and said that maybe I would have a drink after all. As he left the room, door wide open, I slumped down in my chair and allowed myself to reflect on the previous hour or so.

Rejoining me quickly, Raymond handed me the soft drink. "I just got a call from Detective Kennedy. He was off duty but insisted he'd be here in fifteen minutes. If it's okay with you, I'm going to leave you and let him handle all this. Do you mind just waiting here for him for a few minutes?"

"No, that'll be fine," I said. And it was. I was glad to be left alone for a short time. I sat drinking my diet cola, not feeling anything like the anxiety I had felt the first time I had been here. The open door helped a lot. People walked by every moment or two, peeking in at me as I peered back at them. My mind was jumping around from Ian to Gretchen to Nathan and back to Ian as I reviewed all I had learned about them in those few days.

Within only a few minutes, I heard a familiar voice from out in the hall, but it didn't quite match the person who came through the door. I had to study him for a second or two to realize it was Kennedy. I had recognized his gait, his body, his general appearance. The foreign part was the lack of a suit. He, too, wore a black polo with his name embroidered on it. I checked it out as he came toward the door, making sure I was seeing who I thought I was: Kennedy looking like an average guy. He somehow looked younger, not as heavy, and friendlier without the suit.

"Where's Appledom?" I blurted out as he pulled out a chair.

"What am I, chopped liver?" He smiled as he took a seat across the table from me.

"I'm sorry," I said, suddenly embarrassed. "I just thought you always worked together."

"We usually do," he offered, "but our workday is really over now, so I told him I'd cover this." He smiled. "If that's okay with you," he added with a note of humor in his voice.

To my surprise, I felt somewhat comforted by his presence. I told him my story. He asked a lot of questions about Ian and Gretchen, about how she had essentially blackmailed him, and about me happening to have a gun in my desk drawer. I told him about how going to the restroom with Chloe had finally made all the pieces fall into place for me.

"Poor Chloe," I moaned, thinking of what she had undoubtedly seen. We talked for a moment about who should contact her parents and agreed that we both should. He filled a number of pages in his tiny notepad, flipping them quickly as he wrote down the details of my story. He was pretty serious about the whole thing, cracking up only mildly when I told him about how my bullet had ricocheted off the floor to hit Ian in the knee.

"Why does that not surprise me?" I heard him mumble as he continued to take notes.

He seemed gratifyingly horrified at my little ride in the trunk of my car and even congratulated me on my narrow escape. By the time I had told him everything he wanted to know, I was exhausted. Obviously, the events that had happened before the interview had a lot to do with that. As we finished our talk, he stood and held the door open for me, escorted me out to the building's exit, and asked if I was okay to drive home. He reached out to shake hands with me, and we shook, looking each other in the eye and even sharing a smile.

"I hope I never see you again, Hannah Hutchinson."

"And I hope the same, Detective Kennedy," I said, laughing.

I slept better that night than I had slept in weeks.

Chapter 36

Saturday, March 23rd

Saturday, thankfully, was a beautiful, sunny day. There's nothing worse than a funeral on a rainy day. But that day was full of tiny chartreuse leaves trying to open up to the sun. Of flowering shrubs giving a glimpse of what was to come. Of cloudless blue sky, and sixty degrees. Of spring, almost. Spring is such a fickle season—making little appearances, then hiding behind the coattails of winter. Or is it just that winter is cruel in its ability to be almost gone, then reappear? I guess that's what makes us love spring so much: Days like this that hold promise of things ahead and allow us to shed the layers of extra clothing. Days that give us that oh-so-human emotion, hope.

I had been dreading this all week, would have loved to skip it, but knew I couldn't for two reasons. The first, and of course most important, was Rosie. The second was political or professional, whichever you'd like to call it. I had to go because it was expected of me.

I dressed with more care than usual, donning a navy-and-white dress and navy pumps, from which I had to wipe layers of dust. They probably hadn't seen any wear since my last funeral. I worked for a few minutes longer than usual on my hair, with the result that it ended up no different than my usual brown Easter grass look. Exactly the reason I don't often take the extra time. Still, I thought I looked pretty presentable as I checked myself out in my full-length mirror. I stood there staring at myself, procrastinating, trying to think of something else I needed to do before I left the house. I sighed, then gave Rascal a pat on the head and his usual "be good while I'm gone" talk, which he doesn't really need.

Funerals are bad enough, but going to the funeral of someone you actively disliked is worse than a trip to the dentist when you know you're headed for a root canal. I put my head down and strode into First Presbyterian, a huge old church I had never been in before. It had unimaginative stained glass windows and dark wood everywhere. Great, a gloomy old church to set the perfect mood. There were lots of people there, probably close to two hundred. I wondered cruelly how many there were like me, attending out of a sense of duty rather than a love for Gretchen. Wow, I thought. Are you really going to be this much of a bitch in a house of God? I turned off my evil thoughts and sent up a silent apology to the Big Guy. It seemed people were just milling around, but after a moment, I realized there was a sort of greeting line up at the front of the chapel, where the family was receiving hugs and condolences. I got in line and within a moment saw Rosie, flanked by her dad on one side and an older couple, probably grandparents, on the other, along with what I guessed were other relatives. When Rosie caught sight of me, she broke out of line and tackled me with a hug. I hugged back, and we walked arm-in-arm back to her place in line, where, surprisingly, Nathan also gave me a hug. I was introduced to grandparents, aunts, and uncles, who all received me with grace as I shook hands and told them how sorry I was for their loss.

I was touched to see how many kids were there. There were at least thirty, mostly sixth-grade girls, kids who had known Rosie since kindergarten. From my little crew, Josh, Megan, and Christie were there, each with a parent in tow. There was also a nice showing of staff from school, including Andrew, the superintendent, and a number of teachers. I thanked each of them for coming, knowing they weren't really there for me but extremely grateful that they had come. We sat down together as the minister started the service. A friend of Gretchen's in a very businesslike suit spoke of her accomplishments. Bible verses were read, prayers were said, a solo was sung, and it was over. Sweet and blessedly short. I got up to leave, looking around to see if I could say a quick goodbye to Rosie. She was up at the front of the church with her eye on me, and when she saw me looking her way, she waved me over frantically. What could I do? I made my way back to the front of the church, excusing myself to get through the lucky folks who were on their way out.

"Please come to the cemetery with us, Ms. H," Rosie said, getting right to the point.

I glanced up at Nathan and my eyes stuck on his, which were imploring me. I looked back at Rosie with a smile plastered on my face. "Sure. I'll be there," I told her.

"Thanks, Hannah. We appreciate it," said Nathan.

Spring Grove Cemetery is one of the most beautiful cemeteries in the country. It is famous for its architectural planning, its beautiful monuments, and especially its gardens. Cincinnatians go there in droves for walks and picnics. I don't take walks there only because it's too far from home for me. If I lived nearby, I'd be there regularly. It's that pretty. So I told myself I didn't really mind going, and I actually believed myself. Since Gretchen had been cremated, there would be no lowering of a coffin into the ground, just hopefully a short little service led by the minister. But things got emotional when Rosie put a rose next to her mom's urn at the end of the ceremony. There was some pretty heavy-duty sniffling going on all around, me included, and Rosie ended up with her face planted in Nathan's stomach, obviously sobbing. I was invited back to the Mitchells' house by Rosie's grandma, but politely refused. The thought of going into their home, the house I had entered illegally and invaded the privacy of, was just too much for me. I told Rosie I'd see her at school on Monday. Nathan nodded his assent, confirming that she would be there. I really had to agree with him that it was the best place for her. She had done okay the week before, so hopefully keeping busy was helping her.

"See you then," I said as I turned to take my leave. Little did I know then that I'd see her sooner than that.

Jamie called late in the afternoon to find out if I wanted to go see a live band with him. It sounded like fun, but I wasn't feeling very jovial. Besides, I was having some pretty big mixed emotions about our weird interlude of Thursday night. As if he could read my mind, he said, "You know, I meant what I said on Thursday night, Hannah."

"You were drunk, Jamie. You don't have to say that. It's okay."

"No. It's not okay. I admit I was a mite liquored up, but I wasn't bullshittin' ya. I meant every word. I know you and I could make a serious run."

This flustered me, and I fumbled for words as he added, "I'm here for ya. That's the truth. I want you to think on that and let me know where I stand."

"Okay," I said. "I will, Jamie. I promise." I hung up and went straight to the pantry. Damn him! I didn't want my life to change. I didn't want to think about it. I wanted everything to stay the way it was. I worked my way through a bowl of cereal, some pretzels, maybe six or seven Oreos, and a diet cola. Then, feeling like I could squeeze nothing else down, I putzed around the apartment for a while, getting nothing done, and finally got the therapy I really needed: I took Rascal for a long walk and decided to put off any more thinking until tomorrow.

Chapter 37

Sunday, March 24th

I woke up Sunday morning feeling the best I had felt in what
seemed like ages. No bad dreams overnight. No murder on my
mind. No big questions in my life. Well, maybe one, but I fought
the urge to give it any thought.

I was a good girl *again*. This was two weeks in a row that I was
getting my schoolwork done early on Sunday. I hoped it was a new
trend. My mother called and I had a nice, civil conversation with
her. Naturally, I had to retell the whole story of Ian and Gretchen,
but I thought of it as good practice for what I would probably have
to do repeatedly at school the next day. In the version for Mom, I
left out the part about Ian coming after me, and me shooting him
in the knee. I had never told my mother about the gun training or
about having the gun in my classroom in the first place. There are
just some things moms shouldn't know. I satisfied her curiosity
enough to give her closure and a sense that I was safe. I know she
really does care about me. Loves me, in fact. We are just so
different that I always have trouble finding common ground with
her. Gretchen's murder, horrible as it was, was an easy thing for us
to talk about compared to things like my career, my lifestyle, my
lack of a partner. When I got off the phone with her, I decided to
get the call to Chloe's parents over with. I knew the police had
already contacted them. I just wanted to sympathize and let them
know I would do all I could to help Chloe get past the incident.

They were wonderfully understanding and insisted that they hadn't noticed any huge changes in Chloe. I could only hope they were right. Hopefully, Chloe hadn't really understood what she was seeing through that wide crack in the restroom stall.

I thought about doing a little cleaning but decided the apartment was at a comfortable level of slovenliness. I settled instead on a trip to the park with Rascal. That day's weather was nothing like the previous day's. In Cincinnati, we always say that if you don't like the weather, just wait five minutes and it will change. But don't they say that everywhere? That morning was windy and cold, no sun in sight, but I don't usually let the conditions outside stop me from taking Rascal out.

Sharon Woods is a bit of a long drive for me, but I love to walk around the lake there, so that's where we headed. The parking lot was nearly empty at that hour, noon on a Sunday. As we walked toward the lake, I shivered, wondering if my hoodie would be enough. The wind was positively whipping around. But down by the water it wasn't as bad. You could see it blowing across the lake, seemingly pushing along a group of ducks who were busy lunching on whatever it is ducks eat. I smiled as I watched their tails go straight up, their webbed feet paddling comically in the air, upper bodies disappearing under the water. Rascal took this in with a lengthening of his neck, a frozen gaze, a stop every few steps to observe them. We worked our way around the lake, a pretty good long walk, but an easy, flat one. At times it was downright chilly, but as I walked the large circumference, we also had moments that were comfortable, and I felt good being out there, somehow feeling free of worries. Almost free, anyway. Rascal trotted along with his tail waving like a banner, occasionally looking back at me with a happy grin. There is something about giving pleasure to this animal who loves me so unconditionally that makes me feel genuinely good.

By the time we had done the mile or so lap around the lake, I decided we deserved a burger and fries, which we got on the way home, Rascal's take being a few french fries and the last bite of my burger.

I found that I had time on my hands that afternoon, and I settled down with a book I had been trying unsuccessfully to read for several weeks. I nestled into my reading chair, got involved, lost track of time, enjoyed myself, and after a couple of hours, when I was almost bleary-eyed, nodded off. The phone woke me, or I might have slept away the rest of the afternoon. What time was it, anyway? I glanced at my cell before answering: quarter to five. Caller ID said it was Nathan Mitchell. That brought me fully awake. I cleared my throat so I wouldn't sound groggy.

"Hello?"

"Hi, Hannah. It's Nathan Mitchell."

"Hi, Nathan. What's up?"

"I'm sorry to bother you on a Sunday afternoon, but I wanted to let you know that Rosemary won't be at school tomorrow after all."

"Oh, I'm so sorry. Is she not doing well?"

"No. She's not doing well at all." Now I heard the strain in his voice. He sounded like he had sounded that night outside of Shrout's Cafe. Stressed. Desperate.

"What is it, Nathan?"

"She's here in Children's Hospital, in the ICU. She's really ill. They have to do the surgery tomorrow. It's become an emergency. They've got her sedated to ease the stress on her heart. She's hooked up to all these machines. It's awful."

"Oh, my God, Nathan. That's horrifying! Can I come down there? Can I come see her?"

"Actually, yes. If you don't mind, I'd really appreciate that."

I wrote down the details he gave me and told him I'd be there in half an hour. I quickly put on clean jeans and a sweater and was out the door in short order. I did some very fervent praying for Rosie as I drove to the hospital. I tried a bit of rationalizing with God: She had just lost her mom. She was such a good kid. She had a kind heart. How about a nice break for her?

Getting to the hospital, I worked through the maze—parking, getting to the right tower, finding the right set of elevators, following directions from a couple of hospital employees—and finally came to Rosie's room. As I was about to walk in, Nathan's parents came out of the room with him as he was giving them hugs and reassurances. To my surprise, first his father, then his mother hugged me, both murmuring words of thanks to me for coming to the hospital.

Nathan also thanked me for coming, then turned without saying another word, walked into the room, and sat down in a chair close to the head of Rosie's bed. I followed him in, stopping short as my eyes fell on Rosie. Was she asleep? Unconscious? I wasn't sure. She was hooked up to a number of machines that glowed and beeped, but at least she was breathing on her own, although she had oxygen tubes taped to her nose. I sat down opposite Nathan and we had an almost whispered conversation as he told me how Rosie had fainted several times at home. He had brought her to the ER, where they had diagnosed her heart as failing due to the increase in the leak, and possibly also due to the stress in her young life. He told me the emergency surgery would be done the next morning at eleven thirty. Rosie was sedated, but only mildly. Nathan was all for waking her up to let her know I was there to see her. I protested adamantly, and he finally gave up the idea.

I sat there with him for over an hour. We talked about the funeral, about what a good mom Gretchen had been (okay, I admit that was Nathan talking, not me), and about what a great kid Rosie is. That part was easy for me to chime in on. I reassured him that she would be okay, which was stupid because, of course, I had no idea whether that was true. But isn't that what you say in these situations? Nathan's parents were coming back in the morning to be with him during the surgery. I was glad he wouldn't be alone. Poor guy. Nothing like burying your wife one day and facing the thought of losing your only child the next. I snuck a peek at my watch and saw that it was after six o'clock. I asked him if he wanted me to stay with Rosie while he got something to eat. He insisted that he didn't want to go down to the cafeteria and eat alone, and in the end, we both went down to eat an awkward dinner that neither of us tasted. Being in a hospital cafeteria, maybe that was for the best. I left him after dinner, knowing he would undoubtedly spend the night on the fold-out couch tucked at the back of Rosie's room.

I had one more visit to make before I left the hospital. I made my way back to the main atrium and consulted one of the maps on the wall, looking for the psychiatric ward. I meandered down a hall, up an elevator, and down another hall, stopping at a nurse's station to ask if I was on the right path. After a couple of miles of hallway, I reached a set of locked doors with a posted sign instructing me to ring the doorbell on the wall for entry. When I did, a voice came over an intercom informally saying, "Be there in a sec."

I looked through the window and saw a young guy in green scrubs headed my way. He opened the door and asked me who I was, and who I was there to see. Then he walked me back to a nurse's station, where he consulted a clipboard.

"Yup, you're on the list," he said, which was a relief after my long trek to get there. "Right this way. I'm sure she'll be glad to see you." I followed him a short distance down the hall. "The list of allowed visitors says you're a teacher. One of Zelda's, I guess?"

"No. Actually, I'm her brother Zak's teacher. Zelda and I are just friends."

"That Zak is quite a character. Zelda seems to really respond to him."

I chuckled. "Yeah, everybody responds to Zak."

He held out a hand, indicating Zelda's room. I thanked him and walked in. Zelda was sitting up in bed, looking out the window. She turned, hearing me enter, and offered her tiny Mona Lisa smile.

"Hi, Ms. H."

"Hi, Zelda. How are you doing?"

"I'm fine," she offered tonelessly.

"Fine? Really?" I asked.

Now she answered with a lot more expression. "Yes. I'm perfectly fine. I'm not even thinking about hurting myself, but they won't let me out of here. Everyone's acting like I'm some kind of suicidal maniac."

I was a little bit surprised by the drama in her voice and fumbled for a minute for something to say. "Umm . . . are they looking at adjusting your meds before you go home?"

"They've already done that, but they say I have to wait a couple days until I'm stabilized," she said with a roll of her eyes and a flop of her head back against the pillow.

"Ah, well, guess there's not much you can do about that." I managed to turn the subject to school, the weather, anything I could think of to make conversation. I'm no shrink, and I didn't feel like I had any business getting into Zelda's problems. When I had called her parents to see if it was okay for me to visit her, they had been happy to put me on her visitors' list but cautioned me that she was going through some pretty wide mood swings. I stayed for about half an hour and then said I had to go. It was with a sense of relief that I left the hospital.

Chapter 38

Monday, March 25th

I got to work early. I actually snuck into my room again, re-locking the door and keeping the lights off. I so wanted my normal back. I just couldn't face the parade of attention I knew would be coming my way after all that had happened Friday after school. I kicked my shoes off to get comfortable and glanced over my lesson plans. I pulled out materials, got things set up for the day, and even straightened the room up a bit. Ahh, order in my life. At 7:40, fifteen minutes before the buses would arrive, I opened my door and flipped the lights on. Pen's door was open, so I headed down the hall for a little extra dose of order.

She looked up from her desk as I walked in. "Good morning, Hannah. How's our hero this morning?"

"Oh, right. Some hero," I snorted. "I'm just so glad it's all over so things can get back to normal around here."

"I'm sure you are. There's nothing like the routines of our lives to make us feel like we're in control of things," she said as she got up to file some papers. (Ahh . . . just the sort of wisdom I had come down the hall for.) I decided that telling Pen about Rosie's situation would relieve a little of my internal stress. She listened intently, even abandoning her filing to come around her desk and give me a hug, which I accepted gratefully.

"I'll be praying for her," she said. "I'm sure it will be all right. I know she's in good hands."

"Thanks, Pen. You're the best. I guess I better scoot. I hear the wild hordes approaching." I stepped out into the hall and decided to stay there. I stood by my classroom door and greeted kids as they came down the hall. I plastered a smile on my face. They smiled back and returned my good mornings. I felt my smile become more honest.

Zak came down the hall and attacked me with a bear hug, saying, "My sister coming home today. She come to school tomorrow or Wednesday."

"That's great, Zak. I'm happy for you."

"I'm happy for me too," he responded as he bounced off to his locker. When April came down the hall, I watched her for a moment at her locker. She got it open okay, but when she started trying to put her backpack in, it wouldn't fit. She stopped, put it on the floor, and unzipped it. By this time, the hall was crowded and she was getting bumped from both sides.

"Hey, April," I called from a few feet away. "Come here a sec, and bring your backpack." She picked it up and followed me into the room. "Remember how you unloaded your backpack here in the room last week?" She looked at me as if she suspected I was trying to trick her. Then she put her backpack on her desk and started pulling out her supplies. When she was done, she looked up at me as if she didn't know what to do next, but surprisingly, off came her jacket. After that she was stuck. I cued her to go put her stuff in her locker, knowing that it would take a few more days for her to accept this as habit.

In the couple of minutes we had before morning announcements, I had a little powwow with Chloe and explained that Mr. Stevenson would not be at school anymore, that someone else would be doing the morning announcements. She sat, pouting at me, as I related this to her. Several minutes later, when the daily announcements started, Chloe looked up at the intercom, then looked at me with a smile on her face as the voice of one of the guidance counselors greeted us.

When I paused to see if she had any reaction, she commented, "He's bad!"

"You're right," I said, thinking I should pay more attention to what my students have to say.

When Christie asked where Rosie was during homeroom, I said I thought maybe she just needed a day off after all she had been going through. We talked a little bit about the funeral for the benefit of all the kids. We got through the morning with a pretty good semblance of what I think of as normalcy. It wasn't perfect, but it never is. Naturally, my mind was on Rosie the whole time. I waited until the kids had headed out at the end of third bell to fill Anne and Ava in on Rosie having the surgery that afternoon. We all got a little teary together and agreed that we'd just keep what we knew between the three of us for the moment.

When I went out for recess duty after lunch, I was more relieved than an ADD kid just done with a stint of silent reading. It was good to be outside. I wandered around the play area, enjoying the sunshine and the soft breeze. I sent up what might have been my twentieth prayer for Rosie. I smiled at all these kiddos who had no idea how lucky they were to be in good health. As I wandered to the back of the pavement, I saw the exact same situation I had seen the Monday before. There stood Zak in the out-of-bounds area under the basketball hoop. A group of kids was playing pickup. Here came Will to get a ball that had bounced out of bounds next to Zak. It was like a bad déjà vu. Will grabbed the ball before Zak could get it. Zak stepped inbounds to guard him as he got ready to throw the ball. Will threw the ball right past him. When Zak stopped, looking disappointed, Will gave him a tiny shove from behind and a welcoming gesture, saying something I couldn't hear. Zak's face lit up as he ran out onto the basketball court. Huh, I thought. Was that a little miracle I had just seen?

The afternoon seemed endless. I knew Rosie was in surgery and was only able to get her out of my mind for a few minutes at a time. When Christie and I went up to Jamie's social studies class together, she told me that she missed Rosie. I knew the two of them usually ate lunch together, so that made sense. But I also wondered if Christie had some suspicions about what was really going on with Rosie. She can be an amazingly astute young lady.

When the kids finally left for the day, Anne, Ava, and I spent a few minutes team-worrying about Rosie even though we knew it was doing us no good. As they left, I assured them that I would call them both as soon as I heard anything.

I debated on leaving early or staying to get some work done. Work seemed like the better plan as I had really fallen behind during the last couple of weeks while I played sleuth. I also knew the work would occupy my mind better than anything else I could do. After a visit to the teachers' lounge, where I stocked up with M&Ms, chips, and a Snickers bar (I knew it was excessive, but I was famished), I got down to business. As I devoured my feast, I dug in hard and got quite a bit accomplished.

I was in a rhythm, reveling in the peace and quiet around me when the jangle of my cell phone nearly made me jump out of my seat. I hoped I knew where the call was coming from. As I held the phone to my ear, I offered one more quick prayer, then listened and smiled at the news I heard.

Acknowledgements

Many thanks....

To my husband Scott, who is funny, wise, kind, and has been tolerant of me for over forty years. Thank you for always supporting me in the things I do, and *try* to do.

To my two wonderful sons, Joel and Justin and my dear sisters, Geri and Judy, who all have high expectations of me. Thank you for quietly prodding me on and encouraging me.

I am fortunate to have lots of "sisters in life", many of whom have been my friends for decades. They have listened to me talk about my writing endlessly, and at least pretended to be interested.

Special thanks go to my first readers Sharon Fogelman, Paula Marcagi, Dana Parker, and Dawn Richards who were gentle, kind and complimentary with their very helpful suggestions.

Thanks also for the thoughts, and ideas on plot provided by Kim Thornton as we walked her neighborhood, and by Vicky Tuten, as we walked the beach. They both helped me work through tough spots in my story. For character ideas thanks to Britt, Paula, Jaime, and a few friends who shall remain nameless.

For technical assistance I want to thank Jeff Love of the Cincinnati Fire Department, and Detective Jeff Shari and Lieutenant Steve Saunders of the Cincinnati Police Department. These patient men helped me understand first responder and police procedures. Clearly, I did *not* follow all of their good advice. Thanks also to Derek Wehman for helping me understand what goes into Concealed Carry training.

A huge thank you goes to my wonderful editors at ProofreadingServices.com, who answered a thousand questions and changed my imperfect writing into something a reader could follow and hopefully enjoy.

And finally, a thank you to my parents who made me a lover of books, especially a good mystery.